Mrs. Gulliver

Mrs. Gulliver

A NOVEL

Valerie Martin

DOUBLEDAY · NEW YORK

Copyright © 2024 by Valerie Martin

All rights reserved. Published in the United States by Doubleday,
a division of Penguin Random House LLC, New York, and distributed in
Canada by Penguin Random House Canada Limited, Toronto.

www.doubleday.com

DOUBLEDAY and the portrayal of an anchor with a dolphin
are registered trademarks of Penguin Random House LLC.

Book design by Maria Carella
Jacket illustrations: (hummingbird) by Vi-An Nguyen;
(lips) by Finlandi/Shutterstock
Jacket design by Emily Mahon

Library of Congress Cataloging-in-Publication Data
Names: Martin, Valerie, author.
Title: Mrs. Gulliver : a novel / Valerie Martin.
Description: First edition. | New York : Doubleday, [2024]
Identifiers: LCCN 2023009605 (print) | LCCN 2023009606 (ebook) |
ISBN 9780385549950 (hardcover) | ISBN 9780593471210 (trade paperback) |
ISBN 9780385549967 (ebook)
Subjects: LCGFT: Novels.
Classification: LCC PS3563.A7295 M77 2024 (print) |
LCC PS3563.A7295 (ebook) | DDC 813/.54—dc23/eng/20230308
LC record available at https://lccn.loc.gov/2023009605
LC ebook record available at https://lccn.loc.gov/2023009606

MANUFACTURED IN THE UNITED STATES OF AMERICA

1 3 5 7 9 10 8 6 4 2

First Edition

So shall you share all that he doth possess,
By having him, making yourself no less.

*

Virtue itself turns vice, being misapplied,
And vice sometime by action dignified.

*

'Tis true, and therefore women, being the weaker vessels, are ever thrust to the wall. . . .

Romeo and Juliet, WILLIAM SHAKESPEARE

Verona Island

1954

*O*ur clients are professionals: doctors, lawyers, bankers, politicians (we've served a few mayors over the years), and, because our city is wrapped around the largest port on the island, a steady supply of seagoing men. My rule is: officers only. Discretion is what we offer. Except for the address in wrought-iron numbers, the front door is unmarked and never used; clients enter via a side door behind a tall hedge, so it can't be seen from the street; a password is required at all times. As the password doesn't change, this is the mildest of security measures. Our clients are encouraged to share it with interested friends or acquaintances. It creates a kind of network, with the charm of inclusion in a select society. Boys love passwords.

In the last few years, bad weather and blight have played havoc with the local economy, particularly among the rice farmers on the windward side of the island. A few of their prettier daughters have made their way to the city seeking honest labor and, failing that, turned up at my door. By that time, they are desperate, hungry, and frightened, and their best option is a charity organization run by nuns in a little town up in the hills. I refer them there. I've taken one or two to work, but they're seldom up to my standard for the house. Occasionally, my sympathy overrules my judgment and I employ a girl who presents what I know will be a challenge. This may be shrewdness on my part, as I would not have been successful in my business were it not for a sixth sense I have about some quality in an applicant that will appeal to certain of my clients. Carità was such a girl.

That summer morning, a hot and humid day with rain, as usual, in the forecast, my majordomo, Brutus (aptly named), came to my office, which is also the kitchen, and planted himself squarely in the door frame. "There's an odd couple asking to see you in the drawing room," he announced. "I don't know what they want. They look like beggars, but they know the password."

"Did you tell them we don't open until noon?"

"They're country girls, Lila," he said. "They're looking for employment, is my guess."

I rose from the table. "Then how did they get the password?" I mused. Brutus stepped aside and I sauntered down the hall.

They sat facing each other, one in a leather chair, the other perched on the edge of the red silk upholstered divan, her back straight and sandaled feet drawn in. They were dressed in plain cotton sleeveless shifts that came to the calf, worn but clean. Two destitute girls, one fair and portly, the other an elfin creature, small-boned, emaciated but not boyish. Even in her unflattering dress I could see she had a shapely figure: long waist, full breasts, excellent posture—that's always the first thing I notice. Her hair was an uncombed thick black mop that fell to the center of her back and partially covered her face.

The blonde looked up as I entered the room, her innocent face flushed with hope. Her friend didn't move, her head slightly bowed and turned away from me.

"How do you come to know the password here?" I asked sharply.

"My uncle gave it to me," she said. "His name was Peter Rizzo. He said you might not remember him, because he only came here once, with a friend."

"Who was the friend?"

"I don't know that," the girl replied. "It was when he came to town. He was a rice farmer. Or he was until the blight came. Now he's dead, and the bank took the farm."

"Where are your parents?" I asked.

"Our parents are dead," she said candidly, with no more emphasis than you might use to make a trivial factual observation—for example, *That door is closed.*

"So . . . you're sisters," I observed. "And you've come to the city looking for work."

"That's right," she said. "My name is Bessie Bercy, and this is Carità. I've already got a job. I'm signed up to shuck oysters at the market restaurant on the wharf. The man there showed me how it's done and then gave me a test, and right off he said I was faster than the two boys he's already got put together."

"Good for you," I said. "That shows enterprise."

"Yes, ma'am," she said. "But Carità won't do that kind of work, so now I need to find a place for her, because I can't leave her on her own and I won't make enough for us both. My uncle said he thought she might be useful to you."

At this her dark sister chuckled. "That's not exactly how he put it, Bessie," she said. Her voice, deep and breathy, vibrated through my chest like a cat purring in my lap. As she spoke, she turned toward me, and I could make out through the screen of her hair that her eyes, half closed, were very light. "What he said," she continued, "was that I'd be better off here than with the goddamned lesbian nuns."

How can I describe the rich velvet of her voice? She could have been a countess or an actress, delivering a scene-clinching line. There was an archness as well, distant and amused, deflecting the crudeness of the information she had just so succinctly passed along. She made me smile in spite of myself.

"Carità," her sister said, "don't talk like that."

"I don't think Mrs. Gulliver is shocked," the girl replied. Again, the deep vibration and archness of tone caressed my ears.

"Would you push your hair back so I can see your face?" I said.

She pressed her palms against her temples, pulling back the curtain of hair.

I caught my breath. Her face was beautiful, a creamy complexion with a natural blush, like an English beauty, her nose straight, her lips full and soft, her chin squarish and firm. But it was her eyes that startled me, heavy-lidded and half closed, with thick dark lashes, and irises like blue glass, the perfectly translucent blue of a glacier. Beneath the dark bird-wings of her brows, her eyes glittered enchantingly. I studied her. Something was very odd about those eyes.

"She's nineteen years old," Bessie said. Carità inclined her head toward her sister's voice, but the eyes didn't move. "She's blind from birth."

I raised my hand to my heart; my brain was racing. A blind prostitute, I thought. What would my clients think? I gazed at Carità, who appeared perfectly comfortable perched on the settee, with her straight spine and her hands folded in her lap. There was something pert, almost willful about her. She listened attentively while her sister sang her praises, as if she might make a correction or addition if some asset was overlooked.

"She's real smart," Bessie continued. "When we had money, my uncle brought in a teacher from the mainland, and she pretty much raised Carità. She taught her to take care of herself, she's very independent, and she can read Braille. She's read a lot. She can memorize fast. She can play the piano. Once she knows her way around a house, she can do pretty much anything a seeing person can do. She can even cook."

"If smart alecks don't put sugar in the saltshaker," Carità said. Then she laughed, revealing her teeth.

Two missing on the top right, behind the canine. Businesswoman that I am, my brain begin running a cost analysis of potential revenue versus dental outlay. I gave my dentist so much traffic I had a standing discount.

"We'd have to do something about those teeth," I said. Carità closed her lips tightly and shook her hair back over her face.

"Yes, ma'am," Bessie said.

The fact was, I'd lost a girl a few weeks earlier. Her name was Lottie, and she'd been with me full-time at the house for two years. She was popular, blonde and blowsy, an easygoing good-time girl as simple as a post and lazy as sin. She had a poor sick son who lived with her mother; all her money went to support them. About a year after she came to me, the boy died, and she went right down the alcohol chute. She was weepy and hysterical by turns, the clients got sick of her, and she was draining my coffers. I was about to let her go when her mother showed up at the door to say a relative had died and left them a little money and a house, so she'd come to take Lottie home. A happy ending. My hands were shaking with relief as I helped them pack up Lottie's things and get into the taxi.

So I had Lottie's empty room, and I had the clients. Three of my girls lived out and worked evening shifts, from six until closing. But desire doesn't sleep, and lunch appointments weren't uncommon, so I needed two girls for the noon-to-four slot. At night, the in-house girls come on at seven or so. They also rotated Sundays off every other week. The house was closed on Mondays.

"She'd have to live here all the time," I said to Bessie.

Bessie nodded. "Could I come on Sunday mornings to take her out? She likes to walk outdoors."

This touched me, but it also made me think I was about to make a decision that required careful consideration. "I haven't said she can stay," I said.

"Yes, ma'am," Bessie said, looking down at her rough hands, folded in her lap.

"I want to have my colleague advise me," I said. "I'll go ask him to join us."

"Yes, ma'am," Bessie said again. I glanced at Carità, who

was silent, sitting very still, her chin slightly lifted, listening closely.

"I'll only be a moment," I said to Bessie. "Mr. Ruby is in the office." Then I went out—leaving the door ajar—and down the hall to the kitchen, where Brutus sat at the table, perusing the racing pages.

"I want you to come take a closer look at this girl," I said.

He folded the paper. "Is it those beggar girls?"

"Yes." I said nothing to him about Carità's blindness. I wanted to see an honest male reaction to the surprise.

He followed me down the hall into the room where the two women sat. As we entered, Bessie looked up, her plain face aglow with hope. Carità had not moved. "Ladies," I said, "I want to introduce you to Mr. Ruby, who is my trusted colleague." I motioned Brutus toward Bessie. "This is Bessie," I said.

Bessie stood up, her hand outstretched. "Pleased to meet you," she said confidently.

Brutus closed her hand in his own and nodded. "Likewise," he said.

I turned to Carità. She rose to her feet in that slow and curiously regal way I would come to know, proffering her hand palm-down, as if expecting a soft press of lips. "And this is Carità," I said.

Brutus took her hand, casting a quick questioning glance at me.

"A pleasure," Carità said, leaning away from him as if he'd caught her unawares.

"The gentleman can't see your face," I said. "Please pull your hair aside."

She smiled, keeping her lips carefully closed, swept her hair back with one hand, and held it in place so that her hairline was exposed. She had a shallow widow's peak, a smooth, unlined forehead. Her strange jewellike eyes seemed to contemplate the lapel of Brutus's jacket. I studied the effect upon him. His brow lifted; his nostrils inflated over a quick intake of air. An expression of pleasant mystification pursed his lips. He was a confident man, big enough to look down on his fellow humans, and, I knew from experience, capable of both cruelty and sympathy. He had a rough, often lewd sense of humor, which suited his profession. His eyes searched Carità's face, shifting between pleasure and calculation, just as I had done. "Your face is your fortune," he said, releasing her hand.

What about the rest of her? I thought. That's money in the bank, too.

"My uncle used to say that," Carità said, giving him the benefit of her caressing voice.

"That's true," Bessie put in. "He did say that. But her face didn't keep her from being as poor as a dog in the street, and just as much abused."

Carità stretched one hand behind her until her fingers grazed the sofa cushion, lowered herself to the seat, and drew her feet in beneath her. She performed this action smoothly; no one who didn't know why she'd made that swift probing gesture with her hand would have noticed. "We weren't always poor," Carità reminded her sister.

Brutus stood gazing down at our applicant, who sat on the

edge of the cushion, leaning forward with her hands resting on her thighs. He brought his palm to the side of her face, near her right ear but not touching her. She turned her head toward the hand; her eyes didn't move.

"She's blind," Brutus said flatly.

"Yes," I said.

He drew his hand away and wrapped his fingers around his chin, rubbing the heavy stubble in a gesture of wonderment. His eyes met mine, and we exchanged a look charged with our knowledge of each other and the exigencies of our mutual endeavor.

I turned to Bessie. "I'll just need to have a few words in private with Mr. Ruby," I said.

"Sure," Bessie replied. "We're not expected anywhere."

Brutus followed me to the kitchen. "What do you think?" I asked, closing the door behind us.

"She's totally blind?" he said.

"From birth. But she can take care of herself."

"Does she know what she'd be doing here?" he asked.

"It seems her uncle told her what to expect."

Brutus wrinkled his brows, pulling in his chin. "He sent her here?"

"He was here once as a client, and, evidently, he liked the operation. When he went broke, he thought this would be as good a place as any for his niece."

"What a bastard!"

"Maybe," I said. "But think about it. What are her options? She could wind up begging in the streets, or in some government home, half starved and neglected. Her sister is shucking oysters for a living; she won't be able to look after her. She'd be safe here, and she'd earn money to put away."

"A blind prostitute," Brutus said. "I never heard of such a thing."

"That's what I'm thinking. Not you or any man on this island has heard of such a thing."

"But can she do the work?" Brutus said.

I knew what he meant. It takes a strong personality to do the kind of work our girls do, day in and day out. My prices are high, and the men who avail themselves of our services expect to be treated with interest, even enthusiasm. Personally, I think it's a gift to be able to do this. It's like acting; you must throw your heart and soul—and, especially, your body—into a role that keeps changing and has little to do with your ordinary life.

"I think you should give her a trial run," I said. "Then we'll know what we've got."

He laughed. "I surely wouldn't mind that," he said. "Would she be willing?"

"I don't know why not. I'll pay her, of course. I'll go ask her."

"You mean right now?"

"Are you up for it?" I asked, teasing him. Brutus was pretty much always up for it.

"Where should we go?"

"Use Lottie's old room. It's all made up. I'll bring her to you in a few minutes."

Back in the drawing room, I found the sisters waiting patiently, evidently enjoying the coolness of the shuttered room. I pulled up a straight-backed chair and seated myself between them. "I have a few questions of a personal nature to ask," I said to Bessie.

"Yes, ma'am," she said, giving me her full attention.

"Is your sister a virgin?"

Carità gave a snort of laughter, while her sister blushed to the roots of her hair. "No, ma'am," she said. "She is not."

"Does she use any method of birth control?"

Bessie cast a frightened glance at her sister, then back at me. "As soon as she had her period, my uncle took her to the doctor and he did something."

"Something," I said. "What did he do?"

Bessie ducked her head, wringing her hands in her lap.

"He clipped something," Carità said informatively. "Right up inside me. I don't feel it, and I still get my period, but I can't ever have a baby."

This uncle, I thought, was a cautious bastard.

"That's fine, then," I said. "Now, before I say you can stay here, I need to know that you'll be able to perform the service we offer. It's not an easy job, by any means. I've asked Mr. Ruby to give you a trial run, if you'll excuse the expression."

Bessie looked mystified, but Carità nodded firmly. "An audition," she said.

"I'm not sure that's a good idea," Bessie offered.

Carità turned to her and spoke patiently, as if to a child. "You had to take a test to shuck oysters," she said. "What if you'd been really bad at it? Mrs. Gulliver just wants to know if I can do the job." Then she turned to me. "I think it's an excellent plan."

I gazed at her, frankly impressed. "Good," I said. "If all goes well, I will give you twenty-five dollars and you will be employed here. If, for some reason, Mr. Ruby determines that you're not suited to this work, then you may keep the twenty-five dollars and pursue employment elsewhere."

Carità smiled so broadly that I was put in mind of the dental bill. "That sounds fine to me," she said.

But the baldness of this proposal struck poor Bessie with such force—perhaps she grasped at last the true desperation of her sister's situation—that she burst into tears.

"She always cries," Carità observed.

"I just want to go home," Bessie sobbed.

"You're a good girl," I said to Bessie. "I know you're trying to do the best you can for your sister." I took up the box of tissues on the side table, and she reached out, pulled a sheet free, and applied it to her eyes.

"I never wanted to live in the city," Bessie continued. "She always did, ever since she was a child. Uncle Peter always brought back presents when he went, and he talked about how lively it was."

Carità put her hand over her mouth and sneezed.

"Bless you," I said.

She nodded, then spoke from behind her hand. "Could you pass me one of those tissues?" she said.

Without thinking, I offered the box to her. She stretched out her hand, missing it slightly. I moved it toward her fingers, they connected, and she snatched a sheet. How did she know it was a box of tissues I was offering? I thought. And then I answered my own question: she'd heard the sound when Bessie took one, that soft, innocuous sound of thin paper against cardboard.

In unison, the sisters blew their noses.

"You've nothing to fear," I said to Bessie. "Brutus is a good man. He makes sure no harm comes to any of the girls who work here."

"Yes, ma'am," Bessie murmured; she folded the tissue and dabbed her eyes.

I turned to Carità. "He's waiting for you in a room upstairs. I'll take you there now. You'll be with him about half an hour. If you have any questions for him at any point, feel free to ask him. He can tell you what to expect."

Carità rose from the chair and stood attentively, without moving. "Should I brush my hair?" she asked. Her voice had a blithe coquettishness that charmed me, as it would many others.

"You're fine," I said, approaching her. Should I lead her by the hand? Her fingers found my arm at once, and she slipped her hand inside my elbow, turning in the direction I was facing.

"How many steps are there?" she asked as I guided her to the staircase.

"I've never counted them," I admitted. "But there's a landing halfway."

She ascended the steps slowly but without hesitation. I said, "We're at the landing," and then, "This is the last step."

"Fourteen steps," she said when we reached the top. "Landing halfway." I led her along the hall to Lottie's old room. "Just so you know," she added, meaning the steps. Oddly, I've never forgotten it—fourteen steps, landing halfway.

"We're at the door," I said, rapping on the wood with my free hand. Brutus opened at once and stood smiling in the frame. Carità released my arm and stepped forward, holding one hand out before her, the elbow bent. This hand found Brutus, rested softly and briefly on his torso, then pulled back. "Oh, excuse me," she said, smiling to herself.

Brutus met my eyes over her head, his expression bemused. He took her hand in his own, drawing her into the room. "First, I'll show you where everything is in here," he said.

"That would help," she replied cheerfully. As he turned her toward the bed, he pushed the door closed behind him.

I stood on the carpet feeling strangely bereft. Is this a good idea? I thought. The businesswoman in my brain, who is ever on the alert, replied, "Oh, shut up." I made my way back down the stairs to the drawing room, where Bessie sat looking as miserable as a wet cat. "Why don't you come to the kitchen with me, and I'll fix you a cup of tea," I said.

Her face brightened. "Yes, ma'am," she said. "I'd like that very much."

"Good," I said. "I want to ask you a lot of questions about your sister."

Half an hour later, when we heard Brutus and Carità on the back staircase, Bessie was on her second cup of tea and her third vanilla wafer, and I was in receipt of the story of her life: the feckless father, dead in an auto accident; the Italian mother, who died after delivering a blind daughter into the world. ("She lived long enough to name her Carità," Bessie said. "It means 'mercy.'") The rich uncle, a confirmed bachelor, absorbed in his rice plantation, who agreed to take in the girls and treated them as his own. He had a big library and a lot of ideas. He brought in teachers; in Bessie's case, she was sad to report, nothing stuck, whereas Carità had a prodigious memory and was interested in everything. She read Braille books at a rapid pace; her teacher ordered them from the mainland. She adored music and learned to play the piano. They had everything they could want: nice clothes, a cook and a maid, two dogs and a house cat; Bessie had a bicycle she rode to the country store to buy sweets for them both.

Three years ago, when the sheath blight came, the uncle thought he could weather it, but the following season, just as the crop was heading, a tropical storm passed through and wiped it out a second time.

"That changed him," Bessie confided. "He became a bitter man. He believed our family was under a curse. Carità was just one more blighted thing in his life."

When the bank foreclosed, the uncle found a job on a farm on the mainland. He would be forced to work another man's land, to live in another man's quarters. The bank auctioned off everything he owned. He despaired of caring for his nieces. He gave Bessie fifty dollars, the password to my house, and two bus tickets to the city.

Then he took his best pistol, went out to the empty barn, and shot himself.

"How long have you been here?" I asked.

"Two weeks," she said. "I was looking for work, and I left Carità at the hotel. It wasn't a good place for her, not a safe place. A mean woman there pushed her on the staircase, and she fell all the way down. Then she found a man in the room going through our bag, and she hit him with a lamp. The manager was mad and wanted us to pay for the lamp. We were about out of money, so Carità said, 'It's time to use that password.'"

"I see," I said.

"And here we are."

We heard footsteps on the staircase; then Carità stood in the doorway. "Oh," she said. "It's a kitchen." She took a step into the room, holding her hands out before her.

Bessie jumped up and guided her to the table. "Are you all right?" she asked.

"Oh yes," Carità said. She had a pleased expression, as if she'd just accomplished a feat.

"How did you know this is a kitchen?" I asked.

"Kitchens have a very distinct feel," she said. Bessie was patting her on the arm anxiously. "It was fine," she assured her sister. "Brutus showed me everything. This is a big house."

I looked at Brutus, who was standing by the door with a dazed expression on his face.

"How did it go?" I asked.

He brought one hand to his neck to rub the flesh just below his ear, his lips parted and his brow furrowed. "We need to talk," he said.

"Is there a problem?" I asked.

Bessie, who had pulled out a chair for her sister and was standing behind her, cast Brutus a wary look but didn't speak.

"No," Brutus said. "Not at all."

"Then I'll stay here," Carità said, turning her ear toward me.

Brutus nodded.

"Yes," I said.

"And I've earned twenty-five dollars," she said, sounding pleased with herself.

"That's right," I said. "And the room you were in will be yours."

"It's bigger than our hotel room," Carità informed her sister. "And it has a sink, a wardrobe, a bed, and a comfortable chair."

"Why don't you take Bessie and show it to her?" I said. "You can wash up a bit and brush your hair. There's a brush in the wardrobe. The other girls will be arriving soon. They'll help you find a dress you can wear tonight. I think Vivien is about your size."

Bessie nodded, looking tense. Carità stood up at once, pushed her chair under the table, and turned to her sister, who led her back to the staircase. "There's a ceiling fan," she told Bessie. "It makes a nice breeze. I won't be so hot at night."

Brutus went to the stove and poured himself a cup of coffee. He drank coffee all day and whiskey all night.

"So how did it go?" I asked again.

He took a sip from the cup, his dark eyes fixed on mine over the edge. "It was about the strangest experience I've ever had," he said.

"But you liked it."

He nodded. "I did. Yes, very much."

"What did you like?"

"Well, you know, she can't see you. But you can see her."

"And that's appealing."

"It's not like she's blindfolded," he mused. "You can look right into her eyes."

"Her eyes are very strange," I observed.

"They are," he agreed. "I found myself just staring into them, and it didn't matter, because she didn't know I was staring."

"So that's what you did? You stared into her eyes?"

"When we were in bed. Yes. Before that, we talked a bit. I led her around the room; she touched everything, and after that she knew exactly how to get around without help. I showed her the sink and how to wash the gentleman's penis. That made her laugh."

"She laughed at your prick?"

"Not loud, just a giggle. She thinks sex is funny."

"Did she say that?"

"No, but she's playful. She checked out the mattress by bouncing on it. She could barely wait to get her dress off, because she wanted to feel the fan breeze on her bare skin."

"How's the body?"

He took a swallow of coffee and set the cup on the counter. "She's beautiful all the way down," he said. "Creamy skin, beautiful breasts, fantastic ass."

"And she's willing."

He nodded, passing his hand through his hair. "She wants to please and she's curious. After we were done, she asked me if she could feel my face; if I wouldn't mind. So I said sure, and we sat on the side of the bed, and she felt my face, just very gently tapping her fingers from my forehead to my chin, then my ears and the back of my neck."

"What did she say?"

He looked away while a blush crept up his neck to his cheeks. "She said I have a strong face."

I rested my chin on my hand, studying my old comrade closely. He turned toward me but couldn't meet my eyes.

"I will be damned," I said. "You fell like a tree."

"It's the novelty of the thing," he said.

"You fell like a tree," I repeated.

It was no surprise, I thought, that Carità had a fine time with Brutus—he was an attractive man with a lovely cock, and he liked women—but how would she feel about some of our less savory clients, and, most important, how would they feel about her? "She's not going to appeal to everyone," I said.

Brutus nodded. "I was thinking of Dr. Minton," he said, and we both burst out laughing.

"I can see her flailing his little whip around the room while he tries to get his sad old bottom in her way," I said.

Brutus wagged his buttocks, muttering, "Here, you idiot, hit me here."

What a vision! We teared up with laughter. But when we calmed down, Brutus seemed subdued and thoughtful. "She's strong," he said. "But she's small. Some jerk could get rough with her."

"Did you show her the buzzer?"

"I did," he said. "And I told her to push it if she felt frightened at all. Even just a little. Just push the buzzer: help is on the way."

"That's good," I said.

The sound of women's voices drifted in from the yard, one

complaining, one commiserating. Then Vivien's sharp-featured face appeared at the screen in the back door, and she pushed into the room, followed closely by Sally. It was time to open the bar and get ready for work. "We have a new colleague," I told them. "She's upstairs. You should go and welcome her."

"What's her name?" Sally asked. She immediately charged up the back stairs.

"Carità," I called out.

Vivien pulled out a chair and flopped down in it. "I need to cool down a minute," she said. "The bus was packed with sweating humanity." She opened her purse, took out a lacy handkerchief, and patted her upper lip.

Late that night, when our last client was gone, when Jack, our bartender, had washed all the glasses and locked the liquor in the cabinet, when three girls were home with their families and two were asleep upstairs, I prepared myself a cup of chamomile tea and sat at the table, going over the receipts for the week. Business was good. The liquor consumption was definitely up, and there was no shortage of clients.

Most of them were regulars, arriving separately and scattered over the hours. They knew what and whom they wanted, but no one was in a hurry, and as it was a hot night and my drawing room one of the coolest in town, they soon had the champagne cocktails flowing.

I hadn't allowed Carità to accept a date, as it was her first night and she was new to the business. Sally and Mimi had done her up like a doll, arranged her hair, put on makeup, dressed her in a flowered silk slip, a matching peignoir, and a pair of feather mules they found somewhere. They are good-hearted girls, and Carità frankly appreciated their attentions. They escorted her downstairs and seated her on a leather chair near the bar. And there she sat, looking ethereal and exotic, the whole night long.

As I sipped my tea and looked over the string of numbers I'd entered on my sturdy calculator, I had a sense of peace and accomplishment. The only sounds were the soft whir of the ceiling fan and the rustle of leaves in the evening breeze that made nights in the city so soothing, even restorative. I stood up, opened the screen, and stepped out onto the wide veranda. I couldn't see the sky; it was a dark blotch among branches. I went down the few steps, across the garden, and out the gate to the sidewalk, where I could see the moon. It was a waning sliver of white, fading in the west. I looked back at the house. The lights were off upstairs. Mimi and now this new girl, Carità, were asleep in their beds. It was my house, a thought that filled me with pride. And all around me the streets of San Alfonso sprawled out from the bay, some of its citizens still awake, no doubt, either up to no good, or heading home after a job, or drinking that first cup of coffee to start another day of work. It was my city. I had a place in it, and if you knew the right people, they could direct you to my door.

San Alfonso is my home, but I wasn't born here. I grew up on the windward side of the island, in a poor village nestled on the slope of green mountains we call "the hills." We were too far from the water for fishing, and the soil was too compact for farming. On the lee side of the mountains, the soil is rich and fertile, and along the riverbanks, the swampy land stays wet enough to grow rice. The farms in this central valley produce most of the vegetables, fruits, wheat, rice, and meat consumed on the island. Everything else, except fish, we import.

So food is cheap, but everything from cooking pots to motorcars comes in by boat, and we pay for the transport. It's a two-day boat trip to the mainland; tickets are expensive. Tourists come because it's always warm, fishing is good, lodging inexpensive, drugs are widely available, and prostitution is legal. In the interior, we have some interesting birds that are found nowhere else in the world. The rivers are dotted with falls and sulfur pools that make for warm, soothing baths, so we get birders, nature lovers, and arthritics. The only thing that keeps our island from being paradise on earth is the large human population, mostly crowded into our only city, San Alfonso, which sprawls around the deep bay on the east coast. Like port cities all over the world, San Alfonso is pleasure-loving, and notoriously corrupt, drawing the world's endless supply of crooks and con men to our shores.

What our island has in excess is fresh water—more than a hundred little rivers traverse it, none of them navigable—and coconut trees. Thus, our biggest export: coconut-oil soap.

In my village, all the adults worked at the soap factory, a vast tin-roofed, clapboard-sided monstrosity set smack on the opposite shore of the bubbling stream that ran past my school, where toxic lye fumes were a daily special on the lunch menu.

Apart from the fumes, I liked school, and my parents' little three-room house, with its wooden shutters, whitewashed walls, and pine floors, seemed fine to me—all my friends lived in similar houses. Chickens ran wild in the streets, and when it rained, the water poured off the tin roofs in sheets. On weekends, we gathered at the baseball field the soap company had fitted out with picnic tables, braziers, and even a small stage with a palm-covered roof where our local musicians practiced together in impromptu bands. The men played ball while the women tended the hot dogs and chicken grilling on the braziers, swatting the hot air away from their faces with palm fans.

Nobody ever went far. A trip to a fishing village was an adventure. But at school, we studied the history and geography of the island. In our book, there was a two-page photo spread of San Alfonso, the capital, with shops and a big open market, a park, two stone churches, a nursing school, and a university founded by the Jesuits, which, our teacher told us, was so highly ranked that students came from the mainland to study there. That all looked interesting, but what enthralled me was the photograph of not one but two movie theaters, both with giant marquees advertising the latest films. This was my dream. I would go to the city, buy a ticket, take my seat in an elegant theater (I'd choose the balcony), and munch popcorn from a paper bag while on the big screen before me beautiful women and dashing men sang and danced and played out magical stories for my pleasure.

My life was carefree, but my parents' life was hard. My father worked at the soap factory, in the mixing room. As soon as I was old enough for school, my mother took a job on the packaging floor. By the time I was twelve, my father was suffering from nasal and throat lesions. In the following year, his lungs were affected, and he was soon so weak he couldn't stand, much less work. Mother couldn't make enough money to feed us and care for him. In her desperation, she wrote to her sister, who lived in the city. My aunt and uncle owned a dress shop and had no children. My aunt wrote back, agreeing to take me in. I would live with them, attend the nearby public school, and work in the dress shop after school and on weekends.

I was frightened by my father's steady decline and anxious for my mother. She was determined to care for him until the end. We both knew this couldn't be far off. I had met my aunt once, on a brief visit she made when I was a small child; I had only a dim memory of a soft-voiced, slender lady in a tuniclike dress and a hat that fit close to her face. She had brought me a tin of violet candies. I had never met my uncle, and I knew my parents disapproved of him. So I had much to think about, to apprehend, to fear. But when I was alone in my bed, what I felt was such excitement I had to keep myself from grinning. My dream had come true. I was going to the city!

One balmy summer morning, after another exchange of letters, my mother packed my bag for me—in truth, I had precious little to take. I said goodbye to my father, who could only gasp, holding my hand with tears in his eyes. Then my mother and I walked five miles to the bus stop. I can still remember the thrill when those bus doors, like a raptor's wings, snapped open before me. My mother embraced me, and I promised to write to her. I turned away, lifting my suitcase as I climbed the two steps to the darkened interior, fiercely clutching in my free hand my one-way ticket to Central Station, San Alfonso.

My aunt was waiting for me at the bus stop, looking anxious and, of course, older than I remembered. I hardly noticed her, so entranced was I by the sights and sounds around me, the novelty of the taxi pulling up at the stand outside the station, the short ride through the downtown; I could smell the sea through the open window. The house was a neat bungalow, painted a soft pink with white shutters and concrete steps to the sidewalk. It was close to its neighbors, all similar structures lined up with narrow passages in between. Inside, my aunt led me past a few bright rooms with open shutters to the one chosen for me, which was windowless. It was the equivalent of a large closet, with a narrow mattress on an iron frame, a desk, a lamp, and a chair. I laid out my few belongings on the desk.

Aunt Irene was a fanatical housekeeper, and she made it clear that I was to confine myself to my closet and the kitchen. The floor of the room she called the living room, which no one ever entered, was covered in a bright-green wall-to-wall carpet with a deep nap she carefully brushed to go all one way. If you put so much as a toe on it, she knew.

The school, however, was welcoming: the teachers were kind yet strict, the students friendly and excitable. They teased me about being a country girl, but not cruelly, and I soon had a few friends who shared my passion for movies.

Within a year of my arrival in the city, both my parents were dead. My father's demise was expected, my mother's, according to my aunt, the result of exhaustion from the labor of nursing him. My aunt arranged to have them buried together in the village cemetery. When my school was out for the summer, she took me with her to lay a bouquet of lilies on the stone she'd had engraved with their names. "What wasted lives," she said, as we stood there in the harsh sun at the treeless cemetery. "I never understood why your mother stayed with him."

This was unfeeling, but I had come to expect universal disdain from my aunt. I also knew that she and my mother had been estranged by their marriages. More than once I had heard my mother observe to my father that she didn't understand why her sister didn't leave my uncle.

My uncle. His name was George. The owner of Paris, a shop for the fashionable woman. Once, when my mother spoke dismissively of her sister's husband, my father observed, "What kind of man runs a women's dress shop?"

Uncle George was that kind of man. The kind who liked to tell women what they should wear, who advised them about what looked good on them, what complemented their figures and coloring and personal styles. The kind who had subscriptions to three fashion magazines, which arrived every month from the mainland and were made available to his customers on a rattan table between two chairs near the dressing rooms. The kind who arranged folds and took in tucks, who kneeled before a woman with pins between his lips, turning up a hem. The kind who offered a line of expensive underwear, panties, and garter belts, push-up bras, and real silk stockings, displayed inside a glass case so that he must first take out the requested item and then, with an indulgent smile, pass it to the hesitant customer. The kind who stood very close, tenderly stroking the fabric of a skirt, while he assured the potential owner that this dress would make her husband wake up and pay attention.

The kind who flirted and flattered and seduced every woman he could, and had a sixth sense for how long it would take, and just how much of a problem each new conquest would eventually be. The kind whose ego was a carnivorous beast, who regarded women as meat, who disguised his raw appetite as sincere, as flattering, as reliable evidence of a particular attraction.

His life was a performance, and he was the star of the show. I had a ringside seat every day after school and sometimes on Saturdays, making tea for ladies who might like a cup while examining the latest fashion magazine, or ringing up sales, and, eventually, helping with the books. My uncle was a monster, and he used me abysmally, but he taught me how to keep books and run a business, and for that I credit him.

He wasn't a large man, but he took up a lot of space. He had a big, handsome head, and dark, burning eyes that felt hot when they focused on you. His conversation was pure aggression, disguised as witty repartee. He addressed everyone, male or

female, by their full name, which was very odd, but felt somehow distinguishing.

The store was an institution, on a busy downtown street that
had become steadily more upscale and desirable. He'd inher-
ited it from his father, who was a tailor and kept a small shop
where several women ran up dresses on sewing machines. This
was before ready-mades were available. George had turned this
shop into a spacious, attractive emporium, with flattering light
fixtures, fetching displays in the long window fronting the
street, racks of beautiful clothes, two curtained dressing rooms
with mirrors and seats, glass cases with displays of gloves and
undergarments, fresh flowers in vases on the counters, the chairs
and table where a friend or the occasional husband might sit while
his wife modeled her selections on a round platform before a big
three-sided mirror.

There was also a storage room, and in it a large couch, with
a side table and comfy cushions. In a little cabinet near the door,
George kept a bottle of whiskey and two tumblers. When he
had a success in his showroom-seduction enterprise, he would
usher his conquest past the curtain, inviting her to join him for
a cup of tea. They could talk privately on the couch. Mind the
shop, he ordered me. And I did.

He treated my aunt with a nosy authority that was exagger-
ated and fake, though she seemed to find it amusing. At first,
I thought she didn't know what he was up to in the shop, but
gradually I realized she had made up her mind not to know. She
never entered the store. He brought her dresses and stockings
and underwear carefully chosen to suit her, to flatter her, to fit

her. "I've memorized *all* your aunt's measurements," he said to
me with a wink.

I was fifteen when Uncle George followed me into the storage room and slipped his hand under my school skirt. My first
lesson in the treachery of uncles, including the unnecessary
advice that it wouldn't be a good idea to tell my aunt. In fact,
I had no desire to tell—I knew my aunt wouldn't believe me.
Or she'd say I'd brought it on myself with the tight skirts and
knitted tops I liked to wear. And maybe she was right. All we
girls talked about at school was sex. A few of us had gone all the
way with boyfriends, and we never tired of hearing the details
of their awkward couplings, in cars on a spit of land near the
sea, or in the park. We sympathized and empathized, wringing
our hands each month as one or another of us prayed for the
prompt arrival of our menstrual cycle. I didn't tell them about
my uncle, because I knew what I was doing wasn't the same as
making out with a boy your own age in a car. For one thing,
I wasn't anxious about my period, because my uncle was very
careful and always used a rubber.

I didn't tell anyone. But my aunt must have guessed, maybe
just by watching the way Uncle George looked up when I came
into the room. She had only distantly registered my presence for
the first year, then she tolerated me, but now she turned against
me. My grades, which were good, weren't good enough. It was
decided I must come straight from school to study in my room.

She declared that my work in the dress shop was just "lolling about," and I should do something useful to earn my keep. On weekends, she undertook deep cleaning of the house and set me to scouring the oven with steel-wool pads, scrubbing the shower stall with a toothbrush, taking down curtains and "airing" them on long rope lines in the little yard at the back of the house. My uncle and I were never alone, which was okay with me, but I wasn't allowed to see my friends, who were, in her view, "hoodlums." When I was seventeen, in my senior year at the high school, I had no money, and I was a prisoner. I had a girlfriend, Maggie, in similar straits—her parents had come down hard on her, and she wasn't allowed even to go to a school dance. We decided to quit school, find jobs, save our money, and move out together.

The most useful course I took in school turned out to be typing. I was good at it, and so was Maggie. We applied to a firm that ran a vast typing pool. No one asked our age, and many of the girls were as young as we were. It was grueling work, eight to six, sitting at a tiny desk in a vast, broiling room surrounded by a hundred other girls at their own tiny desks, clacking away at their machines. The noise was deafening, and the pay was pathetic, but it was respectable, and the firm required nothing but a typing test to be employed. My aunt didn't object to my leaving school to take a job. Of course, she added, she was sure I realized I'd have to pay room and board for the closet and my meals, now that I was gainfully employed. Uncle George said not a word. Sometimes I stared hard at him, but he wouldn't meet my eyes. Once, as he was eating his breakfast alone, and I was passing through the kitchen, I turned over a plate of scrambled eggs and bacon onto his lap. Without so much as a peep, he put the plate back on the table and carefully scooped up the eggs with his fingers.

Maggie and I typed all day, until our hands and forearms ached. After work we went to various clubs near the port, where men bought us drinks and we ate bar snacks for dinner. On the weekends, we studied the rental ads in the paper. In this way, in six months, we were able to put down two months' rent on a two-room flat with a kitchen and bath over a dive bar in a very run-down block near the water. We had a rickety balcony from which we could view the backs of warehouses and, farther downtown, the statue of the Virgin Mary atop Our Lady of Good Hope Church. She faced our way, pregnant and trium- phant, one hand slightly raised, inviting us to join her up there. We were free.

We shared one ambition: to get the hell out of the typing pool. One night, finishing a bottle of bourbon at our kitchen table, we agreed that there was almost nothing we wouldn't do to escape that mindless job. The one exception, the one thing we made a solemn vow neither of us would ever submit to, was the exchange of our liberty for the prison of marriage.

I found a job as a waitress in a fish restaurant, equally demeaning and low-paying, but at least it was relatively quiet, and one could speak to one's co-workers. One of these told me she had made a lot more money at the fishing tackle shop on the wharf, which had been converted to a brothel. The original sign was the new name—The Tackle Shop—which suggested that the owner had a sense of humor, though this turned out not to be the case. Inside, it was fetid and dirty and dark. All the lightbulbs were red, and there were no windows. The store space had been divided up into cubicles with curtains for doors and walls that ended nowhere near the ceiling. Each little room had a bed and a small table with a pitcher and washbasin. The sheets were changed once a week.

The patrons were mostly sailors, the crudest of men, who could imagine no greater pleasure than getting blind drunk and ramming their cocks into the nearest female they could find.

My interview with the harridan of a madam took ten minutes. Her cut was more than half, and as the sailors were poor themselves, tips were rare. Still, it was a lot more than I could make waitressing, and I was interested in the financial potential of the enterprise.

I saved my earnings, with the idea of having a house of my own instead of being at the beck and call of the tyrannical madam, who made my life miserable. She was worse than the men; they at least paid for my services. Mean and shrewd is one way to run a brothel, but I pictured something different. In my off-hours, I went downtown and saw rich men on the streets. If I had on some makeup and a pretty summer dress, they gave me the eye. But they never came anywhere near my place of work. They wouldn't be caught dead there, I thought. But what if there were an anonymous house in a good neighborhood where they could drop in for an hour or two, be treated respectfully, served decent liquor, guaranteed absolute secrecy?

When this house came up for sale, I knew I would have to act fast. The neighborhood was moving toward rather than away from respectability, and the house, though in need of repair, was commodious and solidly built, with a large double drawing room and a kitchen at the back. A wide veranda wrapped around one side. Upstairs were four bedrooms, two so large I could divide them each in half without having the effect of cribs. Brothels are legal on this island, so, once I drew up my business plan, I had no difficulty securing a mortgage. My first two girls were friends from The Tackle Shop. They got the word out, and I soon had a steady stream of applicants.

I introduced myself to Brutus Ruby, part owner of an upscale bar around the corner, another advantage of the neighborhood. It was well established, an island fixture listed in the tourist brochures, perfect for supplying my house with alcohol and customers. He understood at once that I would need a strong man for protection. After a bit of haggling about the split, and a brief, very pleasant affair, he settled in, and we've been together ever since.

My staff comes and goes—it's the nature of the business. When Carità joined us, I already had four girls I could rely upon.

Charlotte had been with me for five years. She was in her late twenties, a strong, healthy, good-looking young woman, with auburn hair and unusual green eyes, a frank manner, and a quick smile that lit up her face. She reminded me of the actress Maureen O'Hara—there was something of the Irish colleen about her.

Charlotte brought in Sally, who was eager to leave her boring job at a sewing factory with long hours and low pay. She was a forceful character, very nosy and pushy at times, full of opinions and advice. She was shapely—large breasts, wide hips, a tiny waist, short legs—and had a baby face with full lips, a snub nose, and thickly lashed dark-brown eyes. In the drawing room, she was always moving around, asking questions of the men, encouraging them to talk about themselves in a way that flattered them. She liked to organize people.

Vivien appeared at the kitchen door in the first week we opened. She'd heard about the house from Brutus, who was on the lookout for possible applicants at his bar. I liked her looks at once: slender and fine-boned, shapely, but nothing overblown, something elegant about her. Her wavy ash-blond hair fell just to her shoulders. Her features were sharp: slanted hazel eyes, high cheekbones, aquiline nose. Her lips were rather thin, and she applied her lipstick a little outside the edges. She had an affected manner, very theatrical and self-important. She struck poses, gazed critically into her wineglass before taking a sip, teased the men with little slaps on the wrist, as if scolding naughty boys.

Mimi, my college student, was the last to join us. She knocked at the clients' door one Sunday morning, and when I opened it, she said, "This is a brothel, right?"

I was taken aback. It occurred to me that she might be a journalist who wanted to write an exposé. "Why do you ask?" I said.

"I heard about it from a guy at the college." She was looking past me at the étagère and coat rack in the hall. "He said it's expensive and posh, so I figured it must pay well."

"I don't understand," I said.

She blushed charmingly. "Right," she said. "I'm not being clear. I'm looking for a job. I'm a student at the college, so I need a job I can fit around my schedule."

"Do you have any experience in this line of work?" I asked.

She gave this simple question a moment's serious thought. "I'd have to say yes," she said. "It's just that I've never gotten paid for it."

This amused me greatly. "Come with me," I said, ushering her into the hall. "We'll have a conversation."

Mimi definitely didn't look like a prostitute. She was as slim as a reed, small-breasted, flat-bellied. She stood with her narrow hips thrust slightly forward; when she sat down, she tended to slouch. She wore her straight black hair cut just below her ears with heavy bangs across her forehead. Her manner was boyish, but her face was strikingly feminine and very beautiful: high, dark brows over wide deep-brown eyes, a straight, slightly long nose, and a full, shapely mouth. To add to my screen-star comparisons, Mimi made me think of Leslie Caron.

Many of my girls came to prostitution the hard way, and often at an early age. Abusive relatives are common culprits, sometimes fathers or stepfathers, occasionally even grandparents, or, as in my case, uncles. I find, in general, uncles are a scourge on their innocent nieces if they can get their hands on them. I am not in favor of leaving girls between ten and sixteen in the care of uncles. It's asking for trouble.

Another path to the brothel, interestingly, is the marriage bed. Two of the girls working for me now, Charlotte and Vivien, made doomed marriages at an early age. Charlotte's husband was a day laborer who was injured on a construction job shortly after their marriage and is now confined to a wheelchair for life. Vivien married an alcoholic who pours every dime she can make down his throat. She has a little son she leaves with his drunken dad while she's working here, so, basically, her life is pure hell, but she can't figure out how to change it. These two go home to the prisons of their miserable marriages every night.

Mimi and Sally are ambitious girls, as I was. They are both saving their earnings to go into some business of their own. Mimi is studying politics, of all things. Sally is an excellent gardener and wants to run a plant shop. Some years ago, I had a strapping farm girl who astounded us all by opening a successful restaurant. Two of her clients from my house were her backers.

Nothing so puts a client off his game as a girl with bad teeth. They come to us with no end of bizarre fetishes, and it's true that some men find a small gap between the front teeth appealing (Sally has that), but missing teeth or very crooked teeth or any serious evidence of decay scares them off. This is why I'm so strict about dental hygiene. Twice-yearly visits to the dentist and the gynecologist: that's the medical insurance I provide for my employees, and they consider themselves lucky to have it.

The morning after Carità arrived, I called on our trusted dentist, Dr. Morrow, and he agreed to see her that very afternoon. His office is only a few blocks away, so I planned to walk her over myself. While I was drinking my second cup of coffee, Carità came down to breakfast in her sad little dress and sandals.

"Do you really have no other clothes than that?" I said.

"I have a suitcase at the hotel," she replied. "Bessie said she didn't think it would look good to arrive here carrying our bags."

I nodded, which I realized she didn't see. "Bessie's no fool," I said. "I'll send Brutus over to pick it up."

"That would be very kind," she said. Her voice, huskier than usual from sleep, had its marvelous lulling effect on me.

"There's coffee in the pot," I said. "The bread and milk are on the table." She put out her hand, resting her fingers on the edge of the counter. "Shall I show you where everything is?" I said.

"If you don't mind," she said.

I stood up and went to her side, guiding her deeper into the room. "The cups are on hooks here," I said, raising her hand to the rack. Quickly, she moved her fingers from one cup to the next, and chose a heavy ceramic mug from the bottom of the rack. "I like a big mug," she said. We moved on. "Here's the pot," I said. "The carafe handle is here. Be careful—the pot is hot." She grasped the handle, lifted the carafe, and filled the mug halfway without spilling a drop. "The table is behind you," I said.

"I remember," she said, turning to the table. She set the cup down carefully on the cloth and pulled out a chair. "May I sit here?" she asked.

"Yes. That can be your place," I said.

"Thanks."

"The bread is in front of you. There's a bowl of cream cheese and a plate of butter." I passed the bread to her, and she wrapped her fingers around the loaf and tore off a piece from the end.

"This is perfect," she said. "We always had a baguette and cream cheese for breakfast when I was a child. My teacher liked to pack the cheese into the end; she called it the nose."

"Are you still in touch with her?"

"Sadly, I'm not," she said. "When she went to the mainland to take care of her mother, I had a Braille typewriter, and we corresponded fairly regularly. But the typewriter got broken, and there was no one who knew how to fix it. In her last letter, she said her mother had died and she would be selling the house. So I don't know where she is, and she doesn't know where I am."

"That's too bad," I said.

"It is," she agreed. "Would you pass me the cheese?"

"I've made an appointment with the dentist for later today," I said. "It's nearby. I'll walk over there with you."

Her fingers strayed to her mouth, pushing into the offending gap. "Do you think he can fix this?" she said around the fingers.

"I do," I said. "He's quite good. Vivien's four front teeth are a bridge. You'd never guess that to look at her."

"Are they?" she said. Then it dawned on me that Carità couldn't look at Vivien's bridge, or anything else about Vivien. She tore the soft bread free of the crust and chewed while she spooned cheese into the nose. When she had swallowed, she lifted the mug and took a sip of coffee. "It's so good to be out of that awful hotel," she said cheerfully.

Dr. Morrow was interested in the story of the missing teeth. "These have been gone for some time," he observed.

"I was twelve," Carità replied. "I was running in a field, and a worker had left some machinery part in the path. The blade of a threshing machine, I think it was. I fell right into it."

"I see you cut your lip as well."

"It wasn't too bad," she said. "Only five stitches."

That was when I noticed that Carità had a thin scar above her lip, hardly visible unless one was looking for it.

"He did a good job," Dr. Morrow observed.

"He did," she said. "But nobody wanted to bother about the teeth, and I didn't care, since I can't see myself."

"Can you fix them?" I asked.

"Oh yes," he said. He was bent over his patient, gazing into the little mirror he had thrust between her teeth. "The gums are healthy. I can hook the bridge to the canine and that first molar. It will be a permanent bridge. I'll make her a temporary one until it's ready." He turned to his side table and began massaging a wad of pink gum. "First we'll take some impressions," he concluded.

As we were leaving, he drew me aside and spoke softly, though I didn't doubt Carità heard every word. "When you told me she was blind, I thought you'd lost your mind," he said.

"But now that I see her, I can understand why you'd want her for your house. She's sexy, and she's charming as well."

"Will you be visiting us soon?"

He smiled, raising his eyebrows and hunching up his shoulders. "I'll wait until I get the bridge in," he said.

"As you please," I said. For the amusement of no one but myself, as I turned to Carità I rolled my eyes.

Back at the house, we found Mimi and Brutus drinking coffee and eating clementines at the kitchen table. Mimi had a grumpy look about her, and I knew why. It was Wednesday, and she had a regular date with Mr. Duffy, owner of Duffy's Hardware and Appliances, a thriving emporium near the city center. Mr. D., as Mimi called him, was a talker. She had no doubt that his endless monologue was the reason his wife had left him five years ago, in the company of a builder who had a business on the mainland. At their first meeting, Mr. D. explained to Mimi that during his marriage he had always come home for lunch on Wednesdays, followed by intercourse with his wife. Why this routine hadn't satisfied her desire for marital relations was a mystery to him, but her parting words had been harsh, including upbraiding him for his insistence on the woeful Wednesday fuck. "I'm never having sex on a Wednesday again as long as I live," she declared, and then she was gone.

So now, on Wednesdays, he had lunch alone at a restaurant on the dock, and then he walked over to keep his appointment with Mimi. "You just have no idea," she told Carità, who was highly amused by this story, "how important it is that the correct screw is near the correct bolt on the counter display."

Brutus shook his head sympathetically. "You poor girl," he said.

"He talks right up to the magic moment," she continued. "It would be impressive if it weren't so boring."

"Do you say anything?" Carità asked.

"No," she said. "He's not paying any attention to me. He has never asked me a single question about myself."

"He pays well," I said. "And he never overstays his time."

"I know," Mimi agreed sullenly. "I shouldn't complain."

One morning after Carità had been with us for a few weeks, she joined me for a late breakfast, as it had been a long night. I was cooking eggs at the stove, and Carità was carefully buttering bread at the table. "How do you like your eggs?" I asked.

"Easy over," she said, "as Uncle Peter used to say." Her tone was cheerful, as at a pleasant memory. She went to the coffeepot, took down her mug, and filled it.

"Tell me about your uncle," I said, turning an egg with the spatula.

She took her place at the table, holding the mug between her hands. "Bessie hates him," she replied. "But he wasn't a bad man. He took us in when we were babies. My father's sister wanted to put us both in a foundling home. Uncle Peter saved us from that. He was my mother's brother, a bachelor, very rich then, and popular with the ladies. The story was, he'd been engaged to a sweet lady once, but she died of the flu a week before the wedding.

"The cook told me my uncle cherished my mother and was so heartbroken when she died he wept for a week. So he took us in and made sure we had nurses and teachers and learned to read and write. I think it amused him to have two little girls running around the property. He gave us free run of the house and the farm. I had a happy childhood. Lots of animals, chickens, dogs, cats, goats. I learned to ride a horse."

I slid the eggs onto a plate and placed it in front of her. "How is that possible?" I asked.

"I had a trainer. We worked in a big ring. I got to Level Three dressage."

I set my plate across from her and took my seat. "Does Bessie ride, too?" I asked.

She reached for the pepper and covered her eggs with a black scrim. "She's afraid of horses," she said. "Also dogs." She handed me the plate of bread.

"Thanks," I said.

She stabbed her eggs with the fork and swallowed a bite. "This is good," she said.

"So why does Bessie hate your uncle?"

"Because of me," she said.

"Because of what he did to you?"

"Well," she said, "what he did is a long story."

"I'm not in a hurry," I said. "Do you want more coffee?"

"Yes," she said, holding out her mug. "Please."

I filled it halfway.

"I guess it all started when I was fourteen. There was a boy who worked in the stable; his name was Jeremiah, and he smelled just like a horse. At first, he teased me, moving things around in the tack room so I couldn't find them. One day, he left a bucket of water in the doorway so I could fall over it. Then he rushed over to help me up and ran his hands all over me. I squirmed away from him and ran for the house, but I didn't tell anyone what happened."

"Not even Bessie?"

"No. I didn't understand what was going on. I didn't know a thing about sex. I just thought he was strange." She paused, cutting up the last of the eggs and swabbing a yolk with her bread, then chewing thoughtfully. "One day, not long after that, I was in the tack room hanging up my bridle when Jeremiah told me he had something he wanted to give me."

"I think I can guess what it was," I said.

She laughed. "You'd be right," she said. "I was such a fool. I thought maybe he had a present for me to make up for the bucket incident. He said, 'Put out your hand, Carità, and I'll give you a nice surprise.' So, I did, and he wrapped my fingers around his cock. It scared the daylights out of me; it was so warm and weirdly stiff, and alive. It moved in my hand, and I screamed.

"It happened my uncle had come in from a ride and was unsaddling his horse just outside the door. He burst into the room, caught Jeremiah with his pants around his knees, and knocked him to the floor. 'Get out of my sight,' he shouted, and then he took me by the elbow and steered me out of the barn and up the hill to the house. 'What did he do to you?' he asked. 'Did he hurt you?' I told him no, he'd just scared me, and that calmed him down. The next day, Jeremiah was gone.

"That night, Bessie told me all about what it was I'd felt, and that men had a hose between their legs that they peed through, and if they put it inside you, you could get a baby. I thought she was making up that last part.

"A few weeks after that, I was sitting at the dining-room table with my Braille typewriter, writing a letter to my teacher. This was after she had gone back to the mainland to look after her mother. Bessie was at the other end of the table, working on a dress pattern. Uncle came in and went to the sidebar to fix a seltzer and whiskey. I felt bad. My head ached, and I had stomach cramps. I pushed the typewriter away and stood up, and as I did, I felt a wet gush between my legs, running down to my knees. I was wearing pedal pushers, and the whole crotch was soaked. I put my hand down there and it came away wet. My uncle turned around and saw me. 'Good God,' he said. Bessie must have looked up then, because she gasped. She pushed her chair back and rushed to my side. 'What's going on?' I said.

"Uncle said to Bessie, 'Didn't you even tell her what to expect?' and Bessie said, 'I never did'; she sounded ashamed. So that was how everybody knew I'd got my period. Bessie told me now for sure I would get a baby if I ever let a man near me with his hose.

"A few months passed, and Uncle announced that he was taking me to the city to see a doctor. I said I wasn't sick, and he said he knew that, but now I was a woman, and he couldn't spend every minute with his eye on me. Every man who saw me was going to want to take advantage of me and ruin my life. He said he'd made up his mind.

"I didn't care about any of that; I was just excited to go to the city. Uncle said we'd stay at a hotel and dine in restaurants. I'd always wanted to go to a fine restaurant. Also, we'd walk along the waterfront where the big ships come in. I'd read about all that.

"So we went, just Uncle and me, in his car, with a driver, and we checked into a hotel near the park. I was in heaven. Everything smelled different, wonderful and strange—the hotel smelled like lavender and cloves. The sounds were all the bustle of people, talking and laughing, and the noise of cars in the streets. We went to the restaurant and had a big dinner; anything I wanted, Uncle said, so I had steak, which he told the waiter to cut up for me, and potatoes, and then crème caramel, and I ate half of Uncle's chocolate cake. Then we took a walk on the waterfront. The gulls were screaming; I'd never heard such a sound. There was a cool breeze, and I could hear the water rushing in and out under the pier. Uncle told me that in the morning the doctor would examine me between my legs, but he wouldn't hurt me, and I shouldn't be afraid.

"When we got back to the hotel, a friend of Uncle's was waiting to take him out on the town. 'You haven't lived until you've visited Mrs. Gulliver's house,' he said. Uncle escorted me to my room, and I went to bed while they came here." She opened her hands, indicating the kitchen. "And I guess they had a very fine time."

"Did he tell you about it?" I asked.

"Not then," she said. "In the morning, we had a big breakfast, and then we went to the doctor's office. Uncle had to stay in the waiting room. The doctor had a soft voice; there was a nurse as well, and she was very kind, helping me undress and put on a robe; and then she showed me how to get up on the table and put my feet in the stirrups. That made me think of my saddle, only I was on my back. She gave me an injection that burned a little, but then I just felt kind of dreamy. The doctor poked around; he kept saying things like 'This may feel a little cold, you may feel a bit of pressure,' and then he said he was finished, and I might have cramps or spotting.

"The nurse helped me dress again and led me out to my uncle. The doctor was speaking to him. When I came in, they fell silent, and I said, 'Is somebody going to tell me what this is all about?'

"The doctor explained he'd clipped some tubes together inside me so that I couldn't ever get pregnant. Then we got in the car and went home."

Carità paused and ran a piece of bread across her plate, mopping up bits of egg. She pushed it into her mouth and chewed.

So, I thought. He had her sterilized. "How did you feel about it?" I asked.

She sipped her coffee, considering my question. "I hardly knew what to think. It was over and done, and I'd had no say in the matter. I guess I wished Uncle had consulted me. But I'm not sure that, if he had, I wouldn't have agreed to it. My own mother died having me, so I have a reasonable terror of childbirth. I'd never had a mother, and I didn't particularly want to be one. Frankly, I'm not crazy about babies. So, in a way, I guess I felt relieved. When I got home, I told Bessie, and she cried, of course. That's when she took against my uncle."

I considered this story. Carità was clearly knowledgeable about sex, and she had come directly from her uncle's farm. "Did your uncle abuse you?" I asked.

She shook her head firmly. "No. It wasn't Uncle. I lost my virginity to my piano teacher, Mr. Percival Marker."

"Really?" I said. "How did he manage it?"

"Very gradually. Just lingering his hands on mine when he adjusted my position on the keyboard. A little pat on the shoulder. Standing behind me and pulling back my hair—a bit impatient in that maneuver. Giving me a quick kiss on the cheek when I did well. Endearments. Compliments. How talented I was. How forceful my playing was for a girl. I knew what was up, that's for sure."

"Did you discourage him?"

"Not much. One day, as he was packing up to leave and I was sitting on the bench next to him, he put his hand under my chin, raised my face, and kissed me."

"This sounds like a romance novel," I said.

"It does, doesn't it? But I wasn't in love. I was just curious."

"So did you have sex on the piano bench?"

She chuckled. "No. It was on the carpet under the piano. It was a baby grand."

"How long did this go on?"

"Once a week for a few months. I didn't like it at first. It hurt. But then it stopped hurting, and I did like it. Percy was terrified that my uncle would find out."

"And did he?"

"Oh yes. The cook came into the music room one day; she didn't hear any music, and she wanted some herb that was in a pot on the windowsill. She just opened the door, saw us, and backed away. The next day, my uncle called me in and said that Mr. Everett would no longer be employed as my music teacher. The next week, I had a new teacher, a lady from San Alfonso who was brilliant. My playing really improved."

"How old were you?" I asked.

"Seventeen," she said. "Not long after that, a big storm destroyed the rice crop. Uncle was in debt from the sheath blight, and that wiped him out. He started drinking a lot, and he was selling things. No more riding lessons, then he sold my horse; no more piano teacher, then he sold my piano. It went on for over a year.

"Then, one night, about a week before he shot himself, he told me about your house and what girls get paid to do here, and he said he thought I might be in demand and I'd be safe, because he saw how you and Brutus keep the men in line. He asked me what I thought about that, and I said I wanted to be in the city, and it sounded all right. I thought I could do it. Then he cried. Everybody was weeping by then. Bessie never stopped; even the cook was weeping into the soup. Everybody but me."

"Why didn't you cry?" I asked.

"Well, not because I can't, which is what some people think," she said impatiently. "I just don't see the point of it. People who are crying are people who need a plan."

This made me smile. Carità was incapable of self-pity. Her

way was: head down, push on. "And is it all right for you here?"
I asked. "Can you do it?"

"Some of the men aren't very pleasant," she said. "It's like
they want to humiliate you."

"That's true," I agreed.

"If I wanted to tell someone they were worthless to me, I
don't think I'd pay them to let me do it."

"They think the fact that you'll take money to let them do
it proves that you're worthless."

She considered this. "That's it, isn't it?" she said. "You
can't win."

"You win if you don't care what they think. And you get
paid."

"Well," she said, "I truly don't care what they think. And I
make a lot more money than Bessie does. So . . . I guess I win."
She arranged her knife and fork on the plate, folded her napkin,
and passed it across her lips. "I like the other girls," she said. "I
feel I have friends here."

"They like you as well," I said.

She stood up and carried her plate and utensils to the sink.
"It's all right," she said. "I can do it." For a moment I thought
she meant she could wash the dishes, but I realized she was
answering my question about the job. Then she turned on the
tap, took up the sponge, and carefully cleaned her plate.

A few months passed, and Carità fell into the routines of
the house. Dr. Morrow fitted her with a bridge that looked per-

fectly natural, and she took to smiling easily. She dressed in provocative costumes at night, but in the daytime, she wore her own clothes and made herself comfortable. She was working steadily enough to get an idea of how much she could earn, so she was motivated. Carità loved money. One afternoon, Dr. Morrow came by, and when I told her he had a standing discount, she was clearly irritated. He kept her an hour and went away saying he was well satisfied. Vivien and I were in the kitchen when she came down a few minutes later, wearing a cotton blouse and a pair of pedal pushers. She ignored our greeting and went directly to the coffeepot.

"Any problem?" I asked her.

"No," she replied, filling her mug. She took a chair next to Vivien and plopped down moodily.

"I've only enjoyed Dr. Morrow's attentions once," Vivien remarked. "What did you think?"

Carità sipped her coffee, then set the mug back carefully on the table, keeping her hands wrapped around it. "Too much licking," she said, wrinkling her nose comically.

Vivien let out a hoot of laughter. "I know," she agreed. "Why does he do that?"

"He talked a lot, too," Carità continued. "He told me he had a daughter who died when she was two, but if she'd lived, she'd be my age."

"I had no idea," I said. "I didn't know he'd been married."

"I think it's creepy that he told you that," Vivien observed.

"He's just kind of sad," Carità concluded.

Dr. Morrow was indeed a sad character, but beyond his patronage and his professional services, he had proved a useful resource for my house. On infrequent occasions, at my request, he arrived carrying a small black leather case that contained a few tools not required for dental procedures.

Like so much of the world, this island is run by hypocritical men whose passion for controlling women's bodies knows no limit. Their own sexual profligacy is a matter of pride, and it's understood that their desires must be gratified without impediment. Hence, prostitution is legal, and abortion is not.

We provide "French letters," and our gynecologist fits the girls with flexible caps, but there is always the cavalier customer who maintains that rubbers diminish his pleasure. Though the caps are effective, they are not foolproof. For this reason, a few years ago, when Charlotte requested a private conversation with me on our closed day, I wasn't entirely surprised. She appeared at the kitchen door and stood gazing through the screen at me, her expression so sorrowful I knew at once what was wrong. "Sit down," I said. "I'll fix you a chamomile."

She had missed two periods.

"Dr. Morrow can do it," I said. I poured boiling water over the tea bag and set the cup in front of her.

She furrowed her brow. "He's a dentist," she observed skeptically.

"He chose dentistry because it's lucrative and he's on his own," I explained. "He did two years of medical school."

"Is it expensive?"

"Very," I said. "It's also dangerous. It can be very painful when the contractions start. If infection sets in, it could kill you."

She sipped the tea while tears silently filled her eyes and spilled over, making thin streaks down her cheeks.

"When I was young," I said, "I worked in a house where two girls died—one in the hospital, the other just bled to death in her room. A midwife came there regularly. The madam didn't care about caps or rubbers, and it was just bad luck if you got pregnant. Those two deaths were out of twenty that went off without a hitch, so the odds are good. Dr. Morrow has done four for me with no complications. It will knock you flat for a couple of days at least."

She took up a paper napkin and patted away her tears. "I can't afford it," she said.

"I'll split the fee with you, and you can pay the rest in installments," I said. "He likes you. He won't press you for cash, and there's no interest. You just pay what you can every month."

She nodded, sniffing, then applied the napkin to her nose and blew hard.

"Do I go to his office?"

"No indeed," I said. "He does it here. Right on this table. He wants to be near the door. If he got caught, he could go to jail. And so could I."

She nodded. "I don't have any choice," she said. The tears had stopped, but her expression was grim.

I wrapped my hand around hers on the table. "I'm so sorry, Charlotte," I said.

"When can I do it?"

"The sooner the better. I'll speak to him today. Early morning is best, six a.m. or so. That way, you can go home and rest all day. With luck, it will be over by the next morning."

"I can come at six," she said. "How long does it take?"

"Not long. Half an hour. The procedure isn't painful. You'll have time to go home before you feel anything."

When I told Dr. Morrow of Charlotte's predicament, he exhibited a thin sliver of human feeling. "Poor girl," he said. "Her husband is in a wheelchair, isn't he?"

"Yes," I said. "And he has no family. She's his sole support. I'll pay you half up front. She can't afford to pay the rest all at once."

"No," he said. "I understand. We'll make a schedule."

The procedure was simple enough. He used a speculum to open the uterus and a syringe to flood it with saline solution. I stood by with towels and encouragement. He told Charlotte that in the next twenty-four hours she would feel some cramping and that she should then sit on the toilet for as long as it took for the "matter" to pass out of her. He packed up his tools and was out the door with a caution that we were to speak to no one and must not call upon him again, even if she wound up in the hospital.

When he was gone, Charlotte propped herself up on her elbows, gazing at the towel between her legs. A little fluid seeped out, but no blood. "That's it?" she said.

"Now comes the hard part," I replied.

She sat up, swinging her legs off the table. "I'm going straight home," she said. "Jamie was asleep when I left, but he'll be waking soon and wanting his breakfast. With any luck, he'll never know this happened."

"I hope so," I said. Then I gave her a box of pads and sent her on her way.

I heard nothing from her that night, nor did I expect to. Vivien had agreed to stop by her house in the morning, and it was a good thing she did, for she found poor Charlotte half naked and semiconscious, writhing and moaning in a spreading pool of blood on the bathroom floor. In his panic to help her, her husband had gotten his wheelchair jammed in the doorway and slid to the floor, where he lay on his side, sobbing and calling for help, unable to reach her.

Vivien ran to the pharmacist near their house and told him her friend was dying. He had an ambulance dispatched from the hospital. By the time they got there, Charlotte was unconscious.

She was in the hospital for two nights. The diagnosis was hemorrhaging caused by a miscarriage. They gave her blood, cleaned her out, and informed her that it was unlikely she would ever bear children. Her response to this last pronouncement surprised them. "Thank God," she said. Then she burst into tears.

One hot night in early September, when there was hardly a breath of air stirring, the clients were lounging about in the drawing room, as limp as sick kittens and just as difficult to please. I put an old samba record on the player to cover the lull in the conversation and told Jack to serve up a pitcher of gin and tonic with plenty of ice, on the house. There was so little action I thought we might have an early closing, but near midnight, two college students appeared at the door. I recognized one of them, an obnoxious youth, strutting and preening, his chest puffed out like a rooster's. He patted Mimi on her buttocks as he passed her on the way to the bar. His name was Ben Betone, BB to his intimates, the son of Marcus Betone, the rich, powerful, soft-spoken gangster who owned a laundry chain where you could get your linen or your money laundered. Marcus didn't deal drugs, but stolen shipments of alcohol and tobacco were in his purview. He controlled a gang of hoodlums whose sworn allegiance he commanded. They were occupied in gun running, graft, and protection rackets. He also enjoyed the confidences of a few key politicians, who relied on him to discredit their opponents around election time. He'd appeared at my door when I was just setting up the house, offering a reasonable fee for laundry service and intimating that certain protections were included in the price. His son, BB, was spoiled, headstrong, vain, and conscious of his position as heir apparent to his father's empire. Marcus's ambitions for his son included what he himself had never obtained: a college education. BB was majoring in business. Without his father's knowledge, he was getting an early start on his career by providing his fellow students with all the drugs and weapons they could afford. He never slept, so he went about with that "Fuck you, don't bore me" edge that girls his age found attractive, though an older woman could see at a glance that what he really needed was a nap.

He had our password from his father, who patronized my house infrequently and always hurriedly. The girls were keen on the father; he left large tips, was neat and clean in his habits, and, though brusque, was never unkind or crude. BB, they despised. Lottie had refused to go with him. Mimi, who was his favorite, was always gloomy when she came down after a bout with him. "He takes forever," she said. "And he's cheap."

Behind BB came a second young man, a fellow student, no doubt, who hadn't been in the house before. He was a lanky, pale boy with shocking, ungreased, shoulder-length, wavy blond hair, and dark, restless eyes, dressed in a loose seersucker jacket over a black T-shirt and white linen pants. He drew his shoulders up and back as he entered the room, and his eyes darted about furtively, taking in the scene: the barman polishing a glass, the paintings of debauched women in various degrees of deshabille on the walls, the girls, also variously undressed, in conversations with overheated men in street clothes who appeared relaxed, a little bored, engaged, one way or another, in being seduced. His gaze wandered to the couples dancing languidly to the dreamy music from the player; to the good carpet and tasteful furnishings; to Charlotte, dressed in a red lace petticoat and a black satin bustier, bending over so as to give a full view of her lifted breasts to an overweight bald man in a too-tight vest seated on the divan; and, finally, to me. I was standing near the bar with a gin and tonic in my hand. I nodded and lifted my glass, summoning him to join me. When he was close, I said, "You're a new face in our midst."

He ducked his head, failing to meet my eyes. "Sure," he said. "May I offer you a drink?"

A double nod, a swallow of air. "Sure," he said again.

"I'm Mrs. Gulliver," I said.

"I'm Ian," he replied.

I touched his elbow to turn him toward the bar. "This is Jack." Jack put his hand out, and Ian was quick to respond. "This is Ian," I said.

"What can I fix you?" Jack asked.

He glanced at the bottles arranged behind Jack's attentive face. "Rum and Coke," he said. "On the rocks."

"Coming up," said Jack.

"I see you came with our friend BB," I said. "That makes me think you must be a student at the college. Am I right?"

"Yes," he said. "That's right."

Sally, who was got up in a blue silk kimono with chopsticks stuck in her chignon, pushed in beside our new customer, her red lips fairly panting with anticipation. "Who is this?" she cooed to me.

Ian took his drink and turned to her coolly. "I'm Ian," he said.

"Aren't you an attractive boy," she said.

I left them, to rescue Vivien. BB was berating her, for some reason, giving her cheek a series of sharp little pats with his fingertips while he repeated, "Listen to me, you listen to me."

"Your friend seems shy," I said. He left off ragging Vivien and turned to me, his eyes narrow, his mouth screwed up in a sullen pout. He looked past me at Ian, still at the bar, treating Sally to his monosyllabic responses.

"He's a baby," BB observed. "The college girls are all over him. He needs a woman with some experience."

"If Sally has to do all the talking," I said, "she's going to get parched. He should buy her a glass of champagne."

Vivien backed me up. "I could use a glass of champagne," she said. "I find it makes me listen better."

For some reason, this amused the mercurial BB. "Order a bottle," he said.

This caused old man Gautier, who was breathing in Charlotte's flowery perfume, to call out, "Put one on my tab as well."

The girls all murmured with pleasure. The evening was rescued. As I returned to the bar to help Jack and Sally serve out the glasses, Ian drifted away. He approached Carità and made some light remark, gesturing to her feathery mules. I wasn't close enough to hear him, but I could observe his face, and I watched to see the moment when he realized she was blind. She made a reply, smiling charmingly, turning her ear toward him as she always did when someone spoke to her. He nodded and laughed nervously—her reply evidently amused him. He sipped his drink, settling his full attention upon her. Another remark, another reply. She lifted her chin as she spoke, and her eyelids dropped halfway. He drew his head back, his expression complicated. He realized she couldn't see him. His eyes darted about the room as if seeking a place to land. He found my steady gaze and, without so much as an excuse, left her side and made a beeline for me.

"Are you enjoying yourself?" I asked.

"Is that girl blind?" he asked.

"She is," I replied.

His brow furrowed dramatically, a parody of concern. "What is she doing here?"

"Her name is Carità," I said. "And what she's doing here is what we all do here."

"It's obscene," he said. "You're exploiting a disabled person."

"She came to me, looking for work," I replied. "She's under no obligation; she can leave whenever she likes."

"But you're making a profit," he snapped.

This caused me to focus closely on the boy. "So—you're a law student," I observed.

"That's beside the point," he said. "She came to you for help. Does she understand what sort of life you've forced on her?"

"Do you?" I said.

He stood looking aghast for a moment, then turned abruptly and went back to Carità's side. He bent over her, speaking softly. She leaned back in her chair, raising her beautiful face to his, exposing her alabaster neck and a tantalizing hint of cleavage to his view. She said something that made him smile. He stretched out his hand and brushed a stray lock of hair from her shoulder. Then he stepped back and brought his fingertips to his lips.

BB, who was opening his wallet to pay for an hour of Mimi's time, called out to him. Ian joined him for a brief exchange. Then, without so much as a nod in my direction, he passed into the hall and out the side door.

It was nearly dawn when I pulled off all my clothes and slipped gratefully between the sheets on my bed. As I drifted to sleep, I recalled the image of Ian bending over Carità, daring only to graze her hair with his fingertips. He'd be back with some cash in his pocket, I had no doubt. He was a romantic, self-righteous boy, and I liked the idea of him with Carità, two healthy young bodies drawn together by sexual attraction and not much else. Brutus had been charmed by her playfulness in bed, but for this boy, this Ian, she would be a revelation. The thought made me smile. She would forget him in a month, but he would remember her for the rest of his life.

Carità slept late the next morning. Mimi had gone off to the library, and I had read everything in the paper but the weather report by the time I heard Carità moving around upstairs. She came down a few minutes later, dressed in her favorite Capris and a short, sleeveless white cotton blouse with a Peter Pan collar. We exchanged good mornings, and she helped herself to coffee. "I slept so deeply," she said, setting her mug down and pulling out her chair.

"We were all up very late," I said. I pushed the bread toward her, and she took it between her hands and tore off half the loaf.

"I had a strange dream," she said.

I wondered what her dreams must be like. "What happened?" I asked.

She reached for the cheese plate. "When?" she said.

"In your dream."

"Oh," she said. "I was in a room, and there was something in there with me, a kind of force. I knew it was there, but it wasn't touching me. Then I tried to open the door, and the knob turned, but I couldn't pull it open. Because of the force. I just kept turning the knob and pulling, but the door wouldn't open."

"Were you afraid?" I asked.

"No. I was just determined to get that door open. Then I woke up." She dragged the knife through the cheese and smeared it onto her bread. "Dreams are weird," she concluded.

I folded my paper and sat gazing at her. She sipped her coffee calmly, then, as she was lifting the bread to her lips, she paused, her face brightened, and she turned her attention to the yard. "Mimi's here," she observed.

I looked out the door to see Mimi locking her bike to the fence, hoisting up her backpack, pushing through the gate, and charging up the porch steps. She threw open the screen, stepped inside, and lowered the heavy backpack roughly to the floor with a loud thump. "God, it's hot out there," she said.

"You've got a lot of books," Carità observed.

"I do," Mimi agreed. "I've got a big econ exam this week."

"I thought you were studying politics," I said.

"That's my major. But I'm thinking of minoring in economics. It's a good combination."

I got up, opened the refrigerator, and looked inside. There was a pitcher of cold tea left over from the day before. "There's iced tea," I said. "Would you like a glass?"

"I would," said Mimi, pulling out the chair next to her friend.

"Is economics about business management?" Carità asked.

"No," Mimi replied. "It's about economic theory. We study theories of production and labor in market economies. That's what it says in the course description. This exam will cover two bigwig theorists: Adam Smith and Karl Marx."

"Karl Marx I've heard of," I said, filling our glasses with ice.

"Do they disagree?" Carità asked.

"They do," Mimi replied. "Though not entirely. Smith is all for competition and rational self-interest. He thinks a division of labor is good. I make a product I don't need—say, a basket or a screw—and I sell it to someone who wants it. We both improve our situation. The standard of living is raised for all classes, and this leads to more freedom and what he calls 'universal opulence.'"

I brought our glasses to the table and set one down before Mimi.

"And what does Marx think?" Carità asked.

I recalled the name from high school. "He was a communist, wasn't he?" I put in.

Mimi gave a wan smile at my ignorance. "Not exactly," she said.

I sat down, feeling the dull anxiety that comes over me whenever talk turns to abstract ideas. Universal opulence, for example, struck me as a good name for a movie theater.

"What does Marx think?" Carità repeated.

"Well, Marx is obsessed with class conflict. He thinks the class division inherent in a capitalist economy creates a chasm between those who own the means of production and those who have nothing to offer but their labor. For example: a car factory. The factory owner determines what the workers' labor is worth. The products these workers produce—in this case, cars—are then sold for profit *by* the owners and *for* the owners. This necessarily results in exploitation of the laboring class, who must eventually revolt, leading to the destruction of the whole capitalist system."

"Those who have nothing to offer but their labor," Carità repeated. She sipped her coffee, nodding her head slowly. "That would be us," she said softly.

"Not exactly," Mimi said. "We're in a service industry, and Marx doesn't have a lot to say about that. We labor, God knows, but we don't produce anything you can take home and hang on the wall or use to make a cup of coffee. There's no viable product."

I tried to think of what viable product my business produced; the only thing that came to mind was sperm. Not something I could sell. I repressed a laugh.

"What does Smith think of that?" Carità asked.

"He thinks service workers are unproductive workers, and the fewer of them an economy supports, the greater the productive capacity will be." She reached across the table and added a spoonful of sugar to her tea. "He's very down on priests, lawyers, and bankers."

"And women like us," Carità concluded.

"Definitely," Mimi agreed. "Lawyers and priests get all kinds of benefits; women like us, and probably actors, too, have to scratch out whatever they can."

"So . . . Smith thinks a market economy will make everyone

richer and happier, and Marx thinks capitalism will end in a revolution of the laboring class," Carità concluded. "Do I have that right?"

"That's pretty much it," Mimi said.

We were silent for a moment. I considered Carità's summary, pleased to find that I now understood the views expressed by Smith and Marx. Both seemed persuasive to me. "So who's right?" I asked Mimi.

She shrugged.

But Carità said, "Marx is right."

The following Saturday, as I expected, BB and his sidekick, Ian, arrived late in the evening. Carità and Charlotte were both upstairs with a banker from the mainland, who had come in with Mr. Smythe, the manager of the island branch and a regular client of ours. Ian went straight to the bar and stood, sipping his rum and Coke, surveying the scene with a knowing air. It was a sultry night with a warm, wet breeze lifting the curtains. The melancholy songs on the player contrasted with the staccato rustling of the plantain trees near the window. Vivien approached Ian, patting her lips with her lacy handkerchief, like some antebellum character in a film. She never failed to tell her dates that she was named after Vivien Leigh. "Is it too hot to dance?" she asked flirtatiously.

He looked down at her, drawing his drink close to his chest as if he thought she might snatch it. "I don't dance," he said.

"It's just as well," she replied agreeably. "It's too hot."

BB, steering Mimi by her elbow, joined his friend. "She's nagging me for a drink," he said. Jack set a champagne glass on the bar and pulled the open bottle from the ice bucket. As he filled the glass, Ian drained his drink. "Have another," BB said. "It's on me."

Mimi laughed. "You two are like a comedy act," she said.

We all heard a shout from upstairs, and in the next moment the visiting banker appeared, his jacket slung over one arm, his shirt unfastened. He paused on the landing to fasten his pants and announced to the room joyfully, "I surrender!"

"Another satisfied customer," Mr. Smythe said to me, slurring every word. He'd been drinking steadily for three hours.

"Those girls," the banker continued, reeling down the steps. "Those girls." He crossed the carpet and collapsed next to his friend on the divan. "There's nothing they don't know," he concluded.

I saw Ian taking in this remark, his eyes making a quick inventory of the banker's cheerful disarray. It dawned on him that the reason he didn't see Carità was that she had been cavorting in bed with this paunchy, red-faced man twice her age. He looked past the two men on the divan, who were refilling their glasses from an open bottle on the side table, to the staircase. His eyes were fixed, a little wild. I'd seen that look before: the young hero on a rescue mission. Was he going to bolt up the stairs to her room? I took a step toward the door and stuck my head out into the hall, where I could see Brutus at his post, ever on the alert. I lifted my chin, and he came along to see what I needed.

I knew Charlotte and Carità wouldn't be down right away.

They were washing up together at the bidet in the big bathroom at the back of the house. I pictured Ian bursting into that lively scene. Carità was like a child at a fountain with that bidet; she'd never had one before and she liked to put her thumb over the spigot and splash water in all directions.

Whereas, I thought, this Ian, with his serious scowl and diffident manner, was incapable of youthful high spirits. What did he imagine he had to offer a working girl?

Brutus stepped into the room and stood blocking the doorway, as calm and inscrutable as a monument. Ian sipped his drink at the bar, where BB was fondling Mimi's breast and nuzzling her neck with his wet lips. He lifted his head to speak to Ian. Vivien joined them, trying once again to engage Ian in some harmless banter, but to no avail. When BB commenced pushing Mimi toward the hall, Ian set his half-full glass on the bar and followed them. At that moment, we all heard voices chattering and then Carità's deep, breathy laughter. I looked up to see her on the landing, leaning on Charlotte's arm. Charlotte whispered something in her ear. They clutched each other, convulsed in laughter. BB pushed Mimi up a couple of steps, unsmiling and distracted. He turned to look back at Ian, who at the sound of Carità's voice had ducked past Brutus into the hall. "Here comes your salvation," BB said to his friend.

Carità released Charlotte and turned to face the group gathered below her: BB and Mimi on the steps, Ian at the foot of the stairs, Brutus and me blocking the drawing room. She touched the stair rail lightly with her fingertips. She knew Ian was there, I thought, though he hadn't spoken.

"Make way," BB commanded, pushing past her. Charlotte

and Carità continued down and across the hall, where Brutus stepped aside to let them pass. Ian, casting me a guarded look, followed closely. Carità returned to the leather chair while Ian went to the bar and procured a flute of champagne, which he carried to her. He bent over her, speaking softly. She smiled as her fingers closed on the glass stem, and she lifted her free hand to touch first her own cheek and then his. He kneeled before her, his face cradled in her hand, speaking earnestly, while she sipped his meager offering. She was fond of champagne.

"This is too sweet," I said to Brutus.

"I don't trust that kid," he replied.

In the morning, I was alone in the kitchen when Bessie arrived to take Carità for her Sunday outing. She was dressed neatly in a skirt and blouse, with a straw sun hat that made her look like a hick. She'd brought a hat for her sister, and a white folding stick, which, she explained, she'd been looking for all over town and finally purchased at a secondhand store. It would be useful to Carità when walking on the street, as people noticed it and were careful not to run into her. "It lets her be more independent," she concluded.

I offered her a cup of coffee. She accepted readily, taking the chair at the table nearest the door. "I'm a little early," she said.

"I see that," I agreed.

"I just wanted to have a few minutes to talk with you about how Carità's doing here."

"I think she's doing well," I said. "But she can tell you that herself."

"She won't tell me anything about here," she said. "She asks me if I want to talk about my job, and I say no indeed, I do not."

"So what do you talk about?"

"Oh, the old days, I guess. And I tell her about what I can see in town. She gets it all mapped out in her head; she's a wonder."

"She is," I agreed. "She makes friends easily. The other girls are fond of her."

"I'm so glad to hear that," Bessie said. She took a sip of the coffee. "It's just a big relief for me to hear that."

I noticed her hand wrapped around the mug. It was rough and reddened, with two unhealed cuts on the knuckles. "And how is your work going?" I asked.

She noticed that I was studying her hand and quickly covered it with its equally unsightly mate. "It's fine," she said. "I do look forward to my day off, I'll say that."

"I'm coming, Bessie," Carità called out from upstairs. We heard her footsteps, quick and sure, descending the stairs. Then she appeared, dressed in a childish cotton blouse with a pattern of ducks on it and a pair of sky-blue pedal pushers—clothes she'd brought from home. I assumed Bessie had chosen them for her. Her hair was tied back in a ponytail, and her face was freshly washed, makeup-free.

"I brought you a stick, sweetie," Bessie said, pushing back her chair. "I finally found one."

"Thank you so much," Carità said; she held her arms out and embraced her sister heartily. "It's a gorgeous day," she added. "Let's go to the park."

"We can do that," Bessie said. "We can have lunch at the sandwich shop there."

And off they went on their weekly adventure, which I knew Bessie dreamed of all through the long days on her feet, endlessly prying open recalcitrant bivalves, and probably during her empty nights as well, alone in a grim, hot little room in a house where none of her neighbors even knew her name.

I was buttering my toast when I heard the back gate close; a moment later, Brutus came in the door. He looked gloomier than usual, and as he seldom visited me on a Sunday, I concluded something was on his mind. I poured him a mug of coffee and set it at his place on the table. "Thanks," he said, pulling out the chair.

"What's up?" I asked.

"It's that fucking BB and his moon-faced friend," he said.

"Ian," I said. "He's got a crush on Carità, but he doesn't have the money to pay for her."

"He's found a better way," he replied cryptically.

"What could you mean?"

"I'll tell you. After he left here last night, he went to my bar. BB came in later, and they had a few drinks together. My bartender told me BB was picking a fight with Joe Shock."

Joe Shock was the dark king of the island underworld. Unlike Marcus Betone, who fashioned himself a man of principle advancing the interests of his organization, Joe was in it for himself, and there was nothing he wouldn't do in the criminal line. His cover was an antiques emporium, but his actual business was dealing drugs and firearms, with a sideline in human trafficking, especially minors and immigrants, and contract murder. His was the force on the island Marcus Betone offered protection against. He had no family, few friends, and contempt for the police, though it was rumored that the police chief worked for him. "That's not a good idea," I said.

"My bartender thinks there was a drug deal going down. At one point, BB pulled out a pistol, just to show what a contender he is, but Joe laughed at him and he put it away."

"Where was Ian during this?"

"He wandered off when things got hostile and didn't come back."

"But you know where he went," I guessed.

"I do," he said. "I'm coming to that."

"Well, get there," I said.

He took a swallow of coffee, enjoying spinning out his story. "After I close up the bar, do the books, it's late, maybe three, three-thirty. I walk back past here to my car, and I hear voices coming from the porch."

"I didn't hear anything," I said.

"Your window was dark; I figured you were asleep. So . . . I come inside the gate, and what do you think I find?"

"I think you're going to tell me."

"It's young Ian and Carità going at it on the wicker chaise."

I considered this unexpected information. "Are you sure it was them?"

"Oh yes," he insisted.

"What did you do?"

"I didn't do anything. I just backed out the gate and went home."

"Then she doesn't know you saw her."

"Not yet," he said.

I didn't like this story. If Carità wanted to take a lover, that was fine with me, but not on my back porch. "I'll talk to her," I said.

Brutus nodded, but he wasn't satisfied. "I hate that kid," he said. "Who does he think he is?"

"He's madly in love," I said.

"Oh, for God's sake," Brutus muttered. "He's just a punk who thinks he's big stuff because he goes to college."

"He's a romantic," I said.

"Right," Brutus agreed. "He's Percy fucking Shelley."

"What do you know about Percy Shelley?" I said.

"I went to high school," he snapped. "We had English teachers."

"Mrs. Voisin," I said.

"You had her, too?"

I nodded.

"That woman worshipped Percy Shelley," he said.

"It's not a bad comparison," I said. "Ian is self-righteous

and thinks he's morally superior to everyone else. Shelley was like that."

"What a joke," Brutus rejoined. "How low do you have to sink, morally speaking, to take advantage of a blind whore?"

I let that question hang in the air between us for a moment, pointing the finger at us both.

"I'll talk to her," I said.

Carità was in a good humor when she and Bessie returned that afternoon. "We had an excellent lunch," she said. "No boring sandwiches."

"Where did you go?"

"It's called La Brise," Bessie said. "Carità insisted."

"Sally told me about it," her sister said. "She has a cousin who works in the kitchen. She said it's popular and has a big patio. I just wanted to sit outside and be waited on."

"I told her she should save her money," Bessie said, looking sternly at me for confirmation.

"I think it's okay to splurge now and then," I said.

After a few more exchanges on the subject of thrift, Bessie allowed that she was working the evening shift and was now so sleepy from the large meal she would need a nap before going to her job. She embraced her sister, shook hands with me, and let herself out the kitchen door.

"Poor Bessie," Carità said when we heard her closing the gate. "She takes life so hard."

"She works hard," I said.

"That's true," she agreed. "And she's not going to meet anyone who can help her on that job."

This was so obvious I made no reply. I was thinking of a way to bring up the subject of Ian. Carità leaned against the counter, looking wistful. Then she smiled. "There must be red honeysuckle in your yard," she said.

"There is," I said. "How do you know?"

"I can hear the hummingbirds."

I listened as hard as I could listen. I heard nothing. "I don't hear anything," I said.

"I know," she said brightly. "Being sighted just ruins your hearing."

That's what we are to her, I thought. The sighted. The ones who can't hear, who can't find their way in the dark. "I want to talk to you about something," I said.

"You sound so serious," she replied.

"Brutus told me he found you and that boy Ian on the porch very late last night."

"I heard Brutus at the gate," she said. "He didn't say anything."

"He thinks Ian is taking advantage of you."

This made her laugh her deep, affecting laugh. "He certainly is," she said. Then her tone changed. "Why does Brutus care what I do on my own time?"

"Good question," I agreed. "He's taken strongly against Ian, I'm not sure why."

"Ian is in love with me," she said. "And he thinks it's you

who's taking advantage of me. He wants to take me away from this house."

So I was right. Ian was on a rescue mission.

"Where does he plan to take you?" I asked.

"I don't know," she said.

"Does he have any money?"

She shrugged. "I don't know," she said.

"And do you care?"

"He's so good to me," she said earnestly. "He's so gentle." She leaned back, holding on to the edge of the counter, chin lifted, eyes closed, lips parted. "He smells so sweet."

She said this last slowly, longingly, stressing each syllable in her throaty alto voice. It went right through me, straight to my hardened heart, and found some vestige of softness there, a long-burned-out but still faintly vibrating memory of irresistible and passionate desire.

They were so young, I thought. They couldn't resist their bodies calling to each other, the sensual signals that flashed between them like fireworks displays, igniting the night sky with flames of desire. Carità had schooled herself to perform sex with all manner of men—the unlovely, the flaccid, the boring, the crude, the rough; Dr. Morrow with his painstaking licking, the banker from the mainland whose heavy application of expensive cologne doubtless concealed a sour smell of pasty sweat. Ian, surrounding her with genuine youth and pulsing vitality, smelled sweet to her. She inhaled him, and he her; with greedy, eager kisses and deep embraces, they were lost in each other. Nothing else mattered.

On my back porch.

"Are you going out with Ian tonight?" I asked.

"It's my night off," she said defensively.

"I'm not trying to stop you," I said. "I think you should go out with him. Get him to take you somewhere he likes to go. Find out what he's like in public."

"He's handsome, isn't he?" she said.

I sighed. No cautioning the young. "He's a good-looking boy," I said. "Where are you meeting him?"

"Here, on the porch."

"That's another thing," I said. "I can't have my girls fucking for free on the back porch. Or in your room, either. If you're going to have sex, go to his room or go to a hotel."

"Why do you care?" she said.

"I don't care, it's my policy," I said. "And I have good reasons for it."

She pushed out her chin, looking stubborn, but she offered no resistance.

"When they come here, they pay," I added. "They have to pay. That's the rule. Otherwise, it's just chaos. Surely you can understand that."

She nodded, but her expression was still petulant. "I understand that," she said.

"Good," I said. "I rely on your good sense."

And I believed that. Ian would have a hard time getting this determined, proud young woman to fall in with his romantic fantasies of escape into the unknown. Love might be blind, and so was Carità, but she had a powerful will to survive, even to flourish, though all the world might be ranged against her.

That night was slow, and we'd closed the house by mid-night. Brutus told me Ian had appeared, as promised, around eight, and stood on the porch until Carità came down the back steps and went out with him. Later, when I finally got settled in bed with a good detective novel, I heard her come in and move swiftly up the stairs to her room.

I was up early the next morning, which suited me. Carità and Mimi would sleep late, I thought, and I could enjoy the time to myself. I made a big urn of coffee and devoted myself to the morning paper, reading from front to back. The house was so quiet I could hear the anoles scampering across the porch. I was halfway through the entertainment section—a fading film star was appearing at a hotel dinner club; a new movie theater was opening near the marina—when I heard the double click of the fence latch. I looked up to see Brutus trudging along the walk, then up the steps to the porch. He stopped at the screen, peering in.

"Good morning," I said. "You're up early."

He came in, careful not to let the screen door slam. "I never went to bed," he said.

"Late revelers?"

Brutus ignored this remark and helped himself at the coffee urn. "I found out something you may want to know," he said.

I made an interested face.

He grimaced over the cup, took a swallow, and pulled out the chair. "Carità's new boyfriend's last name is Drohan."

"Really," I said. This surprised me on a number of counts. The Drohans were a powerful family on the island. They owned the water-bottling plant, a big local employer, and they had fingers in all sorts of operations, including import permits and liquor licensing. One of them was a judge.

"Ian is Mike Drohan's only son," Brutus concluded.

Mike was the judge.

"Well, at least Ian has some money," I said. "I was thinking he was a deadbeat wastrel."

"His family has a mansion on the park."

I indulged myself in a little fantasy: Carità, dressed in expensive designer clothes, a silk blouse and gored skirt that showed off her figure, but discreetly, tastefully; her hair expertly coiffed, her nails manicured; perched at the top of a grand staircase, a staircase so familiar she had no need to count the steps. "He's coming on pretty strong," I said. "He wants her to run away with him."

Brutus sniffed. "You don't seriously imagine that Mike Drohan is going to let his son marry a prostitute."

My rich and elegant fantasy Carità evaporated like steam from a cup. "No," I admitted. "Not likely."

"Not bloody likely," Brutus agreed. He went to the door, opened the screen, and looked back at me. "He's going to break her heart," he said.

An hour later, Mimi came down, groggy from sleep, wearing her favorite flowered muumuu, with a notebook and a heavy textbook under her arm. I moved the newspaper pages aside to make room for her. "Morning," she said.

I nodded. Mimi didn't much like to talk in the morning and neither did I, so we suited each other. She poured her coffee, tore off a piece of bread, and took the chair across from me. I pushed a clean plate toward her.

"Thanks," she said. She opened the book and the notebook and placed the mug between them. Then she settled down to reading attentively, pausing to take careful notes. It pleased me to see her in this, her preferred identity. To have a serious student in my employ somehow did honor to my house. She was like a secret agent, just passing through on her way to an important mission. I thought about her explanation of the difference between Karl Marx and Adam Smith, two names that now meant something to me. She was smart and ambitious, but she didn't flaunt her knowledge. Knowing her clients couldn't have cared less, she never let on to them that she had a thought in her head. What man wants to know that the pretty girl he's paid to pleasure him has seriously considered the likelihood that capitalism leads to class warfare?

Mimi's pen scratched against the paper; outside, a seagull shrieked; the fan whirred monotonously overhead, ruffling the scattered pages of the newspaper. My thoughts turned to what Brutus had told me, that Ian Drohan was a rich man's son. I should have guessed, but I had taken him for one of BB's hangers-on, an indolent youth looking out for some opening in the enterprises of a crime family. Mimi laid down her pen and took up the butter knife.

"Does BB say anything to you about his friend Ian?" I asked her.

"Not much," she said, slathering a thick pat of butter onto her bread. "He thinks Ian is an innocent and he's showing him the real world."

"I wonder how those two became friends," I mused.

"They're dorm mates at the college," she said. "They're also cousins."

We heard a door open upstairs, and then footsteps to the bathroom.

Mimi glanced at the clock. "She came in late last night," she said.

"She was on a date with Ian," I said.

"Is that what you call it?" she replied, raising her eyebrows sardonically.

We heard the toilet flush, the water running in the sink, and then Carità's deep voice humming a slow tune I didn't recognize as she made her way down the stairs. At the doorway she paused, as if she were looking at us, though her eyes were glassy and unmoving, as always. "Good morning," she said. "It's a beautiful day, isn't it?"

"It is," I agreed. Mimi said nothing, but scooted her chair to one side to make room for her friend.

Carità took up her mug and poured her coffee. She was wearing a long, sleeveless white cotton gown with tucks across the bodice. It made her look ghostly. When she joined us at the table, it struck me that her eyes were a little sunken in their sockets.

"You were out very late," I observed.

"I was," she said.

"Did he take you to the Raven's Club?" Mimi asked. "I heard the singer there is good."

"No," Carità said. She had a simpering know-all expression that didn't suit her. "We went someplace much better than that."

Mimi shrugged. This game of guess-where-I-went held no interest for her.

"Where did you go?" I asked.

"Can't you tell by looking at me?" she said, holding up her left hand. There was a wide gold band on her ring finger.

"Carità," I said. "What did you do?"

"Is that a wedding ring?" Mimi said.

Carità gave a hiccup of laughter. "Ian had everything arranged," she explained. "We picked up Bessie and then drove a long way up into the hills to St. Roch's school. A priest—he was Ian's teacher when he was a boy—was waiting for us at the chapel there. His name is Father Dugan; he's such a dear, kind man. He asked me a few questions, and Ian filled out a form. A lady who worked in the church office came in; she and Bessie were our witnesses. Ian had two rings. We made our vows. We exchanged rings." She propped her elbow on the table and fanned her hand from side to side, fingers open wide. It was a simple but expensive-looking ring.

"I didn't think you wanted to get married," Mimi observed dryly.

"That was before I met Ian," Carità replied, closing her hand. "He's changed my life."

I sat there, rubbing my eyes in disbelief, unable to determine how I felt about this turn of events. The only sound was Mimi chewing her bread. Carità was certainly right: marrying Ian Drohan would change her life, no matter what happened next. She definitely wouldn't be working for me anymore. "Do Ian's parents know anything about this?" I asked.

"He's going to tell them today. He didn't want to bring me back here, but we couldn't stay in his dorm room, because BB would be there, so I insisted." She turned to Mimi. "I wanted to tell you myself. Also, I need to pack up my clothes. He'll come fetch me before dinner. Then he'll take me to meet his parents."

"His father's a judge," I said. "He can probably have the marriage annulled."

"Oh, I don't think he can," Carità said. She was dreamily rubbing her wedding ring with her thumb.

"What makes you think that?" I asked.

"Because of what the priest said," she replied.

"And what did he say?"

"He said"—she laid her palms flat on the table and straightened her spine like a schoolgirl giving a recitation—" 'What therefore God hath joined together, let not man put asunder.' "

Carità spent the rest of the day preparing for her new role as Mrs. Ian Drohan. She bathed, washed her hair, then asked Mimi to cut it for her so that she would look respectable when she went to meet her in-laws. Mimi obliged and trimmed her thick locks to just above her shoulders with a froth of bangs over her forehead that made her look like a fashion model. Then they raided both their wardrobes and came up with a presentable outfit, a black calf-length pencil skirt, a plaid cotton blouse, and a brown silk vest that gave Carità a schoolmarmish air. "You need some decent shoes," Mimi said. "All you have is sandals and feather mules."

"You're right," Carità agreed. "I can't go meet my in-laws in sandals."

Mimi said, "How about we go to lunch at Starfish and stop by the shoe shop on Palm Street on the way back?"

"Perfect," Carità agreed. "Lunch will definitely be my treat."

Carità pulled on the sandals and they went out the door, arm in arm. Watching them talk animatedly as they passed through the gate, I thought one couldn't find two brighter, more respectable girls on the island.

When they were gone, I tried to finish reading the paper, but my thoughts kept turning to Carità's sudden marriage. I knew it was foolish, but my feelings were hurt by her secret and sudden decision. It appeared that she hadn't given a thought about the place she had in my house. This wasn't surprising—girls seldom give much notice when they find a way out of this business—but I felt I'd taken a bet by hiring her, and I'd been fair about the money split, more than fair. Clearly, she planned to pack up her scant belongings and walk out of my life as abruptly as she'd entered.

I thought it likely that Ian would mistreat or abandon her pretty quickly, and then she'd be back at my door. She might not even get out of my door. His father would naturally oppose the marriage and threaten to disown Ian if he didn't give up on it. Ian, impulsive though he was, wouldn't walk away from the money and position afforded him by being the judge's only child. The family were Catholics, but they could have the marriage annulled with an application of cash to the right ecclesiastical offices.

No matter how I looked at it, the likelihood that Carità would simply be discarded was high, and the thought of her suffering in the face of this inevitable rejection made me angry. "For God's sake," I said to my empty kitchen. "She's brave, she's smart, she works hard, she deserves a break." As if to answer, a bird in the mimosa tree outside the window cried out, "Too late. Too late."

Mimi and Carità returned in the afternoon, eager to show me their purchases. The shoes were good-looking, square-heeled black patent-leather pumps with a low vamp. They'd also bought a chiffon scarf the color of Carità's eyes, which Mimi tied around her neck inside the collar of her blouse. The final purchase, to my surprise, was a pair of tortoiseshell sunglasses. "Mimi says smart women always wear these on the street," Carità explained.

"She's completely incognito," Mimi put in. "A woman of mystery."

Carità slipped the glasses on and turned her head one way and then the other. "How do I look?" she asked.

I had to admit, the glasses were transformative. Her eyes were so startling and strange, at first glance they took all one's attention, but with the glasses and the new haircut, she looked older, wiser, colder. "Elegant," I said. "You look like an aristocrat."

Carità drew herself up, brushing her hair back on one side with the back of her hand. "And so I am, my dear," she said. "And so I am."

It occurred to me that, in fact, she now appeared to be what she genuinely was, an educated woman accustomed to wealth and liberty. Maybe, I thought, just maybe, she'll be able to pull this off.

After the girls went upstairs, I cleared up the kitchen and took down the accounts book. Jake, the barman, had left an order for supplies. We were low on champagne, vodka, gin, and, as usual, maraschino cherries, which the girls ate like candy. I decided to take the order over to Brutus. He'd be setting up by now, and I wanted to tell him about Carità.

As I was going out the door, Mimi came down the steps and called out to me. I waited on the porch with the door open. "Are you going to the college?" I asked.

"Right," she said. "I've got a class."

We walked down the steps to the gate, where her bicycle was chained up. "It was kind of you to take Carità shopping," I said.

"I just hope this guy shows up," she said. She bent over the bike and turned a small key in the lock. It snapped open with a pop.

"Do you think he might not?"

"I don't know what to think. I just don't trust rich boys in general."

"That's a good rule," I said.

I was thinking about rich boys in general as I walked along the shady sidewalk to the bar, which was called, for reasons obscured in history, the Saxophone. It had kept the name through various owners; no one dared change it, because it was in the tourist guidebooks. Brutus amused himself by hiring a saxophone player to come on Saturday nights and play moody, sexy tunes. Brutus maintained, and I agreed, that a lone saxophone on a sultry night is a powerful inducement to one more drink.

The street was part residential, part increasingly expensive shops, including a small produce store displaying its melons and oranges on wooden shelves beneath a striped awning. Past it, a sheet of water poured down from a balcony that covered the sidewalk. I dodged that and crossed the street.

Mimi was right, I thought. Rich boys couldn't be trusted. And rich families protected their wealth. Ian's announcement that he had impulsively married a poor girl might spur his parents to furious action. They could refuse to let him leave the mansion, start the annulment proceedings, pack him off to the mainland. How would Carità respond if Ian didn't come to claim her? She was persistent, and she had cause. I realized I'd never seen her angry.

From somewhere above me, the plaintive sound of a violin repeating a delicate phrase wafted across the air. I passed beneath it, turned a corner, and arrived at the covered portico of the Saxophone. I could see Brutus through the double glass doors. His back was to me; he was talking to a patron. I pushed open the door and was well inside before I realized that this customer was Joe Shock, whose face I never wanted to see. He spotted me past Brutus's shoulder and nodded lazily in acknowledgment. He knew me, though he didn't frequent my house, which was fine with me—I had him pegged for a sadist.

Brutus was talking and didn't stop, though Joe's half-hearted greeting made him turn to see who had come in. It was dark and cool in the bar. Ordinarily, I would have taken off my sunglasses, but I decided to keep them on. I never could tell what Joe Shock read in my eyes, but I knew he didn't like it.

He looked like his name. He was tall and powerfully built, his complexion freckled and drab—he disliked the sun—and his white hair stood out straight a few inches from his skull. His eyes were a washed-out gray, his nose clearly previously broken and more than once, his mouth a colorless slash. He dressed well, always in a jacket no matter the heat, expensive shirts, and tight-fitting jeans. He had no ass at all.

Brutus finished his sentence: ". . . someone should tell him." Then he addressed me. "You need to hear about this," he said. His expression was so serious that as I approached, clutching my purse with the bar order in it, the news of Carità's marriage fled my brain. "What's happened?" I asked.

Joe Shock narrowed his dead eyes at me but said nothing. "BB and Ian Drohan got into a fight near the park last night,"

Brutus said. "BB was picking up a package from one of Joe's carriers, and he accused the guy of cutting the product. He got aggressive and pulled out that gun he's been showing off. That scared Joe's guy, and he shot BB."

"Is he okay?"

"He's dead," said Joe flatly.

"Jesus," I said. "Does his father know?"

"It gets worse," Brutus said, ignoring my question. "When BB dropped his gun, Ian picked it up and fired at Joe's guy."

"This is awful," I said.

"My guy is in the ICU," Joe said.

How was this possible? I thought. Last night, Ian and Carità were out in the country with Bessie and the priest, tying the knot. Right now, Ian was at the mansion on the park, informing his parents he'd married a prostitute. "It couldn't have been Ian," I said. "He and Carità were out late last night. He didn't bring her back until after midnight. When did this happen?"

"Around three," Joe said.

"It was him," Brutus said. "He came here after he dropped Carità off at your house. He and BB left together when I was closing. It was just after two."

Joe gave me one of his empty stares. "So . . . this Ian character is dating one of your girls," he said.

The words "He's married to her" rose to my lips, but I bit them back. The less Joe knew about Carità, the better I felt.

Brutus said, "He's got a crush on one of them."

Joe smirked, including Brutus in a bond of male condescension. "What sorry asshole has a crush on a whore?" he said.

Brutus shrugged.

"Was Ian arrested?" I asked.

"No," Brutus said. "He ran away before the police got there."

Joe turned to me again. "My guy told the police BB's friend shot him. He didn't know who he was. Then he passed out, so that's all they know for now. If he dies, they'll figure it out, and your boy's looking at a murder rap."

"But surely Ian fired in self-defense."

"Maybe so. I don't much care. It'd be fine with me if he was missing, presumed dead. The fewer witnesses the better. The police picked up the product, the money, two guns, and a dead Betone. I'm out a lot of cash, and Marcus Betone's son is dead. It's going to be a world of shit. You should tell your girl, if she wants to keep her sweetheart alive and well, she should get him out of town." With this parting wisdom, he left us.

I blew out a puff of air and shook myself as if I'd just been released from a spell. Brutus stood slack-jawed, his back to the bar. "Stupid fucking BB," he said.

"This will break his father's heart."

Brutus nodded. "It's going to be bad blood between Joe and Marcus Betone."

"There's a complication you don't know about," I said.

"What is that?"

"Ian took Carità out to St. Roch Chapel last night. He'd arranged to have a priest he knew meet them to marry them."

"They got married?" Brutus said.

"She's at my house right now, in a new outfit, waiting for Ian to take her to meet his parents."

"Damn," he said. "That poor girl."

Surely, I thought, Ian's father would protect his son. If Joe's guy lived, he would say he shot BB in self-defense, which was probably true. Ian could make the same claim.

"I'm going to have to tell her what happened," I said to Brutus.

He nodded. "You have to tell her."

I walked back to my house with a heavy heart. For the first time, I felt I knew exactly what this expression meant: my heart seemed to weigh in my chest, to pull my head down and my thoughts inward, so that I was indifferent to the charms of the natural world. Birds chirped and hopped about in the trees; a gentle sea breeze wafted the fragrance of gardenias past my indifferent nose. How was I going to tell Carità? Exactly what was I going to tell her?

I let myself in at the kitchen, went to the sink, and filled a glass with water. I stood, quietly drinking. The house was still around me—presumably empty but for Carità, who was in her room. I walked down the hall and paused at the staircase, strangely unwilling to take the first step. When at last I did, I heard three quick footsteps; then the door to Carità's room flew open, and she burst into the hall. She stopped at the rail, facing me, holding her arms out before her. "What's wrong?" she exclaimed. "What's happened?"

"I'm coming," I said. "We'll talk in your room."

She made no reply, just stepped back into the open door-way. When I got to her, I said, "What makes you think something's wrong?"

"You came in the house so stealthily," she said. "I could feel that you didn't want to."

"Let's sit down," I said.

She went to the bed and perched gingerly on the edge, pressing her hands flat against the mattress. I pulled the chair near the wardrobe to face her on the wide floorboards and took my seat. "It's true that I have some bad news," I said.

"It's Ian," she said. "What's happened to him?"

"I'm afraid he's gotten into some trouble."

"But he's alive," she said.

"Yes," I replied. "As far as I know."

She took a slow, deep breath. "He's alive," she repeated, comforting herself.

"He and BB went out after he brought you here last night. They got into a fight with another man, a drug dealer, near the park. The dealer shot and killed BB. Then Ian shot the dealer and ran away. No one knows where he is."

"Ian would never shoot anyone," she protested. "And he doesn't take drugs. I don't believe this story."

"Nevertheless," I said, "it's true. The man Ian shot is still alive, but he's in the hospital and may not live."

She bunched up her shoulders and covered her cheeks with the palms of her hands. "I don't care about this," she said. "I don't believe it."

"I'm sorry," I said. "But his father may be able to help him. He's a judge."

She lowered her hands and crossed them over her chest. "He won't go to his father. He despises him."

"I thought he was taking you to meet his parents tonight."

"Father Dugan persuaded him we should go. Ian only agreed because he feels sorry for his mother."

The plot was thickening. Ian wasn't just on a rescue mission, he was also in revolt against the patriarch—a not unusual combination, in my experience. Marrying a penniless blind girl would certainly put the judge to the test.

But this was all moot now. Ian was a fugitive, and he would need legal counsel, the sooner the better. "Ian should turn himself in to the police," I said.

"No," she said. "He won't do that."

Carità appeared to know a great deal about her new husband's views. He despised his father, pitied his mother, didn't like drugs or guns, wouldn't turn himself in to the police. By my reckoning, they had yet to spend twenty-four hours in each other's company. He must have talked all the way to the wedding and all the way back. "Where do you think he'll go?" I asked.

We both heard the *tap-rap* of the screen door opening and closing, then heavy footsteps in the hall.

"He's here," she announced, rushing into the hall. I followed and stood in the doorway as Ian, haggard and wild-eyed, appeared at the foot the stairs. Carità rushed to him, her feet scarcely touching the carpet. They crashed together on the landing, sliding to their knees, face-to-face, kissing greedily and murmuring endearments.

Hell, I thought. What a drama!

Ian repeated his pledge to Carità. "I've come to take you away from here." She hid her face against his chest. Then, raising his eyes over her bent head, he addressed me. "It was an accident," he said. "I never meant to hurt anyone." His face was distorted by emotion, his eyes were red-rimmed, his skin was pallid. His hair hung in lank strands about his ears, and his shirt was wrinkled, the collar open and askew. He'd been out all night. And what a night—he'd married a prostitute and wounded, possibly murdered, a drug dealer. Where he spent the morning was anybody's guess, but it didn't look like he'd found a bed or a shower.

"The man is still alive," I said. "You should turn yourself in to the police."

He narrowed his eyes, as if trying to squeeze me out of his view. "I don't need advice from you," he said. "I've come to get my wife."

"Oh, really?" I said. "And where are you going to take her?"

"Why would I tell you?" he retorted.

Ignoring his impudence, I addressed his wife, who still had her face pressed against his shirt. "Carità," I said. "Listen to me. Ian is in trouble; he can't protect you. The police may want to arrest him. A drug dealer wants him to disappear. It's not safe for you to be with him now."

"Shut up," Ian snapped at me. He spoke softly into her ear. "Don't listen to her. She doesn't care about you."

"If *you* care about her," I said, "you'll leave her here. She'll be safe with me."

Ian gave a mirthless laugh. "Oh, right," he said. "I'll leave her here so you can rent her out by the hour to any pervert on this island who has fifty dollars in his pocket. Good God, woman, what do you tell yourself? You run a whorehouse. No girl is *safe* with you." He tightened his arm around her shoulder, turning her away from me. "We'll be fine," he assured her. "I know where we're going. My car is outside."

"Should I bring my bag?" she asked.

"You don't need anything," he said. "It's all taken care of." He drew her to her feet and guided her down the stairs. She was wearing the new clothes she'd bought to meet his parents. How long ago that seemed now.

"What should I tell your sister?" I asked.

"Oh, poor Bessie," Carità said.

"Tell her she's with her husband," Ian replied curtly. "Where she belongs." They were at the bottom of the stairs now, while I stood helplessly at the top. "Let's go," he said to Carità, urging her down the hall.

"Tell Bessie I'll write to her," Carità called back to me.

I bent over the stair rail, watching them go. Carità was pressed close to his side. She didn't look back.

Well, of course she didn't look back. Carità, by definition, never looked back.

I heard the screen door open and close. I rushed to the back bathroom and leaned out the window. I could see them crossing the yard, then heading out through the gate, along the fence, and out of sight. My throat felt tight, and there was a stinging pressure in my eyes. All I could hear was Ian's harsh rebuke— "No girl is *safe* with you."

I sat on the toilet seat and had a good cry. It had been a long time since anything had moved me to tears. I found it oddly reassuring. So—my heart wasn't yet a stone; I could still be wounded by the casual cruelty of a smart-mouthed boy. Gradually, I regained control of myself. I went to the sink and bathed my eyes with cool water, took a lipstick and a powder compact from the cabinet. I heard the sound of heavy footsteps on the street, and when I looked out the window, I saw Brutus trudging toward the gate. Mimi came whizzing up on her bike. As she dismounted and locked the bike to the fence, they greeted each other. I put the cosmetics away, brushed off the front of my dress, and headed downstairs to give them the news that the newlyweds were on the run.

It was our closed night and there was no food in the house, so we agreed to go out to dinner at a neighborhood café. Brutus was much vexed that Ian had taken Carità to parts unknown, and I had the sense that he blamed me for letting her go, though I couldn't have stopped them.

"Carità is impulsive," Mimi observed. "And she's made a strong commitment to Ian. She's going to stick with him for as long as she can."

None of us felt strongly affected by BB's death. "He's been stuffing a lot of cocaine up his nose lately," Mimi said. "Nervous as a cat, and spoiling for a fight. Talking nonstop. Deeply boring."

"He was definitely coked up last night," Brutus said. "He was lecturing Joe Shock. He was shaking his finger at him."

"Unwise," I said, and we all nodded.

Mimi and I went back home and finished a bottle of champagne. All around us, the big empty rooms were so quiet the house seemed to be brooding. When I finally got to bed, I couldn't sleep. I tossed and turned while I went over and over the events of the unusually eventful day, from Carità's announcement at breakfast to her hurried exit with her fugitive husband. Toward dawn, I fell into a deep, dreamless slumber. It was after eleven when I got up. Mimi had gone to the college, but she returned at noon to be available for callers. As there were none, we made a lunch of cheese sandwiches and coffee. Then she went to her room to study.

I busied myself with house matters, feeling the hours drag by. At last the sun grew less intense and the light took on an afternoon sheen. I heard women's voices from the yard; first Charlotte and Sally, and then Vivien, arriving for work. I asked them to gather in the kitchen until Jack came in. I wanted to address them as a group. I had a lot to tell my staff.

Though my audience expressed varying degrees of concern and regret about the sudden elopement of Carità and Ian Drohan, the news of BB Betone's demise barely provoked a reaction of surprise. "He was out of control," Jack observed. "I heard his big ambition was to be a powerful dealer so he wouldn't have to pay for drugs."

"I feel sorry for his father," said Charlotte. "He never fails to mention his son is in college. He's so proud of that."

"Marcus is a gentleman," I said.

"Truly," Charlotte said. "He's so courteous he makes me feel like I'm doing him a favor. And he always leaves a good tip on the dresser, with a few of those Italian candies—the white ones—what are they called?"

"Torrone," said Sally.

"Right," Charlotte said. "He knows I like them."

"I guess the police will tell him BB's dead," Sally speculated. "That will be hard."

"I wouldn't want to be the cop bringing that news," I agreed.

The girls went upstairs to change, and Jack opened the bar. The clients came and drank and chose their dates, filing up the stairs in twos and threes, flaunting their inebriated gaiety, offering their feeble jokes. My eyes kept drifting to the leather chair where Carità usually held sway, and my ears strained to hear the deep, thrilling sound of her laughter.

I had a gin and tonic, and then another, and another after that, but my spirits stubbornly failed to lift. The little clock on the mantel was standing still. Vivien's date, an overweight optometrist, surprised her by proving an excellent dancer, and she kept the sultry, broody music going on the player.

At last, the clients and the girls were gone. Jack closed up the bar, and Mimi went to her room. I sat at the kitchen table to go over the receipts, but I was so agitated I pushed the account book aside, went to the fridge, and poured myself a full mug of vodka.

Where had Ian taken Carità? And what would happen next? Would the police be looking for Ian? Joe Shock had been vague—he'd prefer Ian missing, presumed dead. Was that a threat? Or did he just want Ian to get out of town? It wouldn't take Marcus long to find out who the dealer in the ICU worked for, if he didn't know already. One thing was clear: Marcus Betone would blame Joe Shock for the death of his son, and the long-standing rivalry between them would overflow into violence.

Joe was scared, I concluded. And Joe Shock scared was a dangerous animal.

When I finally closed my books and climbed the stairs to my room, I paused on the landing, picturing Ian and Carità madly embracing there, clinging to each other as if they felt cold, indifferent hands trying to pull them apart.

I continued up the steps to my room, switched on my fan, stripped off my clothes, collapsed on my bed, and fell into a deep and mercifully dreamless sleep.

Unsurprisingly, I woke with a vicious headache. It hurt to move my eyes. I could hear Mimi in the kitchen; she had an early class on Wednesdays, and I lay very still, trying not to look at the ceiling fan whirring softly over my bed, until I heard the screen door slap closed. I was thinking of Carità, that she wasn't in her room, that she wouldn't be joining me for breakfast.

Where was she?

I got up and pulled on my robe, slipped my feet into a pair of satin mules, and headed for the bathroom, where I drank three glasses of water before I dared look at my face. It was reassuringly fresh-looking. Perhaps I should switch to vodka. I applied minimal makeup, brushed my teeth carefully, and spritzed my neck and wrists with my favorite cologne.

Then I went downstairs to the kitchen, where I knew I would find a fresh pot of coffee and the morning paper, left for me by the thoughtful Mimi.

I decided to have my coffee au lait, so I filled the milk warmer and set it on the burner. I took down a plate and tore off the end of the bread. As I opened the refrigerator door, I was startled by a sound that filled me with misgiving. Someone was rapping the brass knocker on the front door of the house. Three times, softly, a pause, then twice more, very hard.

As anyone who has any business at my house knows perfectly well, we never use that door. I wasn't dressed; I wasn't fully awake; it was an easy decision. I ignored the knocking. A few moments passed, during which I buttered the bread and poured the coffee. I could hear quick footsteps on the sidewalk alongside the house. Good. Whoever it was had given up and gone on, I thought, pulling the newspaper in close to my chair.

Then I heard the gate creaking open and more steps, to the porch door, which was behind me. I turned, feeling an odd chill along my spine. A man I didn't recognize stood looking in at me through the screen. "Are you Mrs. Gulliver?" he asked.

"You're certainly persistent," I replied.

"Why didn't you answer the door?" he retorted.

"Because there's no one in this world I want to see at the moment."

"How do you know that until you see who it is?"

I leaned toward the screen, taking him in more clearly. He was tall, lean, wide shoulders, narrow hips—the kind of man who looks good in his clothes and even better without them. He had strong features: dark, thick brows over hooded eyes; a nose that announced Spain in his bloodlines; a full, wide mouth; a heavy, jutting jaw. His black hair, silver at the temples, had been cut by a stylist, not a barber. It fell just over his ears and waved neatly across his forehead. He was dressed in a short-sleeved white cotton shirt and well-fitting black linen trousers. A good-looking man, I thought. Just my type. "What I see," I said, "is that I don't know you."

"Would you like to?" he replied.

A chortling sound from the stove announced that I'd left the milk on the burner. I leaped to my feet, leaving my mules under the chair, and grabbed the pot handle, which was hot, just as the milk bubbled over the top. I cursed but held on long enough to shift the pot to the sink and drop it into the dish drain, leaving a trail of milk drops across the counter.

"Did you burn yourself?" my visitor asked.

"No," I said. "I'm fine." I opened the faucet and stuck my hand under the cool water.

"Are you sure?" he persisted. I looked back at him. His expression was all fake concern.

"Oh, for God's sake," I said. "Come inside."

He pulled open the screen and stepped into the kitchen, careful to close the door behind him. Then he just stood there, smiling at me.

This is truly an attractive man, I thought. I pulled a dish towel from the hook next to the sink and wrapped it around my hand.

"Did you burn your hand?" he repeated.

I opened the towel and examined my palm. It was reddish, but nothing serious. "I'm fine," I said again, raising my eyes to his.

His eyes. His rueful, questioning eyes, and that smile—so knowing that it nudged a helpless response from my own lips. We were still for a moment, smiling at each other.

And we knew.

"I can offer you some coffee if you take it black," I said. "That was the last of the milk."

"That would be very welcome," he said.

I took down a mug and filled it halfway.

"Do you mind if I sit at the table?" he asked. All his questions were rhetorical, I thought; everything he said had an ironic edge to it.

"Make yourself at home."

He pulled a chair out far enough to accommodate his long legs and reached for the mug I held in my slightly trembling hand. "I think I'd like that," he said.

I leaned against the counter, making no comment, while he glanced around the kitchen, nodding his head approvingly. "It's very cozy here," he said. "Not at all what I expected."

"What did you expect?" I asked.

"Decadence," he said cheerfully.

"That's hard to bring off in a kitchen," I replied.

"And you are Mrs. Gulliver?" he asked.

"I am."

"You're not what I expected, either."

"I see that," I said.

"I expected someone garish and crude. But you're lovely."

"You should see me when I'm dressed," I said.

"No," he said. "I like what you're wearing."

I pulled the front of the robe closed a bit, which made him frown. What a lot of expressions on his long, handsome face. He could be an actor, I thought. "Have we got to the part where you tell me your name?" I asked.

"Ordinarily, I'd prefer to remain mysterious," he said. "But I did come to see you for a reason. I'm Mike Drohan."

Ian's father, I thought. How much did he know about the shooting? And what was he doing in my kitchen? "The judge," I said.

"Don't be concerned," he assured me. "I'm only judgmental when I'm on the bench. Some people think that's a problem."

"If you're looking for your son," I said, "he's not here."

"My sources tell me he's been seeing a girl who works here."

"And if he was?" I said.

He drank his coffee, and his sharp eyes went soft and out of focus. "That would surprise me, Mrs. Gulliver, because my son is a very puritanical young man."

"He came here with his friend BB Betone."

"The deceased BB Betone," he said.

"I know about the gunfight," I said.

"News travels fast."

"So does your son."

"That's why I'm here. Do you know where he is?"

"I don't. But he was here Monday."

"To see that girl," he said. "What's she like?"

"Very beautiful. Very headstrong. Her name is Carità."

"Can I talk to her?"

"She went with your son, wherever he went."

"Why would she do that?"

"Because they're married," I said. "He took her out to his old school chapel Sunday night, and the priest there—his name is Father Dugan—married them."

"Dugan," he repeated. "My nemesis." His eyelids dropped halfway, and a slow breath escaped his lips. "I never should have sent Ian to that school," he said.

"There's something else you should know," I said.

"Does this get worse?"

"You'll probably think so."

He propped his elbows on the table and rested his chin in his hands, looking up at me, the picture of manly misery. "I'm braced," he said.

"Carità is blind," I said.

His chin came down and his fingers crept up his face to his hairline, pressing hard. "Mother of God," he said.

I couldn't repress a chuckle.

"Don't laugh at me, Mrs. Gulliver," he said without looking up.

"You can call me Lila," I said.

He raised his face and gave me a look of pleading. "My son hates me, Lila," he said. "He always has."

"Surely not when he was a baby."

"Even then. He always screamed when I offered to hold him."

"Was that often?"

He shrugged. Sipped his coffee. Set down the cup. "This is excellent," he said. "But I'm wondering if you have something stronger."

"There's a full bar in the drawing room," I said. "We can raid it, if you like."

"How nice," he said. "That's so convenient." He pushed back his chair and followed me out the kitchen door and down the hall. I flicked on the fan switches as we went along. The shutters were partially closed in the drawing room, filtering the sunlight into a pattern of stripes across the walls and the carpet. It was a dreamy atmosphere, and I could see it affected him strongly. He's one of those men, I thought, who live from minute to minute.

"It's so pleasant here," he said. His eyes scanned the provocative paintings on the walls. "I've heard of this place, but I had no idea it would be like this."

"I've been here for ten years," I said.

"The only brothel I ever visited—I was very young—was by the docks, in an abandoned tackle shop. It was a filthy, disgusting place. Grim, actually. I was terrified the whole time I was there."

I crossed into the second room and flicked on the light over the bar. "I got my start in that place," I said.

"Did you?" he said.

"I did," I replied. "And you're right. It was grim. What can I fix you? A Bloody Mary is a good morning-drink."

"Just the thing," he said.

"Have a seat," I said. "I'll bring it to you."

He looked about and chose the silk divan. "So . . . the men come here and have drinks. Do the girls line up for them?"

"No lineup," I said. "That's humiliating. The clients come in here, have drinks, there are some canapés and music. It's more like going to a party. They talk with the girls, sometimes they dance. Some of them are regulars and come for the ambience. It's not that unusual for a man to come in, have a drink, maybe a dance or two, chat with the girls, and then leave. That's what your son did." I dropped a celery stick into the drink and came out from behind the bar.

"Ian dances?" he asked. I handed him the drink. "Aren't you having one?"

"He didn't dance," I said. "And I have a hangover; also, it's a bit early for me."

"It is for me, too," he agreed. "This business with Ian has unhinged me." He sipped the drink despondently.

"Are the police looking for him?"

"Not yet. They're trying to put it all together. The chief had to go out and tell Marcus Betone his son is dead. Everybody knows the dealer worked for Joe Shock. They've got two guns, and they know someone else was there."

"How did you find out it was Ian?"

"He left a scrawled note at my office, saying he was 'involved' in the murder the other night and that he was 'on the run.' He told me not to follow him."

"He was pretty frantic when he came to get Carità," I said.

He rubbed his chin with his palm. "He must be traumatized," he said. "He's a gentle kid. He worries about poor people and animals. I didn't get what the attraction to Betone's boy was all about, but it was important to him. And it sounds like BB died right in front of him."

"Do you think he'll try to get to the mainland?" I asked.

"No," he said. "Ian will never leave the island. I tried to send him to America or even England for college, but he refused. I went to Yale Law, and he thinks that's what ruined me."

"It seems to me you've been rather successful," I said.

"Given my family, it would be hard to fail. That's part of what Ian holds against me."

I was still standing in front of him, and when he looked up, his eyes were level with my breasts.

"What perfume are you wearing?" he asked, his voice catching a little in his throat.

"Orange blossom," I said.

"It's intoxicating," he said. He stretched out his arm to set the drink on the side table. Then he gently wrapped his hand, cool from holding the iced drink, around my knee. "Mrs. Gulliver," he said.

"Lila," I corrected him.

"Lila," he said. "I'm very attracted to you."

I bent over him, bringing my hand to his cheek. "I know," I said.

He smiled; then his eyes widened, as if a thought had struck him. "Should I pay you?" he asked. "I'd be happy to do that."

"This is my house," I said. "And I'm not for sale."

His hand edged up my thigh. "Good to know," he said.

Our eyes met just before our lips. I had not succumbed to such a deep and irresistible thrill of desire in many years.

The orgasm is a powerful force in human society. People don't give it enough credit as a motivating factor, though in some cases it drives the world. What's clear is that once a human experiences the orgasm, they're going to want that experience again. For boys and girls coming of age, this results in masturbation, a sad and solitary practice that generates the fantasies they will come to recognize as peculiarly their own. Then, whether consciously or not, the youth is driven to realize these fantasies as far as possible during sexual congress with a partner. The fantasy will predispose the choice of the partner.

This creates havoc, confusion, and despair, especially if the desire for a sex partner is coupled with the quest for a life mate, as is so often the case. Then other factors must influence the selection—the desire for children, a family life, stability—and the fantasy must be repressed. Soon that repression serves to exacerbate the imagination; the fantasy takes hold powerfully and will brook no resistance. That's when money enters the equation, and money, as it will, changes everything.

People who are willing to pay for sex are, by definition, not particularly interested in any gratification but their own. When a woman agrees to be paid, she understands that the goal of the encounter is not her pleasure but her client's. Her job is to enter his fantasy, to gratify some secret, possibly shameful vision he has of himself. The sex worker's job, all in all, is to assist her client in achieving the orgasm. That's not always as easy as it sounds.

Charlotte once had a poor client, a little man with a foppish mustache and bulging eyes, who required a complete education in the field. He came in early, around eight, and went straight to the bar, where he ordered a wine spritzer. He was clearly nervous; his hand shook as he took the glass; he barely raised his eyes when Jack made some welcoming remark. I was about to come to the rescue when Charlotte caught my eye and, with a lift of her chin, told me she was willing to take him on. She was wearing some silly red silk harem pants and a push-up bra, and had her long hair tied up so that it looked like a fountain. She approached the poor, nervous creature—Freddie was his name—and introduced herself, remarking that she hadn't seen him in our house before. He bobbed his head and blushed to the roots of his thinning hair. "It's my first time," he said.

The girls usually try to get a date to buy them a drink or two—they divide half of the bar take—but Freddie's extreme shyness touched Charlotte, and she said very pleasantly, "Would you like to come upstairs with me?"

He nodded, then shrank into himself as if to take back his assent. His hand rattled the glass as he set it back on the bar.

"Bring it along," she said. "We can talk a bit while you drink it."

He nodded again, taking up the glass. Charlotte slipped her hand into his. "It's this way," she said. As they passed me,

I heard her say, "Don't you think my pants are funny?" The expression on his face was stark terror.

As soon as she closed the door to her room, Freddie confessed that he was thirty-six years old and had never gotten so far as a first kiss. Charlotte was unfastening her bra, but she hooked it back up and drew him to sit beside her on the edge of the bed. She took his hand again and said, "Don't worry about that."

"It's because I'm not very attractive," he said. "Women sometimes like me as a friend, but I never get further than that."

"You're just shy," Charlotte said. "That's perfectly natural. But you were right to come here. I like shy men. Where do you work, Freddie?"

"At the Constant Bank. I'm a teller."

Charlotte said she saw his whole sorrowful little life in that sentence, and she felt such sympathy for him that she put her arm around him and said, "Everything is going to be fine."

She took her time, encouraging him to ask questions as they went, treating him like a student, and, to her satisfaction, he turned out to be a very apt one. Also, she said, when she finally got his clothes off, he had a perfectly presentable, neat little body, nearly hairless, which he was ashamed of (Charlotte disparaged hairy men), and a very adequate prick, which, she pointed out, was always going to be a nice surprise to future partners. Of course, he was so excited by this first experience of intimacy that he came almost as soon as she touched his cock, and was ashamed of that, too. She got him past that, showing him how to excite a partner manually. "Do all men know this?"

he asked at one point. That made her laugh and she said, "They all think they do, but most don't have a clue." Then he was attentive until she told him he had acquitted himself very well. This aroused him, and he was able to have a second orgasm inside her. His success in this endeavor so moved him that he wept in her arms. Charlotte petted him until he was calm again and sent him on his way. "He was actually a natural," Charlotte concluded. "All those wasted years."

The next day, two dozen long-stem roses came in a box for Charlotte from Freddie. She expected to see him again soon, but he never came back. Six months later, she received a card with a newspaper clipping of a wedding announcement inside, and a message in big block letters: "YOU SAVED MY LIFE." "This is so touching," Charlotte said. "I did a good deed for his bride."

Prostitutes seldom have orgasms on the job. They have to keep their concentration too keenly on giving satisfaction to think of their own. Vivien told me that when she goes home to her drunken husband after a night on the job, she wakes him up to have "real" sex with her. Poor woman. She admits she married him because something about him aroused her passion, and though he has destroyed her life with his alcoholism, he still excites her as no one else can.

It's the orgasm—that curious overpowering spasm—that closes down the agitated brain long enough for the world to rush in, that drives poor humans together and sometimes apart. If one has many partners, one understands how rare the much-prized and storied simultaneous orgasm is. Rare, but it can happen, and when it does, it's like a sudden revelation of harmony; the parties lie dazed and sated with only one thought—*This is it!*—repeated like a mantra in the paralyzed brain.

At least, that's what happened in my brain some time— who knows how long—after Mike Drohan put down his drink and wrapped his hand around my knee. We were half on, half off the divan, naked and entwined, sweating, panting, and laughing from exhaustion and amazement. "My God," he said. "I think I dislocated my shoulder."

"My knees got rubbed raw on the carpet," I said.

"I'm sorry," he said, lifting his torso and looking under his arm to see my knees. "Why didn't you say something?"

"I didn't notice until just now," I replied.

He dropped back over me, nuzzling against my neck, pressing little kisses along my sternum. "Shall we pull ourselves together?" he asked.

When we were straightened out and dressed, we sat back on the divan, and Mike took up the abandoned Bloody Mary, in which the ice was thoroughly melted. He took two big swallows and held the glass out to me. "Have some," he said. "It's still good."

"I will," I said. "My headache is completely gone."

"I've cured you," he said.

I drank the still-cool liquid—it was marvelously refreshing.

"Lila," he said, "promise me we'll do this again soon."

I handed the drink back, half empty. "You can count on it," I said.

He studied me, holding the glass between his knees, his

expression bemused, as if his own thoughts puzzled him. "I should be ashamed of myself," he said. "I need to find my son."

"Where do you think he is?"

"I don't know," he said. "But I think Dugan may know. He may even be hiding them. He loves manipulating Ian."

"Will your wife go with you?" I asked.

"My wife is hysterical. I told her about the shooting, but I didn't know about this marriage. When she finds out, she'll go through the roof. She'll want to have it annulled."

I thought of Carità. I could see her plunging down the stairs with her fugitive husband. She was about to have her future decided by a priest, a husband, and a judge. The full force of the patriarchy. It was nearly biblical.

"When will you go?" I asked.

"This afternoon, if I can get an appointment with the priest."

"I should go with you," I said.

"Why would you do that?"

"For Carità," I said. "I'm an interested party."

He considered this. "I'm not sure that's a good idea."

"That's okay, because I'm sure it is. This Dugan clearly thinks he can do what he likes with other people's lives. I don't like the idea of you two sitting around talking about how to get the marriage annulled. Carità deserves an advocate."

He gave a weak smile. "You're very confident," he observed.

"And you're intimidated by the priest. You need me. I'll buck you up."

We were silent for a moment, sitting side by side, his hand

resting on my knee, kneading it through the robe. I studied his profile, willing his consent. He turned his head and looked at me, right in the eyes, with an expression combined of deep suspicion and irresistible curiosity, like a child contemplating some new life-form in his limited experience. I held his gaze, raised my eyebrows, tilted my head. . . . Take the bet, I thought.

"All right," he said. "Come with me."

By the time Mimi got back from the college, I was dressed in my most conservative suit, a yellow cinch-waisted peplum jacket over a navy-blue pleated skirt. I had on nylon stockings and high-heeled black pumps. My banking outfit. I turned before the mirror, checking out the look, and I was pleased with what I saw. My makeup was subdued, I'd put my hair up in a severe French twist, and my earrings were single cultured-pearl studs. I had a pair of expensive sunglasses in my best leather clutch bag. No one, I thought, would mistake me for a madam. I looked quite the prosperous matron.

I blew myself a kiss and went downstairs, where I found Mimi in the kitchen, eating an apple and a piece of cheddar cheese. "Is that really you?" she said when she saw me.

"You're not the only one with two personalities," I said.

She chewed the apple, studying me. When she had swallowed, she said, "I thought you were pretty depressed last night, but now you look radiant."

"It's true," I said. "I've been transformed."

"What happened?"

I could feel the smile plumping my cheeks, my eyebrows lifting, all-knowing and coquettish. "I've fallen for a man I know nothing about," I said.

She laughed. "That's so great. Who is he?"

I set my purse on the table and pulled out a chair. "I can't tell you yet," I said. "It has to be a secret for a while."

"Is it someone I know?"

"No. I only met him myself this morning. He's coming to pick me up in a few minutes. I won't be back to open; can you handle it?"

"Sure. What should I tell Brutus?"

"Don't tell him anything," I said. "Just say, um, just say . . ."

"I'll say you're looking for Carità and Ian."

"That's the truth," I said.

"Best policy," she pointed out.

"Right," I agreed. "Tell him that."

"Where do you think they went?"

"Maybe to the priest who married them. That's my guess."

I got up, went to the sink, and poured a glass of water. Why was I keeping my plans a secret? I wondered. Why didn't I want Mimi to see Mike Drohan? I drank the water, set the glass in the sink, went to the door, and stood looking through the screen at the gate. We'd agreed that he would pick me up at four. I glanced at the clock—it was 3:58—then back at the gate. A sporty white convertible pulled up at the curb, and Mike, calm and confident at the wheel, raised his hand in greeting.

"Here's my ride," I said to Mimi as I pushed open the door.

"Good luck," she called after me.

As I approached the car, its roof gave a groan and, with a

creak and whir of gears, lifted out of its accordion fold behind the rear seat. Lurching and flattening across the front like a diver worried about the depth of the pool, it closed noiselessly at the top of the windshield. Mike reached up to snap the locks into place. Good, I thought. I dislike driving long distances in convertibles with the top down. It can be fun in town when you want to see and be seen, but on the open road you get blown to bits, and you can't hear to have a conversation.

I crossed in front of the vehicle, glancing down the street in both directions, then pulled open the passenger door and slipped inside.

"You look fantastic," he said.

"But do I look respectable?" I asked.

"Definitely," he said. "I'm in awe."

"You're teasing."

"That's true," he agreed; he shifted the gears and pulled out into the road. "I was in awe when you leaped out of the chair in that plush blue robe to stop the milk from boiling over."

"You admired my quick reflexes," I speculated.

"Something like that," he said. He turned onto the main street that runs from the docks to the end of the town, effortlessly shifted gears, and picked up speed. The buildings along the road gradually thinned out, becoming lower and farther apart, until they were just shacks squatting over unmowed fields with tattered plantains and dusty mimosa crowded together like lurking thieves in their yards. We came to the turnoff for the highway that runs up into the hills and straight across the island. Another shift of gears, and we leveled out at a steady speed. The traffic was light out here, more lumbering farm trucks than cars. Mike's hand left the gear shift and settled on my knee. "It's only been a few hours," he said, "but I couldn't wait for them to pass."

"What did you do?" I asked.

"I went to my chambers, got one of the secretaries to make an appointment with the priest, examined the docket, read the police reports about the Betone murder."

"What did you find out?"

"Not much. The only witness is the guy in the ICU. When the cops got there, he was still conscious. He said BB threatened him with a gun and he fired in self-defense. BB dropped the gun, and BB's friend picked it up and shot him."

"He didn't identify Ian?"

"No. But the cops have the gun, so they've got his fingerprints. It may take them a day or two to identify him."

"Is Joe's guy going to live?"

"The doctors say it's fifty-fifty at this point. He's unconscious now, and they think he may go into a coma."

"If he was still holding the gun when Ian fired, doesn't that mean Ian fired in self-defense?"

He shifted his eyes from the road, giving me a quizzical look, then returned his attention to the road. "It could," he said. "If Murdoch lives. That's his name, Dizzy Murdoch."

"Dizzy." I snorted.

"If he lives, he'll be charged with murder. I think Ian would get off on self-defense."

"And if he dies?"

"It gets more complicated. There are no witnesses."

"I see," I said.

"It's also possible—I think it's even probable—that BB's father will have Murdoch taken out at the hospital. He could just not regain consciousness forever."

"Marcus was crazy about his son," I said.

"Because BB was just like him," Mike said.

"That's not true," I said. "BB was a cheap hood, and vicious as a rat, whereas Marcus is a calculating player, very discreet, and capable of common courtesy."

This made Mike smile, and his eyes flashed approval. "You're good at summing people up," he said.

"In my business, it's a survival skill," I replied.

He crossed into the right lane and steered onto an exit ramp.

"Isn't the school much farther on?" I said.

"We're taking a detour," he replied. "I think you'll like it."

We came out between a gas station and a cotton field, then took a dirt-packed side road that descended into a true tropical forest. Everything was green; even the air was green, and thick with oxygen and fragrances, some like exotic perfumes, others the sickly-sweet of rotting fruit. "I've never been to this part of the island," I said.

"Were you born in the city?"

"Oh no. I was a hick. I was born in a village on the windward side, south of here. Everybody worked at the Virgin Soap factory. When I was a girl, all I wanted was to get to the city." A brightly colored bird swooped low over the road ahead, and I watched as it disappeared into the green curtain of the forest. "This is beautiful," I said.

"It is," he agreed. We turned onto a dirt road so narrow that I might have touched the glossy foliage from the window.

About half a mile on, the road opened into a clearing, and in that clearing stood an old-fashioned bar-hotel, with a semicircular portico and potted palms on either side. The second floor had long single shutters that opened from the bottom. Iron tables and chairs gathered under a pergola on one side.

"How did you find this?" I exclaimed.

"I get around," he said. He swerved into the gravel lot, where two cars and a motorcycle were parked, and turned off the engine. "We don't have to meet Father Dugan until seven-thirty," he said. "I thought we could stop off here and plan our strategy."

"I admire that fine legal mind," I said, pushing open my door.

Mike got out on his side and grinned at me over the roof. "And you don't believe a word I say," he added.

We met at the back of the car. He passed his hand around my waist and bent over me for a brief kiss. When our lips parted I said, "Is there some reason why I should?"

"I can't think of any," he replied. Then we sauntered, holding hands like two teenagers, under the portico to the double screened doors. Nailed to the cypress lintel was a brass plate engraved with the word "TROPICALE." "Original name," I observed, as Mike pulled open the screen. Inside, it was all pale cypress, large potted palms, and a line of ceiling fans, with a long bar down one side and three tall, deep-silled windows looking out into an emerald dreamscape on the other. A few iron tables with wicker chairs were scattered across the tile floor. At the back was a counter under a printed sign that read "Hotel Registration" hanging by thin white chains from the ceiling. Two men sat drinking at the far end of the bar, and a young couple leaned toward each other, speaking softly, over one of the tables. "Table or bar?" Mike asked me.

"Table," I said. We took the one nearest the door.

The bartender, an elderly man with wild white hair and a drooping white mustache, folded the newspaper he was reading and came out to greet us. "Good evening, Judge," he said, his dark, cheerful eyes fixed on me. "We haven't seen you in some time."

"Too long," Mike replied. "But nothing has changed here, thank God."

"No," said the barman. "We don't keep a clock here, so time passes us by."

"Is that the secret?" Mike said.

"What can I bring you?" the barman asked.

"Just white wine for me," I said.

"I'll have a Bloody Mary," Mike said. As the bartender nodded and turned away, Mike added, "It's my new lucky drink."

It was pleasant and cool in the open room, with the line of fans whirring overhead and all things green pressing in at the open windows. I pushed my purse to one side and rested my elbows on the table. "What else is lucky for you?" I asked.

"Not much, frankly," Mike replied. "I'm not a lucky guy."

"You seem to be doing all right," I observed. "You've found a place where time stands still."

He slid his hand across the table and grasped my elbow. "Let's pretend that's true," he said, "and we have all the time in the world." Our eyes met and held. I felt again a strong pull, as of recognition, combined with a deep pang of sadness. The bartender came toward us, carrying a bamboo tray with two sweating glasses, which he set carefully before us. From somewhere behind the bar, a soft hiss of static resolved into low and languid dance music. I disengaged my eyes and made no reply, allowing my fingers to stray to my glass and lift it by the bowl.

"Lila Gulliver," Mike said softly. "It's an odd name."

I tasted my wine; it was crisp and dry.

"Is there a Mr. Gulliver?"

"No, sadly," I said. "I'm a widow."

"I wish I could say I was sorry," he said. "How did your husband die?"

"I'm not sure. He may not even be dead. He was an explorer. He went on a voyage and never came back."

"How did you meet him?"

"I met him when I was very young," I said.

He sipped his drink, eyeing me suspiciously over the rim. "Where was this?"

"It was in a comic book," I said.

He sputtered, then swallowed.

"He had just returned from a long voyage among some very interesting islands."

"The ones with the little people and the very big people," he suggested.

"Yes," I agreed. "And another with talking horses."

He rubbed his cheek with his forefinger, stretching his neck as if to clear his throat. "So—you're the girl Lemuel Gulliver left behind."

"I figured there had to be one."

"What's your real name?"

"Macpherson," I said. "Evelyn Macpherson."

"That explains your red hair and amazing skin."

"I haven't said that name in a long time."

"Shall I call you Evelyn?"

"Oh, please, no," I said. "I wouldn't like that at all." I applied myself to my wine, feeling disconcerted, as if I'd been caught in a lie when, in fact, for the first time in years, I'd told the truth. Mike signaled the barman, making a little circle in the air with his index finger. "I think we have time for another round," he said.

"How far is it from here?"

"Maybe an hour and a half."

"How well do you know this Father Dugan?"

He gave his face a quick little shake. "Never met him."

The barman arrived with our drinks. As he set them down before us, his hands trembled, and I had the sensation that all three of us were doing our best not to notice. When he was gone, Mike turned his glass slowly in place, staring down into the little red sea with the celery stick poking out like the mast of a sunken ship. "I'm dreading this interview."

I said nothing.

"He's close to my wife," he said, "and he knows I tried to keep Ian out of that school."

"I don't think priests are allowed to hold grudges," I said.

"I'm the one with the grudge. He's always meddling in my life from afar. Ian thinks he's Jesus incarnate. My wife probably confesses *my* sins to him."

I chuckled and took a swallow of wine. "What's she like?" I asked.

Mike lifted his glass, holding the celery stalk aside with his index finger while he sucked in a big gulp of vodka-infused tomato juice. When he put the glass down, he scowled at it, then raised his eyes to mine. "My wife," he said, "is an equestrian. Do you know what that's like?"

"She likes horses," I said.

"She lives for horses. She's up early and off to the stable, and she comes back late for dinner, unless a horse is sick—they get sick a lot—and then she stays out all night and sleeps in the tack room."

"Horses get sick?" I said.

"They do. And the vet bills are staggering."

"I can imagine," I said.

"The first time I saw her, she was dressed all in white, astride a huge black horse, this blonde, blue-eyed goddess coming straight at me at a gallop across a field. There was a hedge midway; the horse sailed over it. Claudia didn't move a muscle. Then they trotted up to me—I was standing on a porch—and she gave me a very fetching smile and said, 'Do you ride?'"

"Do you?"

"I don't," he said, shrugging off the bright recollection. "Horses terrify me."

"How did you distract your wife from the horses long enough to marry her?"

"I didn't have to do a thing. She had her sights on me. The day we met, she knew who I was and how much I'm personally worth, and what my family is worth. Well, none of that is a secret on this island."

"That's true," I said.

"She tried to make the horse thing look like a pastime, but the truth was, she and her sister were running a little stable—that was all they had—and they were barely making ends meet. Her dream was to be an international dressage champion."

"And did she realize that dream?"

"She has four horses. She takes them around to various competitions. She even ships them to the mainland for big events. She has a wall of ribbons and trophies."

"This is very odd," I said.

"I think it's crazy, but no one cares what I think."

"I agree with you. But what's odd is that Carità rides horses, too. She told me she could compete in dressage, whatever that is."

"I thought she was blind."

"She is. But she's fearless, and she had a trainer."

"Claudia will like that," he said. We sipped our drinks, thinking about what Claudia would like. Then he shrugged, setting his drink down carefully. "How did we get on this topic?"

"You were dreading Father Dugan," I said. "And his influence over your wife."

"She went to the sister school, St. Agnes. Dugan was a young priest then, a teacher. She adored him. Now he runs the boys' school. She gives money to the benefits and goes to all the reunions."

"It has a good reputation," I observed.

"I didn't go to a Catholic school and I didn't want Ian to, either, but the three of them ganged up on me, and I gave in."

"Are you a Catholic?"

"I was raised Catholic, like everybody on this island. Weren't you?"

"My father was a Scotch Presbyterian," I said.

"Right," he said. "Macpherson."

I nodded.

"What about this Carità? Is she Catholic?"

"Her mother was Italian, so she must have been, but she died when Carità was born."

"That's so sad," Mike said. He signaled to the barman, making a checkmark in the air.

In the parking lot, he put his arm around my waist; at the car door, he kissed me, and I was dizzy with desire. "We can come back here after this meeting," he said. "The rooms are fine. Shall I get a key before we go?"

"Yes," I said. "I'll wait here."

"Great," he said, and he executed a little leap of joy in the air as he turned back.

"I can't stay all night," I called after him.

"I'll have you home before dawn," he promised.

I opened the car door and sat on the seat with my feet on the ground.

You struggle and work hard to make a life, I thought, and you go along, and it's just fine, it's interesting, you're making a comfortable living. Then somebody pulls a switch somewhere, and there's a knock at the door that blows your world wide open. I'm thirty-eight years old, I concluded, and it looks like I don't know a thing about myself.

We drove a few miles without speaking. Then Mike said, "Why do you think Ian did this?"

"What part?" I said. "The marriage or the shooting?"

"The marriage," he said.

"I think he sees himself as a savior. He decided Carità needed to be rescued. He's definitely cast me as the villain."

"Did she want to be rescued?"

"She came to me looking for a way to make a living without being killed," I said. "It's not an easy life, but she was safe in my house. She's an amazingly resourceful young person, and she doesn't complain or feel sorry for herself. I was surprised she fell so hard for your son."

"Why do you think she did that?"

"I think she was knocked out by the sex. They both were."

"That can be very persuasive," Mike agreed. He lifted his hand and patted my thigh before settling it back on the gear shift. "Would you like to be rescued?" he asked.

"From what?" I said. "I like my life just the way it is. And if there's one thing I dislike, it's being expected to feel gratitude for something I never asked for. Rescue is the last thing I need."

We drove on in silence. I was thinking that, sooner or later, Ian would expect Carità to be grateful, and that he would be disappointed in that expectation. It was pretty clear that the helpless party in their union was him, with his reckless crashing around in other people's lives. It wasn't an accident that he was with BB at a drug deal within hours of persuading Carità to be legally bound to him. He'd made those choices, but if you asked him, he'd say he was rescuing his true love from bondage and trying to save a friend from harm. Carità wouldn't be fooled by any of that; she had a very strong sense of her own worth. She might have some complex feelings about Ian Drohan, but one of those would never be gratitude.

The jungle curtain enveloping us thinned gradually, and the road opened, wider and less encroached upon by tropical flora. We were heading down into the midlands of the island. It was still very green, but it was the bland green of grass and deciduous trees, a temperate valley where the air was crisp, unruffled by the sea, and the cultivated fields of beans and grain, the deep, fenced grass lots where sheep and horses grazed mindlessly, made one think of nothing so much as pictures of the English countryside. Scattered villages were tucked in among the slopes, each with a parish church. Two of these were connected to well-reputed schools, one for boys and one for girls.

"It's St. Roch," Mike said. We arrived at a crossroads, and he turned off toward the west.

"I've heard of it," I said.

"Have you ever been there?"

"No," I said. "I don't know this area at all. I must have passed through it in a bus twenty-five years ago, but all I noticed was that it wasn't the city yet."

"It is bucolic," he agreed. "It looks like a good place to be bored right to death."

He's like me, I thought. We need life and turbulence.

The road wound down until we were in the midst of the farming community, passing through a village of perhaps a dozen houses and outbuildings, then onward between two fields of beans. Small brown birds rose up in sudden clouds as we passed, then spread out and settled again. "Even the birds are different here," I observed.

Mike nodded. "They're all brown or black," he said. "Parrots can't take all this peace and quiet."

"Parrots are far too sociable," I said, and we laughed.

After two more valleys, we turned into a narrow lane lined with pawpaw trees, then headed up a long gravel drive. The church came into view from the ground up, a solemn sandstone edifice with arched mahogany doors, stained-glass windows, and a square bell tower. Mike pulled into the circle and parked next to a battered pickup truck in a four-car lot on one side. I was thinking of Carità, arriving here with her lover and her sister, crossing the circle arm in arm. A well-tended herb garden in a plot near the stairs perfumed the air with scents of rosemary and thyme. She would have noticed that. Birds were everywhere, hopping about on the redbud bushes that flanked an open tiled porch on the far side, swooping in and out among the crepe myrtles at the back of the parking lot, picking about in the bright-green grass patch. Mike turned off the engine. "Well," he said. "Here we are."

I was about to have a conversation with a priest, I thought, an occasion not exactly in my line. "Does Father Dugan know anything about me?"

"Only that Carità was in your employ."

"Okay," I said. "That's good."

"Are you afraid he won't approve of you?"

"I think he's obligated to disapprove of me."

"You forget Mary Magdalene," he said. "She was a particular favorite of Jesus."

"Right," I said. "But she had to give up her job and follow him everywhere."

Mike considered this. "Jesus rescued her."

"Again with the rescue," I said.

As we walked past the church, under the porch to the vestry door, I was thinking about Mary Magdalene. "Didn't she wash his feet with her hair?" I asked Mike.

He looked puzzled. "Who?"

"Mary Magdalene."

"Did she?"

"Some men like that," I said.

Mike gave me a look of mild alarm. "Do they?" he said.

"Would you like that?" I asked.

"If it was your hair," he said. He touched the base of my neat French twist, then my cheek. "Damn, Lila," he said. "Now I'm getting an erection, and I have to talk to this priest about my son."

"Just imagine your son is standing on the other side of that door," I said.

He nodded, paused before the door. After a moment he said, "Yes, that's working." Then he raised his hand, made a fist, and knocked three times on the dark wood.

The small man who opened the door looked more like an owl than a priest. Though his costume was correct—black cassock with brown rope sash, huarache sandals over black socks—his features were avian. He tilted toward us as if his toes were wrapped around a perch. His eyes were round and black with heavy white brows, and his white hair stood out in two tufts on either side of his head. His sharp, beaklike nose jutted over the thin, colorless line of his mouth. He had that stunned readiness of an owl caught in a sudden flash of light, and as his eyes moved from Mike to me and back again, I had the sensation that his pupils were dilating. His voice, for he spoke at once, was thin and chirpy. "Judge Drohan," he said. "We meet at last." Then, eyes back to me: "And you are . . ."

"This is Mrs. Gulliver," Mike said. "She's Carità's employer."

A simper rearranged his lips; then his owlish eyes ran over and through me with such cool penetration that I took a step back. He saw right through us, I thought, and he knew at once how things stood between Mike and me.

"Do come inside," he said, pulling the door wider. We followed him through a gloomy, narrow hall, with faded toile wallpaper and a worn sisal floor mat. In an arched alcove cut into the wall stood a painted wooden statue of a man dressed in a knee-length robe and tall boots, reaching down to comfort another man, in tattered clothing, who knelt before him. A dog, holding some sort of parcel in his mouth, leaned against the skirt of the standing man's robe, staring alertly at something outside the alcove that only he could see. "St. Roch," Father Dugan remarked.

I paused to examine the statue. "Why does he have a dog?" I asked.

"It's a very ancient story," he said. "He was a virtuous man who devoted himself to caring for the sick and the poor. When he fell ill with the plague, he hid in a forest, so as not to infect others. A dog found him there and brought him a loaf of bread every day until he recovered. After that the dog never left his side. He's the patron saint of dogs now. There's a dog on the altar at St. Peter's Basilica in Rome, thanks to St. Roch."

There was something compelling about this statue, and I stood before it a moment longer. It seemed to me mysterious and aloof, yet ordinary, like finding an old, sealed letter, never delivered, containing some urgent message from long ago. It glowed with an aura of holiness. I touched the dog's head; it was smooth and hard. "It's a fine statue," I said.

"I call the dog Fido," Father Dugan said, ushering us on with an open palm. "Which, as you know, means 'I am faithful.'"

We came to an opaque glass door that opened into a white-plastered office. A desk facing two wooden armchairs, and a crucifix placed strategically so that the occupants of the chairs must confront the crucified Lord, constituted most of the furnishing. Bare as it was, there was something inviting about the room. Perhaps it was the electric kettle and the big teapot under a quilted cozy arranged on a rattan table in one corner. Above it a triangular, glass-fronted corner cabinet filled with small, white-labeled brown bottles suggested a pharmacy. The sun was low, and a diffuse golden light filtered in through the long, shuttered window. Father Dugan went directly to the desk, indicating with two quick bobs of his head that we were to take the armchairs. I could feel Mike's nerves as if they were my own; he was seriously on edge. I wondered that he should be. Father Dugan struck me as eminently harmless and of a cheerful disposition, more comic than threatening.

"Now," he said, "what can I do for you? I'm assuming you've come about Ian and his bride."

Mike, as lawyers will, sprang directly to offense. "Why didn't you tell them to consult their parents?" he said.

"I did," he replied. "Of course I did. But they were very determined. Ian said he was certain you and his mother—how is she, may I ask . . . ?"

"She's fine," Mike said.

"He was certain you would object. Carità, as *you* know"— he bowed his head to me—"has no living parents. They had brought their birth certificates; they're both of legal age. Carità's sister had come to be a witness. I saw no reason to turn them away. I've been a friend and adviser to Ian for many years, and I know him to be a strong-minded and quite determined young man. He and Carità are clearly very much in love."

"They've known each other a few days," Mike snapped.

Father Dugan blinked his eyes, making no response.

"Claudia is going to demand that this marriage be annulled," Mike said. "You must know that."

"That wouldn't be in my power to do," he said. "Nor is it up to Claudia."

"Do you think she's going to forgive you for this?"

His bushy eyebrows quivered. "I can't see that I require forgiveness, as I've done nothing wrong. Ian and Carità came to me seeking the sacrament of marriage. It would be a sin for me to deny that sacrament to earnest petitioners."

Mike brought one hand to his cheeks and dragged his face down between his thumb and forefinger, raising his eyes pleadingly toward the ceiling. Then he got to the point. "You've married my son to a prostitute."

There was a nice moment of total silence, while the three of us processed this heartfelt exclamation. The priest lowered his eyes, then flicked them to me as if he expected me to speak. His face was so poised and curious that I smiled at him. Taken by surprise, he smiled back. Then he turned to Mike with an expression of serious concern. "Yes," he said. "Ian told me that he had found Carità in a desperate situation."

A desperate situation.

This remark gave me the pip. I looked from one to the other, the judge and the priest—a perfect pair of hypocrites. Who did they think created a world in which an impoverished, beautiful blind girl could escape rape and possibly murder only by working in a brothel? Carità was desperate *when* she came to me, not *because* she came to me. Obviously, her life would be better married to a rich man's son, if he cared for her. I didn't begrudge her decision for a second, though I feared for her. Mike was clearly worried only about his cantankerous wife and his self-righteous son. Father Dugan was on the save-the-fallen-woman tack, trimming sail. And what would he be willing to do if Ian decided Carità was a burden he wanted to be rid of? Offer her asylum? Send her to a nunnery? Outrage busied my brain while the two men regarded each other warily.

"I need to find them," Mike said. "They're not in the city. Do you know where they are?"

"Not exactly," the priest replied. "It seems Ian is in some kind of trouble. An accident with a gun. They came here this morning, seeking my advice. Of course, I told them Ian must go back and turn himself in to the police."

"It was a drug deal," Mike informed him.

"Oh dear," said the priest. "He didn't tell me that."

"No," Mike said. "Why would he?"

"Oh dear," the priest said again. His pale hands riffled a stack of papers on the desk, as if searching for a place to hide.

"I want to help him," Mike said. "I want to tell him what his options are. I think he can get off on self-defense."

Father Dugan's face brightened. "Then there's hope," he said. His eyes fell on me—I was rubbing one of my knees, which was sore from my encounter with Mike on the carpet. "As I said," he repeated, "I don't know exactly where they went. Ian had it in his head that they would go to the west coast and he could find work on a fishing boat. He mentioned a fellow student from there, an odd name, Makoditch or Bakowich."

Mike nodded. "Bakovitch. His first name is Dario. They were roommates, his freshman year."

"Do you know where he's from?" I asked Mike.

"No," he said. "But I can find out. They'll know at the college."

"Good," said Father Dugan. "I have every confidence you will find them."

Mike sighed. "It's just like Ian to imagine he's going to run away and be a fisherman."

"Does he like boats?" I asked.

"He doesn't know a thing about them," Mike said. "And he's a vegetarian."

The priest nodded in agreement. "He's always been a passionate boy," he said. "He feels such outrage at injustice of any kind."

I was thinking of Ian's parting words to me: "No girl is *safe* with you." Just how safe would Carità be stuck in a shack in some benighted fishing village while her husband was out catching fish he was too pure to eat?

Mike was straightening his legs and bending them again. Clearly, he was ready to leave and looking for an exit line. Father Dugan, quick to sense this impatience, leaned back in his chair and produced a small canvas bag from some hidden chamber of his desk. He raised his eyes to the glass case on the wall. "You'd best be off in search of your poor son," he said. "But no visitor can leave my office without a sample of my medicaments." He rose from his chair, moving past me, holding a small golden key, which he turned in the lock of the case. Mike stood up, giving me a look of mock alarm.

"I noticed when we came in that you have a thriving herb garden," I said. "Are you a serious herbalist?"

He looked back at me over the rim of his glasses. "You're very observant, Mrs. Gulliver," he said. "I am indeed an ardent student of the homeopathic medical arts." He turned back, rummaging among the little bottles and jars on the shelves. "This one," he said, "and this one: these are for Claudia. She knows what they are and will be happy to have them."

"Is she ill?" Mike asked incredulously.

"Nothing serious," he said. "Just female troubles." He

pulled a sheet of brown paper from a roll mounted on the side of the case, wrapped the bottles carefully, and placed them into the bag.

"Now, this one is for you, Judge Drohan. I have an intuition that you have trouble sleeping. Just a few drops in a small glass of water before bed. It's very effective." He gazed at his shelves as he wrapped the sleeping potion. "And this is just a general cure for stomach upsets of all kinds, good for the whole family. It has a very pleasant flavor. Just a tablespoon as needed. The instructions are on the label." Into the bag went the sleeping medicine and the stomach cure. "And finally . . ." He moved a bottle aside and took down a white glass jar. "This is for you, Mrs. Gulliver." As he wrapped it, he smiled upon me beatifically. "It's for your knees. Very healing. Just rub it in once in the morning and again once at night."

When we were in the car, Mike handed me the bag and said with mock seriousness, "Don't let anything happen to this."

"Really," I said, "he's like a talking garden gnome."

"Oh dear, oh dear," said Mike in a perfect imitation of the wide-eyed priest. "A drug deal!" He turned the key, and the car rumbled into life.

I opened the bag, extracted one of the little bottles, and unwrapped it. It was carefully labeled in small, neat print, with instructions, indications, and ingredients. "The one for sleep has belladonna in it," I observed. "That should work."

Mike steered past the billowing herb garden, down the

driveway, to the open road. "How does he know I don't sleep?" he said.

"He's like me," I said. "Very observant."

"I think he knew about us," he said.

"He knew about us before we sat down." We drove a few miles in silence. I was brooding about the tacit assumption that Carità wasn't good enough for the useless Ian.

"He'll tell Claudia," Mike said.

"About the marriage?" I said.

He smiled, moving his hand from the gear shift to my thigh, without looking at me. "About us," he said.

By the time we got to the hotel, it was dark, and the road was so black the headlight beams were like golden rails guiding us through a jungle crammed with eyes. When the hotel appeared, the portico glowed from the flickering gas torches set among the glossy leaves of the giant potted ferns. "Shall we have a drink before we go upstairs?" Mike asked, turning into the parking lot. There were a few cars, and when I opened my door, I could hear voices, soft laughter, and guitar music floating out from the patio.

"Sure," I said, stepping down onto the gravel. "There's no hurry."

He laughed. "I don't know, Lila," he said. He crossed behind the car and wrapped his arm about my waist. "I don't want to hurry, but I can hardly wait."

"You'll be fine," I said.

We went into the inviting bar and took the table we'd had earlier. "We should probably eat something," Mike said. "Are you hungry? It's mostly bar food."

"I live on bar food," I assured him.

The bartender joined us. "Welcome back," he said. "What can I bring you?"

"Vodka martini," Mike said. "Olives. Dry."

"I'll have the same," I said.

"And some food," Mike added. "What do you have?"

"We have gazpacho," he said. We both wrinkled our noses. "I can give you a charcuterie plate with cheese and salami, bread, grilled pineapple, cornichons."

"That sounds fine," I said.

"We'll have that," said Mike.

When he left us, Mike said, "Do you actually live on bar food?"

"Pretty much," I said. "I don't cook anything but eggs. Breakfast is my main meal. We're open by appointment from noon to four, then open generally around six, like a restaurant, except we stay open until the last customer is served. I snack in the afternoon, and at the end of the night, when I'm doing my books, I finish up any canapés left from the drawing room."

"What an odd business you're in," Mike said.

"It's the oldest profession."

"Right," he said.

The drinks arrived.

What did we talk about? I hardly remember. We were getting to know each other, though, in an important way, we already knew everything we needed to know, and we knew we knew it. I've always thought sex first, rapport later, is a rational sequence, because, if the sex doesn't work, no amount of earnest friendship is going to fix the problem, and one party or the other is going to end up feeling cheated. I already had a hunch that Mike was a difficult man, and he was clearly on the brink of some kind of crisis; he was in a throw-all-the-cards-in-the-air frame of mind.

We did ascertain our age difference: he was forty-eight, exactly ten years older than I. Our birthdays were a week apart: both Leos. So—it's going to be a roaring match, I thought.

After we'd finished a couple of drinks and all the food, we agreed to go upstairs. I was looking forward to it. The sexual spark between us was electrifying, and I could feel it all over the surface of my skin. His hand around my elbow as we crossed the room to the staircase, on the small of my back as I ascended before him, on my shoulder as we entered the third door on the right of the narrow hall—each touch relaxed all tension like a magic wand, and a welcome dreaminess came over me, washing away every distracting concern. He closed the door, flipped the latch. I turned to him. He laid his palms on either side of my skull, loosening my hair as he pulled me in gently for a five-alarm kiss. My knees buckled, and he held me up, backed me into the bed.

When we floated back up to the surface, our clothes were scattered across the floor, and a soft breeze lifted the gauzy curtain over the open window. In the distance, I could hear voices and recorded music, a song I recognized about sailing away in a boat. Mike's big head, facedown, was lodged between my neck and shoulder. The ceiling fan came into focus. The thought that vibrated like a hummingbird in my brain was: "This is it."

What the songs are about. The connotation of words like "obsession" and "ecstasy." Why the word "carnal" is so much more thrilling than "spiritual." Mike nuzzled my ear and whispered, "What do you think: is it pheromones?"

I laughed, and he lifted his face to smile at me. "Something like that," I said.

A glance at the bedside clock told me an hour had passed. I looked about the room. Whitewashed walls, stone floor, rattan furniture except for the bed, which was brass with vertical bars you could grasp above your head to keep from getting jammed against the wall. There was a framed print of a parrot on one wall, a watercolor of a palm grove on another. The ceiling was high; there was the fan, and plaster cornices. "It's nice here," I said.

Mike groaned softly as he rolled off me. "It's our hideaway," he said. "We can come here regularly."

"That may not be so easy to arrange," I said.

"I don't see why."

"You work days; I work nights."

"Surely not every night. What about Sundays?"

"Sunday is busy all day and night," I said. "Clients come straight from communion to my house."

"You're kidding me," he said.

"No," I protested. "I wish it wasn't true. Monday's our closed day."

"Mondays, then."

I moved my legs to the edge of the bed and pushed myself up to sit. "We'll see how it goes," I said.

We were quiet on the drive back to the city. The birds were settling in for the night, blanketing the forest with a cacophonous racket that made us smile. When we got to the main road,

Mike flicked on the radio to a station that played local jazz. The group playing featured a singer I particularly liked, with a breathy voice, like that of a man exhausted from fast living. Just one more dance, he sang. Just one more, before the sun rises, before we have to part. Mike rested his hand over mine, and the night rolled over us. I was thinking about what we'd just done in the hotel room, the astounding naturalness of it, the sense of having arrived at last at the true destination, the right place. The road opened before us; the traffic thickened; we could see the lights from the harbor. Mike turned the radio down as we left the highway. "I'll put my clerks on finding what town Bakovitch is from first thing in the morning. It won't take long. Then I'll try to track them down. Will you come with me again?"

"I don't know," I said. "Ian really doesn't like me."

"He doesn't like me, either, but I'm thinking it would make it easier for Carità if you were there."

"Maybe so," I said. In truth, I wanted to see Carità.

"I'll come by as soon as I find out," he said. "And we can make a plan."

We were approaching my street. Mike downshifted, turned at the corner, glided up to the curb. The lights were on downstairs, but upstairs was dark. It wasn't that late, I thought. "What time is it?" I asked Mike.

"Almost midnight," he said, consulting his watch.

"They must be closing up," I said. I felt a mild urgency to be in my house, to talk with Brutus and Mimi about the events of the night, to sit at the kitchen table with my tea and my books, attending to the details of my business. As I opened the door, Mike brushed his fingers against my cheek. "I'll see you tomorrow," he said.

I looked back at him, and we smiled knowingly at what we now had between us. No one knew what we knew about each other. I stood up, closed the door, and crossed the sidewalk to the gate.

I found Brutus and Mimi at the kitchen table. He was drinking whiskey, and she was finishing an open bottle of champagne, doubtless left over from the night's customers. As I pushed open the screen, Brutus raised his eyes and gave me an appraising look. He seldom saw me dressed for polite company, and something in the style amused him. "Did you find them?" he asked.

Mimi, who had her back to me, stood up and reached for a wineglass on the wall shelf. "Will you join us?" she asked.

"I will," I said, pulling out the chair next to hers. Then, to Brutus, who was sipping his whiskey, patiently waiting for me to answer his question, I said, "No, not yet. But we have a lead. They're on the west coast."

"That's not much of a lead," he observed.

"True," I agreed. "But I think we'll know the name of the town tomorrow. We know Ian has a friend there."

Mimi carefully poured the wine down the side of the fluted glass and set it before me.

"How was business?" I asked.

"Pretty slow," she said. "Sally's banker came in with a friend around eight. Then things picked up a bit around nine. That Navy guy came in looking for Carità. He went up with

Vivien and Charlotte and seemed pretty satisfied. I had two customers; I think Charlotte had one other. They all cleared out by eleven, and we started closing down."

I sipped the wine, feeling strangely irritated.

"Did you get dinner?" Mimi asked. "There's some sandwiches left."

"I did," I said, lifting the glass. The champagne was flat.

"Joe Shock's guy died," Brutus said abruptly.

I put my glass down. "He's dead?" I said.

"He never came out of the coma."

"Do you think Marcus had anything to do with it?"

"Definitely. The doctors told Joe his guy was stabilized, and he'd be out of the ICU in the morning. Then a nurse checked on him and he was dead."

"What I'm wondering is how they know Ian was even at the scene of the crime," Mimi said. "The only witnesses are both dead now, right?"

"They have the gun, which will have Ian's prints on it," Brutus said. "Joe and I saw BB and Ian go out together an hour earlier."

"So it's all circumstantial," Mimi observed.

"Detective Mimi," said Brutus.

I nodded at Mimi, and she met my eyes with the look of candid skepticism all women share when a man dismisses the salient details she has called to his attention. We were silent for a moment while Brutus refilled his glass. "Rich boys never serve time," he opined.

"That's probably true," I agreed.

Mimi yawned, drained her glass, and rinsed it at the sink. "I'm going to bed," she said.

"Thanks for taking over," I said.

She turned to me, yawning widely. "Glad to be helpful," she said.

Brutus was frowning. When Mimi had disappeared down the hall, he said, "So . . . what I don't get is why you had to go with the judge to track down his son."

"How do you know I was with the judge?" I asked.

"He came to the bar wanting to know where your house is. He knew his son was seeing a girl here. Mimi said you left with a mystery man."

His peevish tone irritated me, and I decided not to let him know anything more about Mike than I had to. "I told him Ian and Carità were married and had left together."

Brutus nodded, lightening up a bit. "How'd he take the news?"

"Not well," I said. "Not well at all. He thought they'd probably run to the priest. I said I wanted to go along so Carità wouldn't get stuck in a fight between father and son."

"But you didn't find them, so the judge took you to dinner."

"We stopped at a bar on the way back."

"Right," he said skeptically.

"What's it to you?" I asked.

He gave his head a shake, trying to clear off the whiskey. "I just don't like that kid," he said. "I wish he'd never come in here. And his father has a reputation for being a jerk, on and off the bench. He's a skirt chaser and a blowhard."

"Is he?" I said, filing this characterization away to be mulled over when I was alone. "He seems nice enough to me. Very concerned about his son, naturally."

Brutus considered this. "His son will get off," he said. "It's Carità who's going to get screwed. They'll have the marriage annulled, drop her at your door, and drive away."

"I don't think they can do that," I said. "The priest said he didn't have the power to do it. They'd have to come up with some kind of cause. If they want to get rid of her, Ian will have to divorce her, in which case he'd be deserting her, and she'd get a big settlement."

Brutus nodded. "That's true," he said. "She could take that little punk to the cleaners."

"You know how she is," I continued. "She's smart, and she likes money. If Ian betrays her, she won't have a scruple, and the law will be on her side."

"She'd be free," Brutus said, savoring the thought.

She'd be free, I thought, and it occurred to me that she had realized this from the start. She could buy a house, get her sister out of the oyster bar, find a teacher, get a seeing-eye dog, and spend her time reading novels, dining out, eating chocolates, and walking in the park.

Brutus put his glass in the sink. "I'd better go close up," he said. "The bar was slow, too."

I picked up the liquor order, which was on top of my red accounts book. "Don't forget this," I said.

He reached out, and as I handed him the form, our eyes met. His were full of questions he didn't dare to ask. "You look great in that suit," he said.

It was just after ten the next morning, and I was eating a scrambled egg at the kitchen table when Mike arrived at the door.

"Don't you have a job?" I asked.

He pushed the screen open and stepped inside, looking pleased with himself. He was wearing a short-sleeved shirt printed with fern leaves, gray linen pants, and huaraches. "Very tropical," I observed.

"I was hoping to catch you in your robe."

"You're in luck," I said. "I just got out of the shower. My hair's still wet."

"I see that," he said. "May I have coffee?"

"Help yourself," I said.

He filled a mug and turned to me, leaning on the counter. "I went in for a couple of hours and got the clerks set up for the day."

"Did you find out the name of the town?"

"I did," he said. "It's San Bosco. Just south of Port Louis."

"I've been on that coast, but I've never heard of it," I said.

"It's a village. Maybe six hundred people. About a three-hour drive."

"You want to go now?"

"Whenever you're ready."

I finished my egg. Mimi was upstairs; I could hear the water running in the bathroom. Charlotte was coming in early. They could manage without me, but I hated to ask them. "I can't just walk away whenever I feel like it."

"If we leave soon," he said, "we can be back before you close."

I pushed my chair from the table. "Let me go talk to Mimi," I said. "I'll see if she's willing."

As I climbed the stairs, I considered my offer. Time was as important as money to Mimi. I'd give her the weekend off with a base pay. I heard the shower cut off, and I went to my room to get dressed. This time, I would be more casual: white silk slacks, a black cotton blouse, my favorite red sandals. I pulled on my underpants and wrestled my breasts into a bra. I heard the bathroom door open, and Mimi, wrapped in a towel, passed my bedroom door. She glanced in at me and paused. "What's going on?" she asked.

"He's here," I said. "We're going to the village where he thinks Ian and Carità are."

"You want me to open," she conjectured.

"I don't like to ask," I said.

"It's okay," she said. "I don't have any classes today."

"I'll give you the weekend off, with pay," I said.

"That would be great," she said. "But you don't have to do it."

"I won't feel right if I don't," I said. "I don't know when I'll get back tonight."

"If I've got the whole weekend off, you can stay all night with my blessing."

I was pulling on my slacks. "Thanks," I said. "That could happen."

She leaned in the doorway, watching me dress. "Do you think you'll find them right away?"

"It's a fishing village," I said. "Six hundred people. Carità is not a woman who goes unnoticed."

"That's true," she said.

I buttoned the blouse, stopped at the mirror to run a brush through my hair, and spritzed my bosom with cologne. "I'm off," I said.

Mimi turned back to her room while I hustled down the stairs, examining the contents of my purse as I went. Sunglasses, a comb, a lipstick, a toothbrush, my wallet, and a checkbook. What else did I need? In the kitchen, Mike looked up and gave me his sweeping appraisal. "I surely do like your style," he said.

"I'm ready," I said.

We both pushed on our sunglasses and headed for the car. As Mike turned the key and the engine whined awake, he grinned at me. "We look like a couple of tourists who lost their way," he said. "The locals won't know what to make of us."

"Have you ever been in that area?" I asked.

"No."

"It's pretty poor," I said. "And they're not happy about that."

"Will they try to rob us?"

"Not so's you'd know it," I replied.

He frowned, shifting gears as we pulled away from the curb. "They won't have trouble taking advantage of Ian," he said. "He's a babe in the woods."

There are several villages on the bay, south of the harbor town of Port Louis. The road comes down steeply from a ridge, then narrows, passing through a marsh where the trees are stunted, and small birds rise abruptly in great clouds for reasons known only to their kind. For the last few miles, we followed a bus plying the coast road. A smattering of tin-roofed clapboard houses painted in pastel colors ended at a dusty square, dominated on one side by a whitewashed courthouse and on another by a general store with a striped awning, flanked by a bar with iron tables and chairs set out on a gravel yard, and two other, unidentifiable shops. A few tired-looking men sat huddled at a bar table drinking coffee. Two women dressed in black emerged from an unmarked storefront—a bakery, I guessed, since each had a baguette tucked under her arm. They shielded their eyes with their hands against the afternoon sun, which was settling down directly over the simple spire of the church on the third side of the square. A parched rosebush clung to a rickety iron-rail fence enclosing a painted wooden statue of a robed man, presumably San Bosco, who raised one hand, blessing his communicants. The square itself was covered in scanty grass and crisscrossed by a concrete sidewalk.

Several cars, two trucks, and a van were randomly parked along the curb. "I guess you park anywhere," Mike said, pulling into a space next to the van. He turned off the engine, and we sat for a moment, contemplating the plain little vista. "Where did they even find a place to sleep in this burg?" he said.

"There may be more to it nearer the water," I suggested.

He nodded. "I hope so," he said.

"Let's ask at the bar," I said.

The bar was a counter. The barman stood before a large framed print of Jesus, his arms raised as if in a cheer, his pink lips lightly parted, and his blue eyes gazing dreamily just over the patron's head. They served beer and coffee. A plate of muffins and another of sandwiches wrapped in paper, arranged behind hand-printed signs proclaiming "Muffins" and "Sandwiches," constituted the food offerings. The floor was chipped, cracked black-and-white tile, and there were a few cane chairs lined up beneath a shelf on the opposite wall. We ordered coffees and stood without speaking while the barman filled two thick white ceramic cups from a tall urn fitted with a spigot. He was a small, wiry man with well-developed forearms, a big head, and oddly small features crowded together beneath a cap of close-cropped wiry white hair.

We were the only customers, and though the barman gave no hint of any interest in our being there, the fact of our otherness, of our not belonging, was as conspicuous as a tiger in the room. He kept his eyes down as he slid the cups across the bar, followed by a slip of yellow notepaper upon which he'd written the price.

Mike took a quick sip from his cup, set it down, and, just as the fellow was turning away, said, "We've never been here before. I wonder if you could help us."

The man paused, allowing his eyes to rest on my face with an expression of perfect indifference.

"I believe my son and his wife may be staying near here," Mike continued. The man's lips moved slightly; perhaps he only pressed his tongue against his teeth; he kept his eyes focused on my face.

"He's a tall blond young man. He drives a white sports car."

Unmoving, the barman blinked.

"His wife is blind," I said.

"They're staying down by the wharf," he said to me. "There's a fish vendor who rents a few rooms over his shop. That's where they are."

Mike glanced over his shoulder at me. "Well, that was easy," he said.

"Can you tell us how to get there?" I asked.

He nodded. "Go out that door, take a right at the corner, and keep on till you see the water."

"Should we take the car?" Mike asked. "Or can we walk?"

"It's not far," he replied. Now he raised his eyes just over my head, and I had the momentary sensation that someone was standing behind me.

"Let's walk," I said. I took up my cup and downed the tepid brew. Mike produced his wallet and laid a bill across the yellow check. "Keep the change," he said. I followed him out into the street. At the first corner, we turned as directed and found ourselves looking down a potholed asphalt road that ended in a wide band of turquoise that was the sea. Thin purple clouds gathered close around the dazzling sun. Both sides of the street were lined with more of the tin-roofed houses, some with porches and garden patches, others with open garages strung with fishing nets, or gravel driveways in which skiffs and small boats perched landlocked on rusty hitches. A few residents were sketchily in evidence, on the porches or walking on the street. Four men, gathered around a table in one of the open garages, drinking beer from cans and slapping down cards with murmurs of confidence or dismay, ignored us as we passed. We walked in the street, as there was no sidewalk.

The asphalt ended in a gravel strip leading to a wooden fishing pier that jutted out over a narrow beach and across the sparkling water. It was unexpectedly solid and appealing, with a wide staircase and sturdy rails. Without speaking, we climbed the steps, crossed to the rail, and looked out over the narrow, curved beach.

And there they were.

They stood side by side, facing the sea, up to their ankles in the receding tide, their arms around each other's waists, her head resting against his shoulder. He was wearing walking shorts and a loose linen shirt; Carità wore a brightly patterned halter-top dress with a full skirt I'd never seen before. Her hair was loose, moving in the light breeze. As we watched, Ian bent his head to press a kiss on her temple. She lifted her face to receive another on her lips. Then she slid away from him, easing free of his waist, her arm gliding along his until they were hand in hand, arms outstretched. He turned toward her, drawing her in. She leaned away, as if resisting, but it was a shy, playful resistance. He released her hand, and she took a few quick steps toward the shore, paused, and turned to face him, smiling. The sun struck her face, and she seemed to bathe in the warmth, digging her toes into the sand. As she turned away, he ran to her and caught her wrist. She allowed herself to be drawn into his embrace, her back to him as he bent over her, swept her hair aside, and planted kisses on her neck.

"It's like a dance," Mike said. His arm was pressed against mine as we leaned on the wooden rail.

Ian released Carità, and she took a few quick steps toward the sea, her arms outstretched at her sides. The water swirled around her calves, her knees. She caught her skirt in one hand and gathered it up to keep it dry.

"She's very graceful," Mike said.

Ian dashed in after her. She was laughing, raising her hands over her head, as if she were about to dive into the waves. He shifted to one side so that he caught her as she let herself fall forward. Her arms folded like wings around his neck. A long kiss followed; their bodies pressed close. When he released her, she ran toward the shore again, stepping high over the waves, and he ran, too, outstripping her and falling to his knees before her in the sand. She held out her hands, resting her fingers on his upturned face.

"It's a shame to interrupt this touching scene," Mike said.

"They do seem carefree," I agreed.

"They're coming back this way," Mike said. "Let's go down and meet them."

They were walking hand in hand toward the pier, their heads bent to each other, talking softly. Something Ian said made Carità laugh, and she raised her face toward where we stood. If her eyes could see, I thought, we'd be directly in her line of sight. Mike strode off toward the waterside staircase they would have to use to get back to the town. I followed. They were out of sight briefly; then, as we arrived at the steps, they appeared, still hand in hand, below us. Ian looked up, saw his father, stepped back abruptly, and said, "No." He caught Carità by the elbow and turned her away.

"What's wrong?" she said.

"Ian," Mike called after him, "wait. I just want to talk to you."

But Ian stalked purposefully through the sand, pulling Carità back toward the water. Mike rushed down the stairs.

I was wondering where Ian thought he was going. The beach ended in a wide stone jetty. A few dilapidated fishing boats lay on their sides in the sand with tattered fishing nets spread over the keels. Mike hit the beach, struck out at a run, and quickly caught up with them.

I followed unhurriedly. I dislike public dramas, and this promised to be one. As I approached, Ian and his father faced off. Carità stood just behind her husband, frowning, her hands on her hips.

"Go home," Ian rebuked his father. "Leave us alone. We're fine. We don't need you." Then, before Mike could speak, Ian spotted me closing in. "What is she doing here?" he exclaimed.

Carità turned her face, her chin lifted in her listening mode. Though I'd not said a word, her expression relaxed, and she said calmly, "Hello, Mrs. Gulliver."

I experienced a surge of affection for this reckless young woman, who always seemed to know more than the people she called "sighted" about what was going on around her. "Hello, Mrs. Drohan," I said.

Ian shot me a chilly look, but Carità straightened her spine, as if accepting a royal address. "She came because she was worried about Carità," Mike said.

Ian flushed bright red with outrage. "She's a whoremonger, Dad!" he exclaimed.

Mike ignored this attack on my character. "Listen to me, son," he said. "The man you shot has died."

"It was an accident," Ian protested.

"I believe you," Mike said. "And I don't think he died of the bullet you fired at him."

This got his son's attention. "What do you mean?"

"I think Marcus Betone had him murdered in the hospital."

"Why would he do that?" Ian wondered.

"In revenge for his son," Mike said. "Though no one will ever be able to prove it."

I was watching Carità, who followed this conversation with an expression of high alert. This was probably not how she had imagined her first meeting with her father-in-law. Like many a poor woman, she had married a man who turned out to be a criminal, though this revelation didn't usually follow so hard on the wedding night. The father-and-son confrontation had erupted without anyone's bothering to introduce her. She stood slightly apart, in the new dress Ian had probably purchased at a roadside stall. The sea breeze played with her hair, lifting it away from her face, then pushing it back across her cheek.

"I'm not going back," Ian insisted.

"That's fine," Mike replied. "I don't want you to come back. That's not why we're here."

I took a step closer to Carità, and she turned to me, glowering. "How are you?" I ventured.

"I'm well," she said.

"Do you like it here?"

She nodded. "It's okay," she said. "I like the beach. But our room smells like fish."

The men had fallen silent, and Mike's attention settled on us. "Carità," I said, "this is Ian's father, Michael Drohan."

She turned toward him, putting out her hand in that aristocratic way she had, as though she expected some obeisance. "I'm pleased to meet you," she said.

I saw the voice hit him, and a needle of jealousy pierced me right between the eyes. Mike was momentarily stymied; then he took her hand lightly in his own and replied, "Call me Mike."

Ian regarded this rapprochement between his father and his bride with deep suspicion. Carità withdrew her hand, brought it to rest against her sternum, and bowed her head, listening for what came next. "How did you find us?" Ian asked. Then, answering his own question, "Father Dugan."

"He doesn't know where you are," Mike said. "You mentioned Dario Bakovitch to him and he remembered the name. I figured out the rest."

"Does Mother know?"

"Where you are? No. But everybody knows about the shooting. It was in the papers."

Ian shrugged moodily. "I don't mean that," he said. "Does she know we're married?"

Mike held his hands out, palms up, in a gesture of frustration. "No, she doesn't."

Ian took this in silence, stepping past me to wrap his arm around Carità's waist and nuzzle his mouth against her neck. She didn't move, but spoke wistfully, as if the vista of how dark her future might be had just opened up before her. "Are the police looking for Ian?" she asked.

"Not yet," Mike replied. "But they will be. And if he gets arrested, he won't be any safer in jail than Joe's guy was in the hospital. Marcus won't be satisfied with offing the dealer. He's going after Joe Shock. It will be a war between them, and Ian could be right in the middle of it."

"Marcus will want to protect Ian," Carità observed. "Which will make Ian a target for Joe Shock. He could be collateral damage."

Mike gave Carità a closer inspection, struck, I thought, by the unexpected directness of her address, the quickness of her comprehension. I'd seen that light dawn before when anyone bothered to listen to her, though this was naturally rare in her profession. Mimi and I had remarked on her aptitude for summarizing the content of a client's character. She liked to listen to the local news on the radio and was adept at predicting the consequences of an alliance or an argument among the local politicians. In spite of her blindness, or perhaps because of it, she was an excellent judge of human psychology.

Mike nodded. "That's right," he said. "And that's why I think you should both go to the mainland."

Ian shook his head wearily from side to side. "No, no, no. We're not going to the mainland."

"It wouldn't be for long," Mike said. "But right now, you need to not be arrested."

"How will they find me?" Ian protested. "There's not even a police station here."

Carità turned to her husband and said what we were all thinking. "As long as I'm with you, dearest, you're easy to find."

"I'm not leaving you," Ian replied.

But Carità was working on a plan, and she laid her index finger across his lips like a mother silencing a child. "Your father is right; you should go into hiding," she said. "You should be disguised. Cut your hair, change the color, let your beard grow, wear cheap clothes, take a bus to some other village. Use a different name. Don't contact anyone. Mrs. Gulliver and I will go back to the city in your car. Once you're settled, send a postcard so I'll know where you are. Then, as soon as it's safe, we'll come get you."

Mike and I looked at each other. "This is not a bad plan," he said.

Without thinking, I said to Carità, "You're welcome to stay at my house until things calm down."

Ian menaced me with a raised palm. "Why is this woman here?" he exclaimed. "My wife will never set foot in that hellhole again. Is that perfectly clear? She will stay at my parents' home for as long as she needs to, until I can come back."

So, I thought, Ian has agreed to go into hiding, and Carità will move into the mansion by the park. She'll be a free woman, and a rich one.

I wondered if she didn't find this result more than a little appealing.

We adjourned to the room Ian and Carità had rented over the fish shop. It was spare and dreary: an iron bedstead with a lumpy mattress, a sink with a cracked mirror and a toilet spliced into a corner, a sprung rattan chair, and a square enamel-topped table with two straight-back chairs drawn up to it. Two cheap beach towels were folded over the back of a chair, probably purchased at the same store where they'd bought Carità's dress. The window looked out over the dusty street. "The shower is outside," Carità informed me. "It's on the ground, inside a fence, and there's no ceiling, so it feels like you're in the sun and the rain at the same time."

It was characteristic of her to find something she liked, I thought.

There was a backpack leaning against the table leg, opened to reveal a bundle of Ian's clothes and a few books. Carità had run from my house with nothing but the clothes on her back.

The four of us stood there, sorting through our uncomfortable, ill-fitting thoughts. I felt oddly superfluous, and resolved to make myself useful. "I'll go check out that general store," I said. "They'll surely have scissors, and they may have some kind of hair dye."

"Good idea," said Mike, too quickly. Well, I thought, they have a lot to talk about.

Outside, the sun was a smear of orange fire shrouded by wispy clouds. I walked along the street, past the flimsy houses and the men stolidly slapping down cards in the heat, thinking of how little I knew about Mike Drohan. Naturally, it occurred to me that he was breaking the law he was sworn to uphold by aiding his son in avoiding arrest. But Carità's proposal was temporary by definition, and Ian would only postpone rather than escape justice. Surely justice wouldn't be served by having Ian found dead in a prison cell. That was the fate his father, knowing what he did about Joe Shock, was wise to fear.

I came to the square and walked halfway around to go in

under the awning of the general store. It was reassuringly cool
and roomy inside. A few racks of clothes and a table covered
with folded T-shirts blocked the front, but behind them were
aisles of shelves with all manner of merchandise. At the back,
behind a long counter, two women stood chatting, while one
carefully folded a pile of brightly colored kerchiefs.

I spotted a section of shampoo bottles along the far wall and
approached it, passing close by the women, who ignored me.
There was a small display of scissors—nail, hair, sewing—and
at the bottom, under the hair spray, a meager selection of hair
dyes—mostly blond—a jar of paint for covering gray, a fast-
acting dye that would result in a dark chestnut, and another
promising a shade described as "ebony." Ian would look ridiculous with black hair, I thought, but the chestnut, if cut short,
would look natural, and not so alarming when it grew out. I
found myself thinking of Carità's notion that Ian should change
his hair color, which, of course, she'd never seen; nor could the
words "blond" or "chestnut" or "ebony" signify anything particular to her. She knew red flowers were in my yard because
they drew hummingbirds. She knew the names of colors she
couldn't distinguish. Her teacher had taught her that some were
warm, some cool. And she knew that Ian's hair was thick and
long, that he was clean-shaven. Her fingers would have told her
that.

I picked up the dye and chose a pair of hair scissors. To
make my purchases appear more random, I added a shower cap,
a box of Band-Aids, and a tube of hand cream. Then I went to
the counter, where one of the sullen women rang up the sale

without looking at me, so intent was she on her companion's description of a family quarrel. I stashed my loot in my purse and headed back to the room where the three Drohans were planning their next move.

I found them subdued. Ian and Carità sat on the edge of the bed; Mike slumped on the chair by the table. They all stood when I came in, announcing that my errand had been successful. I laid out my materials on the table, adding the comb I had in my purse. I'd imagined I would cut Ian's hair, but Mike took up the scissors and motioned his son into the chair. "I used to cut his hair when he was a boy," he said.

"Always in a bowl," Ian said. "Can you do something not a bowl?"

"I'll do my best," Mike promised, combing through his son's wavy locks. It appeared that father and son were somewhat reconciled. Mike pulled up a lock over Ian's forehead and cut it close to the scalp. "I'm going to make it all very short," he said.

It took about twenty minutes of steady snipping before the last curl drifted to the floor. Mike stepped back, surveying his handiwork. "Not bad," he said. Ian stood up, dusting hair from his lap, and crossed to the mirror over the sink. He looked, I thought, like a shorn sheep. His eyes, unprotected, seemed to bulge; his ears, now revealed, were long and fleshy. "This is awful," Ian complained, passing his palm over his skull.

"Let me feel it," Carità said. Ian went to her, bending down while she ran her fingers from his neck, over his head, down his face, to his chin. "Oh," she said. "All your lovely hair."

I took up the box of dye. "You can do this yourself," I said. "Instructions are on the box. I bought a shower cap. It takes half an hour."

Half an hour felt like a long time to me, and evidently Mike thought so, too. "They sell sandwiches at the bar on the square," he said. "Lila and I can get a few and bring them here. While we're out, we'll check on the bus schedule. The less the townspeople see of you two, the better."

Ian agreed at once, and I thought I knew why. While he was in the shower cap waiting for the dye to process, he and Carità could have a parting fuck. "We can stop at the general store while we're there," I said. "They have T-shirts. We could pick up a couple for the road."

Ian was incapable of acknowledging me as anything but a force for evil in his life, so he directed his reply to his father. "A couple of shirts would be good," he said. "Get something plain. Black, if they have it."

And take your time, I heard directly from his brain.

"Will do," said his father.

Mike and I walked along without touching, each experiencing, I did not doubt, seriously mixed feelings about our mission. My own thoughts warily circled the question of the possible reception Carità might expect to receive in her husband's home. Would Ian's mother be kind or suspicious, curious or indifferent? Did Mike intend to tell her where her son had met his bride?

We passed the card-playing locals before Mike revealed the character of his own ruminations. "I have to admit," he said, softly, as if thinking aloud, "I didn't think Ian had it in him."

I drifted closer to his side. "Had what in him?" I asked.

"To take off and marry a girl like that."

"He was very determined," I said.

"To make that commitment," he continued. "He hardly knows a thing about her."

"What do you think of her?"

He glanced at me, his expression perplexed, as if my question had come out of the air. After a moment of thought—what *did* he think?—he answered, "Well, I can certainly see the attraction."

I repressed an impulse to slap his handsome face. Why did this reply irritate me? It was an honest answer delivered in his most bemused and spontaneous manner, no stress on any syllable, no leering complicity at the end. Why did it sting me so? I changed my tack. "What will your wife think of her?"

He rolled his eye heavenward. "She's not going to think it's good news, that's for sure."

"Is she very close to Ian?"

He shrugged. "Only in the way a queen may be close to her valet."

"Is Ian content with that?"

"He tries his best to give his mother the service she requires; we all do. But the truth is, she can never be satisfied, and he can never be anything but a disappointment to her. Perhaps he's begun to realize that."

"You make her sound like a terrible bully."

He nodded. "That's an excellent description of my dear wife," he said. "She *is* a terrible bully."

We had arrived at the square and turned our attention to our errands.

By the time we returned to the runaways, we had laid out a plausible plan. Ian would take the 4:00 p.m. bus to a town farther south. I would drive Carità in Ian's car to my house, while Mike drove home to prepare his wife for the arrival of her daughter-in-law. Carità would pack her scant possessions, and I would then deliver her to the Drohan mansion. Once she was inside, Mike would arrange for a cab to take me home.

And that was exactly what we did. In the plain T-shirt and jeans, Ian was indistinguishable from a wide range of gawky young men. He and Carità both had the unfocused gaze and giddiness of after-sex. They ate the sandwiches hurriedly. Mike would accompany Ian to the bus stop while Carità and I loaded up Ian's car. Money changed hands from father to son. Mike suggested that it might be a good thing if Ian's mother didn't know where he and Carità had met. To my surprise, Mr. Honesty agreed at once. They quickly concocted a cover story. Ian had met Carità at a party; she was the cousin of a friend at college, visiting her aunt in the city. The lovers' parting, a long embrace at the door—tears from him, promises from her—touched me only slightly. I was eager to be on the road.

Ian's car, a sporty British-made two-seater, was parked on the square. As Carità settled into the passenger side, I adjusted the driver's seat, which was pushed back as far as it would go to accommodate the long legs of its owner. I studied the dashboard. Ian had handed the keys to his father, unable to make the gesture of putting his wife once more under my toxic influence on the long ride home. "Nice car," I observed to Carità.

"Is it?" she said. "It seems awfully cramped to me, and you feel every bump on the road."

"It's a young man's car," I said.

"Ian is crazy about it," she agreed. "He drives very fast." This obviously pleased her.

I started the engine, shifted gears, and pulled out from the curb. "I'm not going to do that," I said.

"Do what?" Carità asked.

"Drive very fast."

She leaned forward and began fiddling with the radio dial. "Do you mind if I play some music?"

"Go right ahead," I said. "It's a long drive."

She dialed past frantic band music, people talking earnestly, a weather report, until she found the island jazz station, where a trio—saxophone, piano, and snare drums—accompanying a singer with a rich baritone voice worked over an old ballad about a doomed love affair. "This is such a good song," she said, leaning back in her seat. I glanced at her. Her lips moved soundlessly, mouthing the lyrics. She didn't seem to have a worry in the world. When the music faded to a close that imitated the sound of waves washing against the shore, I said, "Are you nervous about meeting your mother-in-law?"

She nodded vigorously. "I'm terrified," she said. "Ian says she's hard to please."

"Did he give you any tips?"

She was silent. She was picking at her skirt with one hand, her jaw set forward in a way I recognized as imminent belligerence. "I don't like all this lying," she said.

"It's not a great way to start a marriage," I agreed.

"It doesn't make sense," she said. "Ian's father clearly knows where we met."

"That's true," I said.

"Would you mind telling me how he knows that?"

"I'm not sure myself," I admitted. "The morning after you and Ian left, he appeared at the kitchen door and said his sources told him Ian was seeing a girl who worked in my house."

" 'Seeing,' " she said flatly.

"I told him you were married."

"How did he take that?"

I recalled Mike's deep groan, head in hands, at my kitchen table. "Pretty well," I said.

Another silence. "Brutus must have told him," she concluded.

I didn't like the idea of Mike and Brutus discussing my business. "Or told someone who told him," I suggested.

The music changed to a solo piano. I was thinking that,

for me, there was a lot to see on this drive. The sun was setting behind me, and the bright world outside was fading to a delicate mauve, but for Carità it was just a long time sitting in a moving chair.

"Do you think Ian looked different enough?" she asked.

"I do," I said. "And I think it's unlikely that anyone will be looking for him on this coast. Even if the police do come up with a warrant, they'll figure Ian went to the mainland."

"A detective will be assigned to the case," she said confidently. "They can be very crafty."

This amused me. "What do you know about detectives?" I asked.

"Sherlock Holmes is very popular in Braille books," she said. "Sometimes I had to wait weeks for the next volume. I read them all."

It was growing dark when we arrived at my house. The windows were ablaze with lights, upstairs and down. Samba music drifted out the open windows on the warm breeze. I was relieved to be home, but not quite in the right frame of mind to play the charming madam in the drawing room. We went in the kitchen door, and Carità disappeared up the back stairs to pack her belongings. Brutus came in from the hall, looking sour. Before he could speak, Mimi rushed in, wide-eyed, like a schoolgirl. "Did you find them?" she asked.

"We did," I replied. "I brought Carità back with me."

"She's here!" Mimi exclaimed.

"She's upstairs," I said. Mimi clattered past me and up the stairs on her wedge-heeled, open-back mules. We heard her shout "Carità" at the landing, then the sound of Carità's deep laughter as she and her friend embraced in the hall.

"She's back," Brutus said.

"Not for long," I replied. "I'm taking her to the judge's house. Her husband is in hiding."

"That's good," Brutus said. "Marcus Betone is out to destroy Joe Shock, and it's all because of that stupid kid."

"Well, BB had something to do with it."

"Right, but he's dead."

"I feel sorry for Marcus," I said.

A shout from the drawing room, followed by general laughter, reminded us of our duties. "How's the house?" I asked.

"It's a little slow, mostly regulars. That first mate you like from the Lykes ship is here."

"Officer Pehling," I said. "He's an elegant man."

"Charlotte's all over him."

"I'd go in," I said, "but I'm not dressed. As soon as I drop Carità off, I'll come back and take over."

"You're taking her to the mansion," he observed, and I nodded, lifting my eyebrows.

"Do you know where it is?"

"I have directions," I said.

"From the judge."

"Right," I said. We were silent, listening to the pleasant hubbub of the house. The bed in the front bedroom had a creaky frame, and we could hear its rhythmic complaint as a client received his service. Someone flushed the upstairs toilet. The samba was replaced by a moody blues tune.

"What's she going to do in the mansion?" Brutus said testily.

"You know Carità," I said. "She'll figure it out when she gets there."

Or at least I hoped she would. I had no idea how Carità would be treated in Mike's house, but I believed he could be counted on to be kind to her.

Brutus went back to his post. I drank a shot of vodka and ate some olives I found in the fridge. Mimi and Carità came down with her two small bags. The three of us stuffed them into the trunk of the little sports car. The girls hugged and promised to meet for lunch soon. Carità and I slid into our seats, and we were off.

The park fronts a wide stone wharf that runs along the waterfront. On the opposite side—beyond the manicured lawns, the gardens fragrant with gardenia and frangipani; past the bamboo teahouse, the taffy vendor's horse-drawn cart, and the children's playground, the cracked, worn asphalt road rises to a line of fine houses secluded behind tall box hedges and iron gates. As soon as I turned into the oak-shaded perimeter of the public garden, Carità breathed in deeply through the open window and said, "We're in the park."

"How can you tell?" I asked.

She smiled. "The smell," she said. "And the sound of the trees. I can hear birds and all sorts of little squeaks and creaks. The air changes; it's heavy but it's cooler. It's a magical place, isn't it?"

"It is," I said. "I seldom come here."

"You should," she said.

I took the most direct road straight across to the outer ring road and turned in at the street with the empty gatehouse, just as Mike had directed me. "It's the third house," I said to myself, as Carità obviously couldn't count them.

"Can you see it yet?"

"I can't see any houses at all," I said. "They're hidden behind gates and bushes."

The gates were discreetly numbered with brass plates. The third one, which was, oddly, number nine, stood half open but was still so wide that the sports car passed through easily. I slowed to a crawl; the drive was gravel and crunched noisily beneath the tires. "Can you see it?" Carità asked again.

"Not yet," I said, as I peered through the lush greenery pressing on both sides. Then the drive curved, and the building came into view.

It was a massive fortress of a house built in the Spanish style: all smooth, creamy stucco, double rows of arched, leaded-glass windows, a tile roof. Two square towers jutted out on either side of a portico entry, as if to enclose anyone who might choose to enter. The triple arches at the center created a wide protected cloister behind which, presumably, one could find the entry door. A carved double door, I imagined, that might open into a glass-ceilinged atrium—I'd seen something like that in a magazine.

The drive curved again, bringing the car up flush with three wide stone steps to the portico. When it rained, one had only a quick dash to shelter. In the parking area beyond the steps, I could see Mike's car. The plan was that I would honk three times and he would come to escort Carità into the house. Then I would park the car and wait for the taxi Mike would have arranged. Dutifully, I pressed the horn. The harsh blasts were startling in the peaceful setting. Carità reached behind her seat for her cane. I got out and opened the trunk. Nothing happened. She had swung her legs out of the car and was rising to her feet. I took out the small suitcase and the backpack, and set them on the gravel. It was cool; there was even a whisper of a breeze playing among the masses of elephant ears that lined that part of the drive. I joined Carità. "Should I honk again?" I said.

"Maybe," she replied. "Let's wait a bit."

"It's a big house," I said. "It may take a while to get to the front door."

Another minute passed. I felt mildly annoyed with Mike. I didn't want to go into the portico. I was crossing in front of the car to try the horn again when we heard the scrape of a door opening and a few quick footsteps. A middle-aged woman in a suit that looked like a uniform appeared, neatly framed by the main arch. I dashed back to Carità as the woman crossed the few steps, her eyes engaging mine, her manner cool and direct. "I'm Mrs. Bracknell," she said. "Mrs. Drohan's secretary."

"This is Carità Bercy," I said. Wrong, I thought. I should have said "Carità Drohan." However, this was clearly of no interest to the efficient Mrs. Bracknell. She had spotted the luggage and marched away to take it up. I said softly to Carità, "Three wide steps."

"Thank you," she said.

"Good luck," I said. Mrs. Bracknell approached, having slung the backpack over her shoulder so that she had a free arm. This she offered awkwardly, but Carità was quick to position herself alongside her guide. She walked confidently, her stick tucked under her arm, accommodating the length of her stride to her companion's. Mrs. Bracknell didn't pause at the first step. Carità stumbled only slightly, then took the next two with ease. I watched them until they disappeared behind the arch. As I got back into the car, I heard the house door open, then close. I started the engine and pulled into the parking space next to Mike's car.

Just as well, I thought, that I not see him, or give my name to anyone who might connect me to this place where I so obviously didn't belong. I felt annoyed by the whole Drohan enterprise, and I recalled Mimi's sage observation, "I just don't trust rich boys."

As I climbed out of the sports car, a cab pulled into the drive. I stepped out of the shadows to greet the driver.

At the house, I slipped up the kitchen steps, changed into at-home attire, and went down the front stairs to take up my post in the drawing room. Everybody, including the clients, was in a foul mood that night. An obnoxious import-export dealer from the mainland was holding forth on the corruption and depravity of all islanders. The locals were always trying to cheat him, but he was too smart for them, every time. The whole room breathed a sigh of relief when he went upstairs with poor Sally, who had captured his fancy. I had a bad feeling, but I attributed it to my frustration with the Drohans. Brutus stood in the doorway as they passed and sent a cautionary glance my way. He had watched the guy's performance with undisguised contempt. They weren't in the room fifteen minutes when she hit the buzzer.

Everyone froze but Brutus, who bounded up the stairs like a panther, burst into the room, and knocked the man to the floor. As he was hustled down the steps and out the kitchen door, the half-naked scoundrel howled his outrage, threatening a swift revenge. I rushed to the bedroom, where I found Sally lying on her back on the bed with her hands tied behind her, frantically shaking her head from side to side. He'd pissed over her hair, her face, and her breasts. She was soaked in urine and gasping for breath.

I got her untied and helped her to the bathroom, where she promptly vomited into the toilet. Then she went to the sink and laved water over her mouth, her face, her chest, sobbing uncontrollably.

"I'm going downstairs to close the house," I told her. "I'll be right back and run you a bath. Brutus will take you home whenever you're ready. Can I bring you anything?"

She waved her hand, dismissing me, unable to form a word.

In the kitchen, I found Brutus looking out the door at the villain, who stood shouting in the yard, demanding his money and his pants. "Should I give him his pants?" Brutus asked without looking at me.

"Absolutely not," I said. "If I find out who gave him the password, *he's* banned, too."

"How's Sally?"

"Not good," I said. "He tied her up and pissed all over her."

Brutus slapped the screen open and charged down the steps. "First, I'm going to smash your face," he declared. "Then I'll escort you to the helpful policeman on the beat around the corner, and he will very politely book you for assault and indecent exposure."

I passed down the hall to the drawing room. The scene there was appropriately subdued; all eyes turned to me. "Last drinks, please, gentlemen," I said. "We'll be closing for the night in twenty minutes." Charlotte approached me, looking pale and strained in the sudden descent of cold sobriety. "Is Sally okay?"

"She will be," I said, with a confidence I didn't feel. "She's a bit shaken." Then I went back upstairs to tend to her. She was sitting on the toilet, wrapped in a towel, weeping quietly.

"Brutus is giving him a beating and taking him to the police without his pants," I said.

She raised her teary eyes to mine and managed a wan smile. "That's good," she said.

I bent over the tub and turned on both faucets. "I've got a nice vetiver oil to add to this. It makes a very relaxing bath."

"What a pig," she murmured.

"You must have been terrified," I said.

"I was," she said. "I started to get anxious when he wanted

to tie my hands, but he was calm then, kind of teasing. Then he started working himself into a frenzy. He said I didn't deserve to live. He punched me in the ribs so hard it knocked the breath out of me. He pinned me down with his knees on my shoulders and started pissing on me. When he tried to hold my mouth open, I bit his fingers as hard as I could. That made him shift a little and I managed to press the buzzer with my foot."

"Thank God," I said.

She stood up, wrapped the towel more tightly about her waist, and examined her face in the mirror over the sink. "Why did he pick me, do you think?" she mused.

"Because you're little," I said. "You're the smallest girl in the house."

Unsurprisingly, I slept poorly. An incident in which a girl rightfully fears for her life shook us all to our shoes. I didn't doubt that Sally was having a sleepless night as well. She might quit the business, and I wouldn't blame her. I was heartily sick and tired of it myself. With Carità gone, I'd be short; I'd have to hire. I scrambled the sheets, obsessively plumped the pillow. When my eyes weren't re-viewing the image of Sally sobbing over the bathroom sink, the thought of Carità disappearing behind the portico on the arm of the efficient functionary agitated me. Why hadn't Mike come to escort her, as we'd planned? How much did her new mother-in-law know about her? Carità imagined she could charm her way past all obstacles, but the place was huge; they could stash her away and never speak to her. It was as if the mansion had swallowed her up. And what of her feckless husband, lying low in some rented room on the coast, pretending he wasn't rich enough to buy the entire village? How long could that last?

Toward dawn, when the birds outside my window cheerfully announced the day, I drifted to sleep for a few hours. I woke briefly when I heard Mimi in the bathroom and then her footsteps going down the stairs. When I woke again, it was past ten. I knew the house was empty. I got out of bed, washed up, pulled on a housedress, and went down to the kitchen. It was hot already, and as humid as a steam bath. I turned on the overhead fan, poured coffee into a glass. I couldn't be bothered to heat it. I opened the back door and stood sipping my coffee, watching the hummingbirds dashing about over the honeysuckle. An anole, appearing, as they do, from nowhere on the arm of the porch chaise, regarded me with its otherworldly, glassy eyes, absolutely still, yet capable, I knew, of disappearing in a millisecond. The chaise made me think of Carità having sex with her young lover, intoxicated by the smell of him.

The double chime of the clients' door sounded from the hall. Who could be seeking sexual services at this hour?

My first impulse was to ignore it; we weren't open yet, and anyone who patronized the house knew that. The chime rang again—it made me smile, because it seemed to say "ding-dong." I set the coffee on the counter, crept across the hall, and peered through the peephole in the heavy mahogany door.

The dark, intelligent eyes of Marcus Betone instantly found mine. Surely not, I thought. His son had not been dead a week.

But bereavement does strange things to people, that can't be denied. I turned the top latch and pulled the door partly open. "Marcus," I said, before he could speak. "We're not open yet."

His big head pulled back and his brow furrowed, as if to avoid a bad odor. "I'm not here for a girl," he said.

Then what? I thought. I opened the door wider, though I stood squarely in the doorway. He looked, as he always looked, a little melancholy, a little tired, but there was something else in his expression that I recognized, a kind of guarded desperation, a plea for understanding, a desire not to give orders, which was his practice, but to communicate an emotional state. He was dressed neatly in a gray silk suit, no tie, a black cotton shirt with a flat collar, brown loafers. His straight black hair was, I observed, going gray at the temples. He combed it back to feature his strong widow's peak. He wasn't a handsome man—his nose was too big, his eyes were too close, his chin was weak, and jowls were commencing around his rather shapely, almost feminine mouth. But he had an air of confidence, authority, and, oddly, kindness about him that engaged the attention of everyone in a room with him. I thought of something Vivien had told me about him—that he always ended the sex act with a few light pats on the butt, as if to register his approval of her performance.

"How can I help you?" I asked.

"I thought I would talk with you," he said. "If you're not busy."

I stepped back, waving him in past me. "Of course," I said. "I'd like that very much. I've been thinking of you."

He followed me inside to the kitchen, a part of the house he hadn't seen and clearly didn't expect. "We can talk in here," I said. "What can I give you? Coffee? Tea? Have you had breakfast?"

He smiled weakly, choosing a chair and pulling it out carefully. "Just black tea, if you have it," he said.

I put the kettle on the stove, took down the tea tin and the china pot, chose a small mug, set the sugar jar and a teaspoon on the table. "I want to offer you my condolences," I said. "I was shocked to learn of BB's death. He was so young."

He nodded, taking up the teaspoon and turning it over in his hands. "Thank you," he said simply.

What could I give him? I opened the cabinet: nothing but rice, noodles, cans of beans, and a box of vanilla wafers. Mimi always kept the bag sealed with a clip; she ate them with coffee when she was studying. Vanilla wafers it would have to be. I took a plate from the dish drain, poured out a small pile of cookies, and set the plate on the table. Marcus was still absorbed with the spoon. I busied myself measuring tea into a ball, affixing it to the pot. I refilled my glass of coffee, added a little milk. The kettle came to a boil. I poured the water carefully over the ball, closed the lid, and lowered the pot to the table next to Marcus, saying, "Just let that steep a few minutes." I grabbed my coffee glass and took the chair across from him. Marcus put down the spoon and our eyes met, but only for a moment. His gaze, suffused with sadness, drifted away to the middle distance. "He liked to come here," he said.

"He did. We were all fond of him," I lied.

"He wanted the fast life. I thought college might get him over that."

"It might have," I suggested. "He was in his second year, wasn't he?"

"He was. His grades weren't great, but he passed."

"What was he studying?"

He rubbed his chin between his thumb and forefinger. "He was studying not much," he said. "He was taking business courses, but they bored him. Last term, he took an acting class—who knows why? He was excited about that. He got an A. He even got a part in a play."

"He was thinking of being an actor?" I said. This made sense to me. BB was always putting on a show.

"I told him: That's not a good plan. What kind of life is that? An actor pretends to be somebody he's not. He's a nobody. Actors are silly people."

"Sometimes they're very successful," I said.

"Not on this island," Marcus concluded.

He was right about that, I thought. "Your tea's ready," I said.

He nodded, took up the pot, and poured a dark stream into his mug. "I wanted him to study law," he said. "When he told me he and the Drohan boy would be roommates, I thought, Good; he'll be living with a serious student, somebody who studies the law."

Be careful what you say now, I advised myself. "Someone told me they were cousins," I said.

"Distant," he said. "My wife's sister's husband's mother or

something like that. A divorce in there somewhere, so they're not actually related." To my surprise, he slid a cookie from the plate, dunked it into his tea, and popped it into his mouth.

"Did you know Ian?" I asked.

"I saw him a few times. BB brought him around. He seemed like a serious kid, kind of a broody kid. He was polite to me, very respectful. BB told me he hates his father. The judge hasn't made my life any easier, but I don't hold that against his son."

I sipped my coffee. Why was this man in my kitchen?

"Do you know him?" Marcus asked. "The boy. Ian."

"He was here a few times with BB," I said. "I hardly spoke to him."

Marcus flicked his eyes to my face, then back to his own hand wrapped around the mug. "He's disappeared," he said.

"Has he?" I said.

He looked past me at the stove, the row of mugs, the kitchen door, and beyond it to the porch, as if he thought Ian might be hidden somewhere on the premises. "He should stay disappeared," he said.

Was this a warning? "Are the police looking for him?" I asked, playing the innocent.

Marcus took another cookie from the plate, slipped it into his mouth, and chewed reflectively. When he had swallowed, he said, "I always liked these cookies. What are they called?"

"Vanilla wafers," I said.

"Right," he said. "Vanilla wafers. I haven't seen them in years." He sipped his tea, gazing into the mug as he lifted it. When he set it down, he folded his hands together on the table and sighed. "The way I see it," he said, "Joe Shock has two enemies on this island—Mike Drohan and me. When he realized our boys were friends, he thought he could set them up for a fall. If they got arrested on a drug charge together, it would be tough for both the judge and me. Two birds with one stone."

"I see," I said.

"His guy was packing serious heat, and he shot BB twice, once in the chest and once in the stomach. The coroner told me he didn't live five minutes." His voice broke over the last word. His eyes were wet. He lowered his face and rested his forehead in his hand.

I felt my heart go out to him. "Marcus," I said, "I'm so sorry."

He spoke from beneath his hand. "BB was a punk," he said. "I know that. But he could have turned around. Drohan's boy was a good influence on him. If he'd stayed in school . . ."

He paused, swallowing a sob of anguish. "If he'd really wanted to go for the acting, I would have been okay with that."

I stretched out my hand to touch his sleeve. "You were a good father," I said. "BB loved you. He was proud to be your son."

He lifted his face from his hand, blinking back tears. "Every Sunday, he came out to the house and we had an espresso together. He said nobody made a better espresso than me."

"You'll miss that," I said.

"I'll miss that," he agreed.

We were silent for a moment while he regained his composure. I didn't doubt this required a heroic effort of the will. Outside, a wren was blasting away near his nest in the porch eaves.

Such a big sound for such a small bird, I thought. Marcus heard it, too, and glanced out at the morning light dappling a pattern on the chaise. "It's nice here," he said. "I don't know why, but I didn't know this house had a kitchen."

"It's my office," I said. "When I bought the house, I knew this would be where I'd spend my free time, and, of course, the girls like to gather here, away from the clients. I bought this big table when the library closed and they sold off the furniture."

"You've built up a solid business," he said.

I laughed. "Well, it's legal."

"Sure," he said. "But that don't necessarily mean it's respectable. Some of these places they have now on the water-front, they're serving tourists who come over from the main-land just to get underage girls and boys. They bring them in from God knows where—kids, they're just kids. They're trapped. They don't even speak the language. It's the saddest thing in the world."

"The island is changing," I said.

"It is," he agreed. "And not for the better."

Another pause. Any minute now and he'll tell me why he's here, I thought. He finished his tea and held the mug between his hands. "The guy who murdered BB died in the hospital. I hear Joe Shock thinks the score is settled. But, you know, he don't have children."

"No," I said. "Who would marry him?"

"Really," Marcus agreed.

"He's more like a lizard than a human," I said.

"Some things may happen," he said.

What things these were I thought I knew. I nodded.

"Ian Drohan just needs to stay disappeared. Just for a little while. Until things calm down."

Mike was right, I thought. The Joe Shock problem was about to be solved.

"I want you to tell his father that," Marcus said.

I leaned away, momentarily stymied by this request. Marcus met my confusion with a stern, perceptive look. How much did he know? And how did he know it? Mike and I had been, I thought, relatively discreet.

"If I see him," I said, "I'll tell him."

"Tell him I have no grievance against him."

"I'll tell him," I said, studying my coffee.

"When you see him," he added.

I looked up and met his tender, almost affectionate gaze. "Mike Drohan don't deserve a woman like you," he said.

So—Marcus Betone knew all about Mike and me. He probably knew about the Tropicale; maybe he owned it. "Some people might say the reverse," I said. "He's a judge, and I run a brothel."

"He's a man who can't even trust himself," he said. "His own son despises him."

This couldn't be denied, and I sat blinking at the fact.

"Thanks for the tea," he said, pushing back his chair. "It was a good idea I had to come talk to you."

I stood up and followed him as he turned to the hall. "I'm glad you came," I said.

At the door, he paused and offered his hand. "Thank you for what you said about BB. It was a comfort to me to hear that."

I pressed his hand with my own. "It was true," I said. "You were the world to him."

When he opened the door, the warm light poured in and we squinted against it. "If the judge makes you unhappy, just let me know," he said.

"Right," I said. "You'll take care of it for me."

He shrugged, pulling the corners of his mouth down and raising his eyebrows in an expression so theatrical it made me smile. "I could have a talk with him," he said.

I drew my head back, grimacing with mock terror.

"Sometimes that's all it takes," he concluded.

"I'll keep it in mind," I said. Then Marcus stepped out onto the stone walkway that runs between my house and the tall, sheltering hedge that hides the door from the street.

I sat for a while at the kitchen table, thinking about fathers and sons. Marcus Betone had one son: poor stupid BB, now deceased. He also had two daughters, both teenagers now, and a devoted wife who had married him fresh out of high school. The family was close; they all went to mass every week; the girls attended a school run by Dominican nuns. The mother was reputed to be a generous, warmhearted woman, happiest when she had her children and her husband at the dinner table.

About the only business dealings Marcus had that weren't criminal were his occasional visits to my house. He'd brought BB along when he turned eighteen—legal drinking age on the island—and stood at the bar talking to Jack while Vivien, who was Marcus's favorite girl, took BB upstairs. After that, father and son never appeared together. In fact, Marcus's visits were infrequent.

What I'd told Marcus was true—BB adored his father. He was eager to tell any new acquaintance whose son he was. "My father says . . ." was a reliable opening for the dispensation of paternal wisdom. He drank the same bar brands his father drank, flashed an expensive watch he was quick to point out was a gift from his father.

Then there was Mike Drohan, the son of a wealthy, powerful family, who had risen in his chosen profession to the highest level, who didn't, as far as I knew, engage in illegal activity. He was too fastidious to patronize a brothel, much less bring his son to one. He was quick-witted and sharp-tongued, ever on the alert for irony, which delighted him.

What explained the difference? Stand the two men side by side, and what did you see? Marcus, a plain man plainly dressed with no pretensions to style, though his suits were expensive and well made. His voice was scratchy; sometimes I had to listen closely to hear him. His affect was extraordinarily calm and grave. He rarely smiled, though minimal movements of the muscles around his mouth, and a softening in the weary straightforwardness of his gaze, suggested that he found the world, and himself in it, faintly amusing. He noticed everything, and he was easily pleased. A homey room, a relaxed conversation, a cookie—all received an appreciative evaluation.

Now, compare him with Mike Drohan. A dashing, fine figure of a man, confident in the power of his physical presence. He knew at every moment how the sight of him affected his audience, and the world was his audience. His manner was irresolute; his mood shifts were sudden and unpredictable, like a barometer in a hurricane. His life was a crisis he was hoping to weather. His marriage, characterized by hostility and distrust, seemed only to heighten his sense of personal grievance. His wife had no use for him. His son hated him. There he stood, with that sly, knowing smile, leaning toward me in my imagination.

But where was he now?

The next day, there was no word from Mike, no news of Carità or Ian. After closing, I went to the Saxophone to find out what Brutus was hearing. He told me that a thug high up in Joe Shock's operation had been charged with sex trafficking, but before the police could pick him up, he was shot dead in a restaurant bathroom downtown. "Marcus told me some things might happen," I told Brutus.

"He's after Joe," Brutus concluded. "It won't be long."

The second day, the police raided one of the tourist brothels on the waterfront and took out four girls and two boys under sixteen. The venue was padlocked, the proprietor currently residing in a cell at the central lockup. "Joe owned that shop," Brutus told me.

In the mail, I found an envelope addressed to me in a handwriting I didn't recognize. No return address. On the stiff, cream-colored card inside only a few lines, and at the bottom his signature. "Dearest," he wrote. "Complications here, but it will be settled soon. Don't be anxious. I'm very much all yours, Mike."

His handwriting was excellent, flowing and even, without a smudge. "Dearest," I thought. "Don't be anxious." All mine. Concise, yet absurdly dramatic. How I missed him.

On the third night, a runner for the Betone clan opened a car door that tripped a bomb. The explosion blew out the windows of the storefront next to the street. The runner lived, but he lost a hand, and they were stitching his face up for hours. The newspaper headline read "Storefront Damaged in Car Explosion," and the lede was "Police fear possible gang war."

The next night, when I walked into the bar, there was a notable hush in the room. Brutus waved me into the small office where he kept his books. "What's up?" I asked as he closed the door.

He turned to me, looking solemn. "Joe Shock is dead," he said.

"He's dead?" I said. "When did this happen?"

"Last night. Not long after the Betone runner got blown up."

"Mike was right," I said.

Brutus disliked all mention of Mike. "What's he got to do with it?" he snapped.

"He thought Marcus might solve the Joe Shock problem."

Brutus nodded. "Right," he said. "His precious son is safe now."

"How did Joe die?"

"Boat accident is how they're billing it," Brutus said. "He had an expensive speedboat he liked to run around the bay at night, just to show up unexpected here and there and spread a little terror. There was a leak in the fuel line, and the gasoline tank exploded. Joe got blown off the back of the boat, right into the propeller."

"Jesus," I said.

"Not pretty," Brutus agreed.

How relieved I felt at the news of Joe Shock's death. His domain of cruelty and vice hadn't overlapped with my little world, but I was always conscious that he was out there, like a toxic cloud that could kill you if it drifted your way. "He won't be missed," I said.

Brutus closed his eyes and nodded. "Sad, but true," he agreed.

Another night passed. Business was slow, which was good, as I was short two girls. Sally had opted for a well-deserved week off, and Carità, I assumed, was ordering servants around at the mansion. But where was Mike? Would he let Ian know it was safe to return from wherever he was, now that the coast was clear? I courted sleep with a murder mystery; then I dreamed a better ending than the one the writer offered. I've read enough in the genre to know the murderer would be a character who had what looked like an iron-clad alibi and/or a grievance that went way back in time.

I slept late and went downstairs to find Mimi at the table, drinking coffee and reading the newspaper. We exchanged brief greetings; I filled my mug and sat across from her at the table. She folded the paper. "I have some news," she said.

"About Carità?" I guessed.

"Right," she said. "I ran into her and her sister yesterday in the park."

The Sunday walk, I thought. "I'm surprised Bessie is allowed in the mansion."

"That's just it. Carità's not living in the mansion. She's living with her sister."

"I thought Bessie lived in a seedy hotel," I said.

"Not anymore," Mimi explained. "She has a little apartment near the restaurant where she works. I spent the afternoon there. Bessie got promoted to waitress, and she's looking very well. She even has a boyfriend; he's a sous-chef."

"Why is Carità living with her?"

"Things were terrible at the mansion. Ian's mother is on a rampage. She and Mike are battling it out, and she refused even to see Carità. She put her in a servant's room near the kitchen. Carità persuaded the cook to get her a taxi, and she went to Bessie's restaurant. She's heard nothing from any of them. She doesn't know where Ian is."

"This is bad," I said. And not what I was promised, I thought. What was Mike doing?

"It is," Mimi agreed. "But you know Carità. She's completely unruffled. She figures Ian will be back from wherever he is soon, and everything will be set to rights. He gave her some money before he left, and she put it in her bank account, so she's not anxious about that. Bessie works the evening shift and doesn't go in until three; they have their mornings free. They seem happy to be together. It's rather sweet."

"So . . . she just walked out on the Drohans," I said.

Mimi nodded. "She says they'll be sorry. You have to admire that woman."

I pictured Carità, shoved aside, in revolt, in the kitchen. She was not going to be cast off or treated like a problem. She just took a cab and left. "That's true," I agreed. "Carità is indomitable."

I spent the rest of the morning reading the newspaper and thinking about what might happen next. It was another warm, sunny, steaming day, with some afternoon rain in the forecast. The report of Joe Shock's death was brief, dismissed as an unfortunate boating accident, and the victim hilariously identified as Joseph Shock, a local importer. Again, I felt oddly comforted by the certainty that the brute force known as Joe Shock was gone from the world. It lifted my spirits. He had been a vicious and unpredictable player in the island's underworld, as dangerous and poisonous as a viper. Now he was gone. Did Joe Shock have a single friend who felt anything but relief at his demise? I doubted it.

Marcus Betone had won the war, and though he could doubtless be tough, and take harsh revenge when he felt betrayed, his nature was essentially warm. He was a warm-blooded creature. His word was his bond. He believed in a code. If you had his protection—and he had made it clear to me that Ian Drohan now enjoyed that privilege—it would be safe to do whatever you wanted to do on the island. No warrants would be issued; he would see to that. The rules were clear.

I went upstairs, took a shower, made up my face, and dressed in street clothes. It was our closed day, and I planned to do a little shopping. A spritz of orange blossom, a glance at the purse contents, and I was off down the stairs. My big house was cool and still all around me, and it gave me a pleasant sense of solidity and ownership. I thought of Marcus Betone's remark, "You've built up a solid business."

In the kitchen, I found Mike Drohan looking in at the screen door. "I wondered when you'd show up," I said.

He pulled the screen open and stepped inside, saying nothing. He looked terrible. His clothes were wrinkled; he was unshaven, disheveled, dark half-moons smudged under his eyes; he exuded an air of dejection and defeat. He didn't move, nor did his eyes meet mine.

"Sit down," I said. "I'll get you some coffee."

He did as directed, pulling a chair out slowly, as if the weight were a challenge to him. I poured the coffee and set it in front of him. As he lifted the mug and sipped the dark brew, I took the seat across from him. "Are you okay?" I asked.

He shrugged. "Claudia's divorcing me."

All I felt at this announcement was surprise. A not unpleasant surprise. "Why now?" I asked.

"She's been having me tailed for four months. She's got a fat envelope of compromising photos. She's got a photo of you and me going up the stairs at the Tropicale."

"Not good," I said.

"There's one that's mildly incriminating, professionally speaking."

"Any money changing hands?"

"You're quick," he said. "A mysterious attaché case is featured, as is a crime boss."

"Will she use it against you?"

"It's one photo," he said. "There's no telling what's in the case. It could be legal papers; it could be my lunch. I could be giving it to him, or vice versa. It doesn't look good, but as evidence it's pretty worthless."

I considered this while Mike finished his coffee. "So . . . what they say about you is true," I observed.

"What do they say?"

"That you're a corrupt judge."

"I'm not a corrupt judge," he protested. "I just don't like sending people to jail."

"That would be a problem," I agreed.

"I've seen central lockup," he continued. "It's a nightmare. If you're not a criminal when you go in, you will be when you come out. So I'm lenient. When I can, I give the minimum sentence. The criminals know this, and so do their lawyers. They all breathe a sigh of relief if they turn up on my docket, and people who don't know anything assume I'm taking bribes. Why would I take bribes? I don't need money." He set his mug down firmly between his hands, and his gaze drifted out past the screen. "Hell," he said. "Here comes your majordomo."

Brutus appeared on the porch and pulled the door open before he looked inside. When he saw Mike, he paused, his fingers wrapped around the door handle. "I didn't know you had company," he said.

"Come on in," Mike said, without looking up. "You can enjoy my suffering."

Brutus cast me an inquisitive glance. "His wife's divorcing him," I said.

"Oh, tough luck," Brutus said candidly. "Lila, I'll catch you later." He backed out the door.

When I heard the gate close, I said, "Do you know where Ian is yet?"

"I've heard nothing. And Carità has disappeared. Do you think they're together?"

"She's living with her sister."

"How did she get there?"

"She took a cab from your house."

"Good for her," he said. "Claudia wouldn't even see her. She turned her over to the secretary."

"What does Claudia know about Carità?" I asked.

"She knows the whole bloody story, but she's got the sequence wrong. She says it was bad enough when I started carousing with prostitutes, but bringing Ian here was an outrage she could never forgive."

Carousing with prostitutes, I thought. "But you didn't bring him here," I said. "He came with BB."

"Of course I didn't. I would never do that. It was Ian who brought *me* here."

"Did she believe you?"

"No." He lowered his forehead and pressed it into the heel of his hand.

"Do you regret that you came here?"

"No," he said firmly. "That's about the only thing in my whole sorry life I don't regret."

I stood up and moved behind his chair. Basically, he'd

just insulted me in several different ways, none of them novel or interesting, but I pitied him. He'd treated his family like a burden he stoically bore, and now they had decided they'd be better off without him. He'd kept his son at a distance so determinedly, the boy was now entirely out of reach. I had no idea if he was corrupt in his professional life, though it was true he didn't need money, so outright bribery seemed unlikely. He knew that his reputation wasn't great, that lawyers held him in contempt.

I put my arms around his shoulders and rested my cheek against the side of his face. He sniffed twice. "Don't be kind to me," he pleaded. "I don't deserve it."

"I can't help it," I said.

Later, I got the whole story. On the way back from San Bosco, Mike had stopped at the taxi stand in the park and arranged a cab for me. Then he went to the mansion to prepare Claudia for Carità's arrival. But Claudia hit him with the divorce news as soon as he was in the door. She wanted him out of the house immediately, and after she demolished all protest with the envelope of damning evidence against him, she followed him to their bedroom and stood in the doorway while he packed the suitcase she'd laid open on the bed for his convenience. He explained that Carità was coming, and she dispatched her secretary to whisk her to the maid's room.

When Mike was packed, his soon-to-be ex-wife escorted him to the stately double doors under the portico and demanded his house keys. "Don't be ridiculous," he said. "You don't have to lock me out." But she insisted, and, in the end, he pulled two keys off his expensive fob, handed them over, and stood gazing out at the driveway as he heard the bolt shooting into the strike plate on the door behind him. Then he threw the suitcase into the back of the convertible and got behind the wheel. His first impulse was to go to his chambers, where he had a couch and a small bathroom. But halfway there, he changed his mind and drove to the best hotel on the island.

As Mike followed me up the back steps to my bedroom, it naturally occurred to me that he was striking back at his cruel and dismissive wife. Score-settling sex serves as a distraction from the pain caused by overt rejection and fulfills the psychological need to get even. It's a vicious, unrewarding cycle. But even in existential despair, Mike noticed his surroundings. He stood in the doorway, taking it all in. The polished pine floor, the expensive linens on the four-poster bed, the massive mahogany armoire with double mirrored doors, the wide-bladed ceiling fan whirring lazily overhead, the striped pattern of shadows cast by the closed shutters on the windows along the wall, the dressing table with my basket of pencils, compacts, lipsticks, the atomizer of perfume, my blue terry-cloth robe hanging from a bronze hook on the door, the carafe of water and the paperback novel in the tray atop the bookcase I used as a bedside table. "This is your own bedroom," he said.

"It is," I said. "You're the only man who has ever been in it." I unbuttoned my blouse as I crossed to the bed and sat on the mattress, facing him. I had an unpleasant flashback to the old days, long ago, when I sat on a bare, lumpy mattress a few times a day, mentally calculating my take, while a man I didn't care about stripped off his pants, eager to tell me what he wanted me to do.

Though I was willing, my expectations for this coupling weren't high. For some reason, I thought of Brutus and the friendly demise, in his office or at his apartment, of our affair, which had gone forward without comment and ended to no one's surprise. Brutus disliked Mike and assumed he'd let me down. I couldn't deny that I assumed he'd let me down as well. Our affair was hot, but that was all it was, and our worlds could only collide on the sly. I was resigned to the inevitable cooling of our mutual ardor.

But Mike, as it turned out, wasn't resigned, and he surprised me by bringing to our lovemaking a new tenderness, a closer attention, and finally an exhilarating sense of communion. As we fell apart to lie on our backs, our heads propped on the pillows, panting with exhaustion, his hand sought mine and held it gently. We lay still and quiet for several minutes. "I wish we could just float away like this," he said.

"Let's do it," I agreed.

Eventually, we got up, got dressed, and went back to our separate lives. Mine had become something of a dull routine. Mike's was a world of trouble.

Another week passed, in which I heard nothing. Business was brisk; the girls were pulling in lots of cash, so they were in a good humor. I felt like I was waiting for the proverbial shoe to drop.

On Sunday morning, it did. I came down to breakfast to find Mimi at her usual post, poised between her coffee mug and a large book. Once I'd armed myself with my ration of caffeine, I sat down across from her. There was an open box of croissants on the table. "Where did these come from?" I asked.

"The café in the park," she said. "I had coffee with Carità there yesterday, and I bought a few for us."

"Very thoughtful," I said, sliding the butter dish closer to my plate. "And how is Carità?"

"She's frustrated," she said. "She hasn't heard from Ian, and she thinks he may have sent a card to his parents' house."

"That was the plan when he went into hiding."

"She's going to the house today to confront the parents until one of them gives her the information."

"His father has moved out," I said. "They're divorcing."

There was a pause while we both bit into the rolls, scattering crumbs across the table, then chewing assiduously with the concentration of two squirrels on a lawn. When we had swallowed, Mimi gave me a look of cool appraisal. "And how do you feel about that?"

"I don't think it will change my life," I said. "Nor do I want it to."

"Learned from experience, have you?" she said.

"Let's just say I'm old enough to have very low expectations."

We applied ourselves to our flaking pastries. "These are good," I said, patting the napkin against my buttered lips.

"They are," she agreed. She brushed a few crumbs from her fingertips. "That's not all the news about Carità."

I sipped my coffee, raising my eyebrows to indicate interest.

"When we left the café, I told her I was going to a lecture by my favorite professor, Dr. Blintz. He's an amazing speaker, very animated, very ironic. He was talking about Thorstein Veblen, an economist, also ironic. Carità said she wished she could be a fly on the wall at a college lecture, and I told her this was a public lecture at the Atheneum on the campus; he gives one every year. She lit up and wanted to go with me, and, of course, I said yes. So we went."

"Did she like it?" I asked.

"She was knocked out by it. Her mouth was open the whole lecture; she barely moved. She was just drinking it in. We were in the front row, and I saw Dr. B. glance at her a few times while he spoke. Curious, but kindly, like he was pleased she was there. When the question period opened, Carità listened closely to a couple of answers, then shot up her hand. He called on her—I nudged her to tell her he'd pointed to her. She stood up and made a very cogent observation. Dr. B. was interested."

"What did she say?"

"Well, you'd have to know something about Veblen. But, basically, Carità said that conspicuous leisure wasn't just a result of conspicuous consumption; it was the goal."

"I don't get it," I said.

Mimi gazed into the middle distance, considering her reply. "It's that rich people flaunt their leisure to prove they don't have to work."

"That seems obvious," I said.

"Yes, well, it is. But it was well put and very apt. He signaled us to come up to the podium. Of course, he'd figured out that Carità is blind. And it turns out he has a grown son who is blind."

"And he wants to get them together," I suggested.

"No. His son is married, has two kids and advanced degrees in sociology. He also runs a program designed to help blind and deaf students who want to pursue higher education."

"So they can go to college?"

"That's just what Carità said: 'Do you mean I could go to college?' And he said, 'That's exactly what I mean.' Carità burst into tears."

I felt moisture gathering in my own eyes at the scene Mimi had conjured. Carità in tears. This was big. "But how can she do it?" I asked.

"This program provides everything: a mentor, recorded tapes of textbooks, a Braille typewriter, a tape recorder for lectures, even a stipend. They'll get her a seeing-eye dog if she needs one."

"Carità can go to college," I said wonderingly.

"She's full of plans," Mimi said. "She wants to get Ian back from the boonies and tell him the news."

I sipped my coffee while an image of Carità strolling across the campus with a backpack and a dog filled my imagination. Mimi finished her croissant.

"What a good friend you are," I said. "You've changed her life."

"I hope so," Mimi said. "I still don't trust her spoiled-brat husband."

"You're right," I agreed. "He thinks he's her savior. He may not be thrilled when he discovers she's his equal."

Later that day, as I was dressing for the evening, I heard a car pull up at the curb and looked out the window to see Carità brandishing her white cane as she skillfully alighted from a taxi. I buttoned my blouse and went down the back stairs. She was halfway up the walk when I opened the kitchen door and said, "Carità."

She made no response, just navigated the few steps, crossed the porch, and passed close to me as she entered the familiar room. She rested her hands on the back of a chair and turned toward me. She looked weary, I thought. Her hair was pulled back in a rubber band; her clothes, a white linen blouse and black cotton pants, were rumpled, as if she'd pulled them out of a basket. Her red leather sandals were dull from dust. "I need your help," she said.

"Sit down," I said. "Let me give you a cup of coffee."

She pulled the chair out and sank into it. "Thanks," she said. "I could use some coffee, that's for sure."

I took down her favorite mug, filled it halfway, with a dash of milk, as I knew she liked it.

"I have a croissant left over from the ones Mimi bought with you yesterday," I said, taking the white bag, now stained with grease, from the pantry shelf.

"Did Mimi tell you about the college?"

"She did," I said. "It sounds like a great opportunity."

"It's fantastic," she agreed. "It's the dream of my life."

I set the mug and the bag before her. She pushed the bag aside and wrapped her fingers around the handle. "Mimi told me you were going to Ian's parents' house to find out where he is," I said, taking the chair across from her.

"I went," she said. "That's why I'm here."

"Did you find out?"

"I couldn't get past the secretary." Her expression was a mixture of consternation and determination. "She said Ian's mother has left strict instructions that I'm not allowed in the house."

"That's pretty harsh," I observed.

"I don't know what we're going to do about his mother," she said petulantly.

"I think she may be preoccupied with her husband," I said. "She's divorcing him."

Carità sipped her coffee, then set the mug down and leaned back in her chair. "Has he moved out?"

"He has."

"Well, that's bad for him, but it doesn't explain why she shut me out of the house. Ian thinks I'm staying there. I think he must have sent a card saying where he is by now. Do you think Mike has it?"

"He hasn't mentioned it," I admitted.

Carità took a big gulp of coffee. "I need to talk to him," she said.

A bird in the mimosa near the porch let out a shriek of terror or joy, who knew which. Then I heard a sound I recognized, the sputter of an engine downshifting noisily at the curb. His car needed a tune-up.

Carità straightened up at the sound of the gate creaking and brisk footsteps on the walk. "It's him," she said.

Mike gained the porch and looked in at the screen. "Here you are," he said, his gaze sliding past me to Carità. He pulled open the screen and stepped inside.

"Have you heard from Ian?" Carità asked at once.

Mike extracted a postcard from his jacket pocket and brandished it before him. "He sent it to my chambers," he said. "Why would he do that?"

"Possibly more anonymous," I speculated.

Mike was holding the card out to Carità, who sat quite still in an attitude of listening. It dawned on him that she couldn't see it. "It's a picture of a beat-up fishing boat," he explained. "The postmark is San Bosco, but what he wrote, and it's all he wrote, is 'Port Justice.'"

"Is that a town?" I asked.

"It is. I looked it up. It's on an inlet called Black Rock Cove. Population: one hundred and seventy-five."

"He should be easy to find," I observed.

"Will you take me there?" Carità asked, turning her face toward Mike.

"I will," he said. "But not today."

"I want to go today," Carità insisted.

"It's too late to start," I said. "It will be dark by the time you get there. Better to go tomorrow."

"I can be free by noon," Mike said. He turned to me.

"Would you come with us to read the map? This place is to hell and gone."

Carità took this in in silence. Doubtless, she was thinking that if she could read a map and drive she'd be out the door and free of us.

"Sure," I said.

"Where are you staying?" Mike asked Carità.

"At my sister's place," she said.

"Your wife turned her away from the house," I informed him.

"It doesn't matter," Carità said. "When Ian gets back, we'll find our own place near the college."

"Carità's going to college," I explained.

Fortunately, Carità couldn't see the expression of disbelief that briefly animated her father-in-law's features.

"I'm majoring in economics," Carità informed him.

We met in my kitchen at noon, ate cheese sandwiches and drank coffee, marked out our roads on the map Mike had obtained, and set off in his car, with Carità perched uncomfortably on the cramped back seat. It was warm, muggy, and overcast. Mike and I talked idly. Carità sat quietly behind us. She didn't ask for the radio, which made me think she might be anxious.

The journey was uneventful. After taking the wrong fork in an endlessly forking road, we went astray by a few miles but found our way at last to a crossroads with a painted sign bearing the words "PORT JUSTICE" over an arrow pointing the right way. That way was down, down narrower roads, some shell, some dirt, a dip here, a rise there. We could smell the sea. Then, after a slow descending curve, lined with an obfuscating wall of shrubbery, we burst into a two-lane gravel road with a view straight out to the bay.

A battered, heaving elephant of a bus, topped by a pallet heaped with canvas bags of what might have been rice strapped across the roof, toiled toward us up the steep incline on the inner lane.

"That must be how he got here," Mike observed.

I noted that there were few passengers. A man leaning out the window gave us a hostile glare as they passed.

"We're almost there," Carità said. Mike shifted to neutral and tapped the brake as we began the perilous descent to the shore.

San Bosco was probably listed in the island guidebooks as a charming fishing community. Port Justice could make no such claim. The sign announcing the village limit was encrusted with brown rust patches and decorated at its rotting base with a moldering car tire.

The gravel on the road thinned over the packed dirt as we approached the water, for there was no village center, no court-house or general store or coffee bar with wrapped sandwiches. Port Justice consisted entirely of perhaps fifty weathered-board, tin-roofed shacks lined up one or two deep at the edge of a dirty brown beach just wide enough to provide parking for a little flotilla of motorless fishing dinghies. These were propped on their sides, or lifted onto wooden pallets, or lashed to car tires half buried in the sand. A few scrawny children squatted on the rocky edge of a breakwater, dangling fishing lines into the shallows.

"A picturesque fishing village," Mike remarked wryly as the road ended. We had arrived at a concrete platform jutting out over the water. Here stood Port Justice's only claim to charm—a wide, open pavilion constructed of dark wooden beams supporting a high, circular thatched roof. A scattering of rattan tables and chairs occupied one side. At the far end, near the water, a man stood at a wide table fitted with a pump and a sluice that emptied into the sea, brusquely cleaning a fish. As we watched, he dropped the finished project into a cooler on his left, shoved the innards and scales into the sluice, pumped a stream of seawater behind it, and turned to open a cooler on his right, from which he lifted another fish.

"What's going on?" Carità asked, leaning against the seat between us. "Are we there?"

"We are indeed," Mike replied.

"What's it like?"

"There's not much to it," Mike said.

"It smells like fish," she observed.

There was space for a few cars at the edge of the platform. Mike steered the convertible into a slot and turned off the engine. We three sat in silence for a moment. The only sounds were the scrape of the fisherman's knife against the surface of the table and the eternally lulling hush-hush of the tide. "I do like to hear the waves," Carità said.

Mike opened his door and swung his long legs over the packed dirt and grass patch. Carità and I climbed out and stood, stretching our legs, on the other side of the car. We all three faced the water. Far out, in a dinghy approaching the shore, I could make out three men—two rowing and one standing near the front, bent over, pulling at something inside the prow. The sun was low and blinding, and the fishermen were mere silhouettes, featureless and flat. Mike crossed in front of the car, looking grim.

"Is there anyone about?" Carità asked.

"Just a guy cleaning fish," he said.

"Let's ask him about Ian," she suggested.

"We might as well," he agreed.

We stepped onto the platform and out of the sun. It was, at once, cooler, and a breeze rustled the thatch grasses overhead. The few tables and chairs looked worn but clean. "This is rather nice," I observed. "Carità and I can sit over there while you talk to the man."

"Right," said Mike. "Best not to gang up on him."

Carità took my arm, and I guided her to a chair. "Tell me what it looks like?" she said. "Are there any nice houses?"

"No," I said. "This is a poor place."

"Is the beach wide?"

"No. It's hardly a beach at all. It's rocks and patches of sandy dirt. There are several boats pulled up with their nets hanging over the hulls." I watched Mike, who had engaged the man at the table. The man put down his knife and listened, nodding his head mechanically as Mike explained our mission. At length, he raised his arm and pointed at the dinghy steadily approaching. Either Ian was on it or one of the sailors knew where he was. "I think we'll find him pretty quickly," I said to Carità.

Mike exchanged a few more remarks with the man; then they turned away from each other, the man to his fish, Mike to us. I liked watching him walk toward me across the concrete slab in this dull, obscure little village. It occurred to me that no one knew where we were.

He appeared, in the casual elegance of his manner, unconcerned and totally out of place.

"He's on that boat coming in," he said as he approached.

Carità gave a little squeak of joy.

"He's calling himself Joe Green," Mike continued. "He got off the bus two weeks ago, said he was an orphan and wanted to be a fisherman. They gave him a job."

Carità stood up and took a step, touching the table for balance. "How close is he?" she said. "Take me to the boat."

"We've got a few minutes," I said. "He'll see us as soon as they're on the shore."

"That old guy looked at me like I came from another planet," Mike said. "He seemed fascinated with my shoes."

I glanced down at the shoes—light-tan leather, thin-soled driving shoes, useless and slippery, not suited for anything that could be called terrain. Then I looked past him at the sea, and the three men in the boat, which was moving swiftly now in the current, the prow lifting as it plowed toward the shore. All the clouds in the sky gathered around the sun, called home to their god after a day of effortless drifting through the ozone layer. Then we could hear the voices of the men as they prepared to drive their little craft onto the beach, shouting to each other, laughing. I could see them clearly, all three bare-chested, wearing only loose-fitting short pants. Though he was in many ways transformed, I recognized Ian in the front, holding his arms up high and wide, laughing at his own antics. They didn't see us yet.

"Let's go," Mike said.

Carità caught my arm and stepped out abruptly. "Let's go," she repeated.

Mike's stride was wide and brisk; in his eagerness to reach his son, he left us behind. It struck me that his feelings must be profoundly complicated, but that one of them had been, until now, fear for Ian's safety. Carità pulled me along, following the sound of the voices. All three of the sailors were in the water, occupied in the task of bringing up their boat, which seemed determined to wallow in the shallows. At last, as Mike drew close to the water's edge, pulling and shoving, they wrested their craft free of the sea. Mike called out, "Ian!"

Ian, the new Ian, with his short dark hair and golden skin, his narrow waist and muscled forearms, raised his head and took in the three of us. He was bent at the waist, holding a rope and some sort of cleat. He dropped these trappings of his new profession on the sand and called out, "Carità!" Then, ignoring his father's approach, he trotted toward us.

Carità pulled at my arm, wanting to be free of me but uncertain what was in front of her. She held one hand out helplessly before her, dragging me along. "He's coming straight for you," I said. "There's nothing between you. You can run."

She released my arm and shot across the sand, her arms raised before her, laughing at the freedom to run until she crashed into her beloved. Ian rushed to meet her, repeating her

name softly now, his arms open to catch her. Their joyful colli-
sion was so touching to behold, my breath caught in my throat.
Ian whirled her around, lifting her off the ground; then her
hands found his face, his arms pulled her in close, their mouths
came together in a hungry, passionate kiss.

I gazed past the lovers at Mike, who stood close to the boat
looking back at me. His expression was bemused, though not, I
thought, surprised. He raised a hand to me in a gesture of res-
ignation. The two fishermen looked on, passing some remarks
between them. Then they turned their attention to unloading
a deep wicker hamper loaded to the top with the still-writhing
silver bodies that constituted the catch of the day.

Carità had pulled her chair close to Ian's so that she could
rest her cheek against his shoulder. Mike and I sat across the
table from the reunited couple. Our chairs were farther apart.
In fact, I'd pulled mine to one side so that I could be an onlooker
rather than a participant in the family conversation. After all, I
thought, it wasn't my family.

Mike explained to Ian that things were calm in the city; Joe
Shock was dead, there was no warrant for his arrest, and no
reason he couldn't return and take up his studies at the college.

"How is that possible?" Ian said. "I killed a man."

"Actually, you didn't. You wounded him in self-defense.
He was recovering in the hospital, and then he died. But he
didn't die of the gunshot wound."

"What did he die of?"

"No one knows," Mike said. "But Marcus Betone had sworn to avenge his son's death."

"Marcus killed him," Ian said quietly.

"Well, not personally. And no one can prove he had anything to do with it."

"So you can come home," Carità said.

Ian rested his hand on Carità's thigh, bunching her skirt between his fingers. "I'm not coming back," he said.

"What do you mean?" Mike asked, though Ian's statement was clear enough.

"I'm not coming back," Ian repeated. "I'm staying here. I like it here. I have everything I need. I have a job, I have friends. It's a straightforward, simple life. I'm outdoors all the time; I work hard. I'm strong. I sleep well, and I feel good. I feel clean."

"If you didn't want to come home," Mike said, "why did you send the card telling us where you are?"

"I wanted you to bring my wife to me." He released Carità's skirt and stretched his arm behind her shoulders in a gesture of such confident possessiveness it chilled my blood.

"Don't you understand?" Carità said. "Everything has changed."

"Nothing has changed," Ian said disdainfully. "Nothing *can* change in that place. It's a sinkhole of greed and corruption."

Mike stretched his legs out under the table, crossing his feet at the ankles, as if to signal that he was settling in. Carità also altered her position, leaning forward from the protective arm her husband had draped across the back of her chair.

"Maybe not everything has changed," Mike said. "But some things have. Your mother is divorcing me, and she won't let your wife into the house."

"I'm living with my sister," Carità said softly.

Ian took this in stonily. "I don't see what difference that makes to me."

"You need to talk to your mother," Mike said. "She's got some big decisions to make, and you should consult with her to preserve your interests. She'll go after me, but I don't think she can touch your trust. She'll probably get the house, and she may want to sell it. That's a decision you two should make together."

"You're not listening to me," Ian said. "I don't care about the house or the trust or any of that. I plan to disinherit myself."

This declaration was met with an awed silence, pierced only by the shrill screech of a gull as it dived into the sea.

Mike lowered his head, looking thoughtful. "Okay," he said, "I get it. You're a fisherman now. You want the pure life, the simple life. You feel clean."

"You disgust me," Ian said. "I hope Mother destroys you."

Mike nodded. "You'll still get this month's allowance," he said, scanning the line of shabby buildings along the shore. "You can probably buy one of these shacks. You may want your car. If Lila will follow in my car, I could drive it out to you. Then you can sell it, or maybe just let it rust, and pull off the tires to decorate your yard."

This caused Ian to shift his focus to me. "Why are you always dragging this woman along?" he complained. "I don't understand what she's doing here." His eyes grazed my face.

"She sold my wife to any brute who could pay for the pleasure. What possible right could she have to be here?"

I decided to answer that question. "They needed me to read the map," I said.

"Oh, for God's sake," Ian moaned.

"Lila is here because I asked her to come," Mike said. "And I asked her to come because she's important to me."

Ian barked a fake laugh. "Well, that's just perfect, isn't it?" he said. "Now that you're going to be divorced, you can marry her."

"I would," Mike declared. "If she'd have me."

Ian leaped at this bait. "Dad," he exclaimed, "what is wrong with you? You can't marry a whore."

Mike thrust out his chin, shifting his gaze to Carità, who sat stiffly, listening, her hands folded in her lap. "Maybe you need to think about who you're calling a whore," he said.

I caught my breath at this. Mike had laid a trap for his son to walk into. Ian's outrage turned to icy indifference. Sarcasm, I thought, is the cruelest form of parental abandonment. The child has no recourse; his feelings have been thrown down and danced upon. Now I understood why Ian despised his father, and though I didn't much care for him, at that moment I felt a glimmer of sympathy for the boy. He was outmatched.

Carità had sat through this standoff without moving, listening, I thought, to her sweet dream of a carefree life swirl down the drain. I felt sorry for her, too, though in some ways she had outfoxed her husband and his family. She was legally bound to Ian, a condition that might become dull pretty quickly, but even if he longed to be a pauper, he wasn't, and by law she had claim to half of his fortune. She was strong-willed and twice as smart as he was. Now she raised her hand and touched his arm. "Darling," she said.

He turned to her distractedly. "What is it?" he said.

"Are you saying you want us to live here?"

"Yes," he said. "That's exactly what I'm saying."

"Well," she said, "if you want to, maybe we could stay a few weeks, but we have to go back in time for registration at the college."

"I'm not going back to college," he snapped. "There's nothing for me there."

She patted his arm, gently holding his attention. "That may be, though I think it would be a shame to quit, but I'm definitely going, so we have to go back."

Now incredulity sat upon her husband's brow, but Carità couldn't see it. "What are you talking about?" he said.

"There's a program I found out about. They help blind students go to college. They'll give me everything I need. I'll have a mentor and a Braille typewriter and a tape recorder. We can get a house close to the college. Isn't it wonderful?"

"How can you go to college?" Ian said, stressing the object, as in "How can *pigs* fly?"

"As I said, it's a program for blind students," Carità repeated. "I'll have a mentor who will prepare me for exams. Some of them will be oral. I might have a guide dog so I can get around quickly between classes. They have it all worked out."

I was so positioned that I could see both Carità's husband and her father-in-law as she described the bright future she envisioned for herself. I had the sense that I was watching a play, a family drama, and that the acting wasn't first-rate, the plot was predictable and banal. The husband would oppose her, the father-in-law would support her.

"Why would you even want to do that?" Ian asked. He was hesitant, clearly unwilling to shift the subject from his self-righteous defiance of his father.

Carità drew herself up, turning her face away from her husband. "I want to be an educated person," she said calmly. "I want to attend lectures by scholars who have read widely and can speak with authority."

"She's majoring in economics," Mike put in, just to needle his son.

"That's right," Carità said. "I'm very interested in money." The lighthearted sincerity she gave to this possibly damning statement amused me; one of Carità's most alarming traits was her honesty.

Ian's reaction was dismissive and reproving. "What I'm trying to explain is that we don't need money. Money destroys community. That's what I've learned here."

"So—it's back to barter," Mike concluded. "You catch a fish and trade it for an egg. Or a dozen eggs. The problem is, who gets to decide what a fish is worth in eggs, isn't it?"

"Don't be an ass," Ian retorted. "Of course they use money here. But it's not an object. It's a means. No one hoards it. No one is trying to corner the market or drive their neighbor out of business. Everyone participates in the community in whatever way they can." Here he turned his attention to his wife—whose expression was uncharacteristically guarded. "Here's the amazing part," he continued. "There's a woman here who's also blind. Her name is Gilda. She's learned to make fishing nets by hand. She lives on that ridge." He pointed to a rock ledge where a few shacks tottered toward each other. "She's elderly, but very lively." He gestured to the beached boats, each with an array of nets stretched over the keel. "She can't make them fast enough. She could teach you how to do it."

A low chuckle issued from Mike's chest. He understood Carità better than his son did, I thought.

"You think I should make nets," Carità said, wonderingly, without hostility.

"It's honest work," Ian insisted, glaring at his father.

"Dearest," Carità said, turning to her husband, her manner patient and cautious, "I don't think you understand."

"What don't I understand?" Ian replied testily.

"When I was a girl," Carità began, "my teacher told me stories about college. She went to a big university on the mainland, and she said those years were the happiest in her life. Even though we all knew I would never be able to go, she took my education seriously, and when she left, she told my uncle I'd completed all the college-preparatory studies I would need. She thought I could do the work. There was some talk of bringing in a professor, but we lived in the country, there was no college nearby, and what professor would give up his position to go live on a farm and teach a blind girl? Then my uncle lost all his money, and he killed himself. We had no family, so Bessie and I had to make our way. She wanted to move to the village and find some way to support me, but I persuaded her to come to the city. I just wanted to be close to a college." She paused, sighing softly, as at a painful recollection. "I never imagined that I could be a student. But now, it's like a miracle, I've found this program. There are people who will help me, who believe I can succeed. They don't care where I came from or what I've been doing for a living. They're offering me the opportunity to be what I most want to be in this world. It's a great challenge—the greatest challenge of my life." She turned to her husband, laying her palm flat across his bare chest. "I can't turn away from it," she said. "Surely you understand that. A door I thought was permanently closed against me has opened before me. You can't ask me to turn away from it."

I'd been riveted by Carità's simple eloquence, but now I looked at her husband. She leaned into the palm she had pressed against his chest, pinning him to the chair. He fairly squirmed beneath her hand, not so much from the physical pressure as from the force of her argument. I glanced at Mike, who looked quizzical and confused, like someone who has stumbled into a house he doesn't recognize.

Abruptly, Ian grasped Carità's wrist, pushed her back into her chair, and leaped up from his own with a sharp cry. "No," he said. "You're all against me. You all just want to control me." Carità sank back in her chair, covering her face with her hands. Ian turned his back on us and lit out across the sand toward the water.

Mike shook his head slowly, addressing the air. "What is wrong with this kid?" he complained.

These men, I thought. And their dramas.

Carità was weeping. I moved to Ian's chair, touched her shoulder, then drew my hand away. "It'll be all right," I said. She continued weeping but nodded her head. Then she coughed, lowered her hands, and sniffed. I opened my purse and took out a handkerchief. "Take this," I said, pressing the cloth against her fingers.

As soon as she felt it, she said, "Oh, thanks," and proceeded to blow her nose.

"He hasn't had to take you seriously before," I said. "Men generally resist that, especially young men."

She folded the cloth and tapped it against her nostrils. "Fishing nets," she said disparagingly.

Mike sat watching us. "You two are priceless," he said.

"What's Ian doing now?" Carità asked.

"He's kicking rocks at the water's edge," I said. "There's nobody around."

"I should go talk to him," she said. "But I left my stick in the car."

"I'll guide you past the boats," I said. "Then I'll come back and wait here."

She rose to her feet and took my arm. I led her across the dirty sand, past the boats, toward Ian, who stood in the shallows, his hands on his hips, gazing out to sea. "Does he see us?" Carità asked.

"Not yet. He's got his back to us."

"Ian," she called out. He turned, scowling, then turned away.

"He's in a snit," I said. "He sees us, but he won't look at us."

"Just bring me close enough so I can walk to him."

We took a few more steps to the edge of the water. "He's standing in the shallows," I said. "Straight ahead."

She stopped, bending over her knees to unfasten her sandals. "You can go back," she said.

I turned away, took a few steps. "Ian," Carità said again, her voice sweet and plaintive. I went a little farther, paused, looked back over my shoulder. He had come out of the water and approached her, one arm out, reaching to take her extended hand in his own.

Back at the pavilion, I collapsed into the chair next to Mike. "What do you think?" he asked.

"She knows what she's doing," I said. "He doesn't have a chance."

"Surely she's noticed she married an idiot," he said.

"Oh, I think she knew that from the start."

"So she *is* after his money."

I called up the image of Carità that morning, only a few weeks before, when she sat at the kitchen table rotating her hand with the fingers outspread to show off her gold wedding band. "Let's just say I don't think she married him for his idealism," I said.

Mike looked out at the couple. "He's holding her hands and talking very earnestly," he said.

"She's a good listener," I assured him.

"She'll need to be," he said. "Do you think they're going to stay together?"

"I don't know. They might. The sex is good."

"Is it?" He perked up, turning his attention to me. "Did she tell you that?"

"I think it's pretty obvious."

"I'm glad to hear it. I didn't think Ian could be up to much. He's so bloody serious and sullen."

"I think the fact that they're the same age is a novelty for Carità."

He considered this. "Right," he said. "I guess she's had to go with a lot of old guys."

I looked out at Ian and Carità. He had his arm around her waist, and she leaned against him, resting her cheek on his shoulder. He was still talking.

"Tell me what you think, Mrs. Gulliver," Mike asked cheerfully. "If the sex is good, is that enough to save the marriage?"

"I have no idea," I said.

He rephrased the question. "Would it be enough to make you stay with me?"

I smiled, gazing past his attentive inspection to the couple near the water's edge. "Look," I said. "They're kissing."

Who knows if sex is enough, but sex won that day for sure. I wasn't pleased with Mike's secondhand marriage proposal, and Carità was insulted by the fishing-net scheme. Ian was focused on defying his father, and Mike seemed determined to prove his son was a fool. Not a lot of mutual respect all round, but Ian and Carità couldn't keep their hands off each other, and

I knew Mike and I had both entertained the thought that our room at the Tropicale was on the way home from Port Justice.

Eventually, the lovers stopped making out in the shallows and ambled toward us, past the boats, over the sand, hand in hand. When they were close, before they could speak, Mike said, "So . . . what's the conclusion?"

To avoid looking at his father or at me, Ian turned to Carità. "I'm going to stay a week," she said.

"That's fair," Mike said. "You're giving it a chance."

"We'll take the bus to San Bosco so I can buy what I need," Carità continued. "I didn't even bring a toothbrush."

"Where are you staying, son?" Mike asked Ian.

"I have a place," Ian replied curtly.

"Right," Mike said. "Running water, has it?"

Ian took in a slow breath, steeling his patience. "Yes, it has running water, Dad," he said. "And it has a bed and a table and two chairs, and even a window."

"Sounds perfect," Mike said. "Sounds inviting."

Carità, ignoring the hostile father-son dynamic, addressed Mike. "Would you come back to get me next Monday?" she asked.

Mike turned his full attention to her. Down came all the frosty superiority. "Yes, my dear," he said. "I will come get you anytime you say and take you wherever you want to go."

"That's good," Carità said. "Because I'm not sure where I'll want to go."

Ian slipped his hand around her waist and bent over to nuzzle her neck. "I'll change your mind," he said. This made her laugh. She raised her hand to touch his cheek.

"Shall I tell your sister?" I asked.

"Yes," she said. "Tell her I'm here with Ian."

"All right," Mike said, rising from his chair. "That's settled. Same time, same place, next Monday."

I stood up as well. Carità skillfully detached herself from her husband and reached out to me. "I need to go to the car to get my stick."

I held out my arm and we connected. "It's this way," I said, setting off. As Mike turned to follow us, Ian said, "Dad. I have to ask you something."

He needs money, I thought. I was pleased to have a few minutes alone with Carità. "Are you sure you'll be okay here?" I asked.

"He's so stubborn," she replied. "I feel like I don't have a choice."

This discouraged me. "You do have a choice," I said. "You can come back with us now. He'll be along once the boredom sets in."

She smiled ruefully. "It's setting in for me already," she said. "I have to go meet the blind net-maker. Ian's sure I'll be crazy about her."

"Do you think he's serious about not coming back?"

"I think he's afraid to come back," she said.

"Why? He's not going to be arrested."

"It's not that. It's his parents. He's afraid they'll try to make him take sides. He's angry at them both."

"I can see why he might be."

"And he's afraid of failing at college."

"He's not doing well?"

"He's doing fine, but he doesn't see the point of it. He doesn't want to go to law school. He's interested in literature, but he thinks the English majors are all poseurs. I think he *really* doesn't want *me* to go to college."

"Why?"

"He thinks I'm deluded. He thinks I'll fail. And maybe he's afraid I won't fail."

We had arrived at the car. Carità yanked open the door, clambered into the back, and liberated her stick from the floor. "He's all tied up in knots about the evils of money," she said. "He wants to give it all away."

"What are you going to do?"

She climbed back to the front and sat on the seat with her feet on the ground, carefully unfolding her stick. "I honestly don't know," she said. "Maybe a lot of sex will bring him around. He's been in this backwater for a couple of weeks, learning to fish and having monkish fantasies of a pure, sinless life."

"That's never good for a young man," I said.

She stood up and swept the ground before her with the stick. "I'm dreading the bed," she said. "I bet it's made of rope and straw."

"At least there's running water," I said. "This way."

She came to my side, and we turned back toward the sea. She stepped along quickly, sweeping the stick before her in a semicircle. She didn't take my arm. "I hope that means a flush toilet," she said.

When Mike and I were alone in the car, I asked him what Ian had wanted.

"Money," he said.

"I figured that was it."

"They don't take checks here, and there's no bank, so he'd run out of cash."

"That's pretty funny," I said.

"What did Carità say?" he asked.

"She doesn't want to meet the blind net-maker."

He laughed. "Well, who can blame her?"

"She's also hoping Ian's room has a flush toilet."

"She's practical. Unlike her husband."

"Some people want to change the world, some just want to come out on top," I said. "Ian's in the first group."

"This is deep wisdom," he said.

"Are you making fun of me?"

"Not in the slightest," he said. "You astound me." He inserted the key and started the car engine. "What group are you in?" he asked.

"I think it's obvious I'm not trying to change the world."

"Me, neither," he said. He turned the car into the road, holding the wheel loosely as we rattled uphill through the potholes. "When do you need to get back?" he asked. "Do we have time to stop at the Tropicale? I could definitely use a drink."

"Tonight's my closed night," I said.

His eyes widened. "That's right," he said. "It's Monday. That's great." We bumped along a bit farther without speaking. Mike rested his hand on my thigh. "That's great," he said again.

That night, after several drinks and a dinner of bar food; after much talk of Mike's impending divorce—he wouldn't contest it—and his son's impetuous marriage—about to undergo its first real trial; after climbing the wide steps to our familiar room; after stripping off our clothes in no particular rush, and falling amiably into each other's arms across the bed; after what might have been hours of lovemaking—tantalizing, teasing, sometimes tender, sometimes fierce, sometimes laughing while tussling, sometimes gasping for breath; after we collapsed at last side by side, holding hands and talking; after taking turns in the bathroom and drinking all the water in the pitcher; after a heavy tropical rain commenced falling torrentially, as if someone had unzipped a cloud containing a lake in the sky, wrapping our room in a cool, hushing curtain of water; after I fell asleep with Mike wrapped around my back; after all that, I woke in the dark, still room and found myself thinking, uncharacteristically, about the future.

Which is to think about the past.

The talk about his divorce had allowed Mike to segue to his proposal—which I had taken to be a joke, designed to antagonize his son—that he would marry me if I would have him. "It wasn't a joke," he said. "I meant it. I mean it. Would you?"

"It's a little soon to think about that," I said. "For one thing, you're still married."

"If I don't fight it, it could go pretty quickly."

"Your lawyers may have other ideas," I said. "And you should listen to them."

"How long could it take? A year?"

"And there's the problem that I'm still married," I said.

"You're married?" he asked, with an expression of such total incomprehension it was as if I'd revealed I was from another planet.

"You amuse me," I said.

He leaned toward me over the table. "You're married," he repeated, as a statement this time.

"To Captain Gulliver," I said.

He snorted, grasped his glass of whiskey, and brought it to his lips.

"He could return," I insisted.

"Now you're making fun of me," he said. "But, Lila, I'm serious."

"So am I," I said. "And I want you to understand this. I've changed my name once, and I have no intention of changing it again."

"I'm just trying to secure you," he protested. "I don't want to lose you."

"Listen to yourself," I said.

He was silent for a moment, sipping his drink, listening to himself. He tried another tack. "Will you come live with me?"

"I have a house and a business to run."

"I'll get an apartment, a big one, downtown. Something with a terrace. When you close at night, you can come to me, and in the mornings, we'll have a leisurely breakfast and read the papers."

"You're seriously running with this," I said.

"It's a great idea. Tell me you'll think about it."

"I'll think about it," I said.

So . . . I was thinking about it.

I hadn't known Mike long, but he clearly had serious character flaws, and some of them weren't easy to overlook. He was deceitful and arrogant, and had no self-control. These were venial, even banal failings. In many respects, Mike Drohan was just an ordinary guy. He was an unfaithful husband, and a truly disastrous father, incapable of seeing that his son craved his approval and hated himself for that craving. Carità had zeroed in on this at once; she understood that her young husband's absurd posturing and pretension masked the force that was driving him, which was fear. Fear of failure. Fear of deserving his father's contempt.

Men are expected to succeed, women to fail. Every woman knows the deck is stacked. In practical terms, this makes it more difficult for women to succeed, but it's more damning for men to fail. Win or lose, defying expectations is heavy going. No one knew this better than Carità.

Ian's fisherman phase would pass. No force on earth was going to keep Carità from going to college, so he'd have to give in to his wife, and it wouldn't be for the last time, I had no doubt. He would never need a job, so he could defy his father by being some kind of artist. A poet, perhaps. He could write sonnets about fishing.

This thought made me chuckle. Mike stirred behind me, snuggling up to my back, one hand finding a breast, his knee slipping between my thighs.

The thing was, I thought, and we both knew it, our sexual compatibility was off the charts. There were no games of power or subjection, no aim for pleasure that wasn't mutual. We had gotten through, with impressive speed, the preliminary diffidence, to the deep sadness of sex, and the hope it inspires of having found for the body that fragile vessel in which it is our fate to navigate the tempestuous seas of sensuality, a safe harbor. This was proved, I thought, by the fact that, when we lay side by side, sated and exhausted, though we shared smug glances and ironic smiles, both of us had tears standing in our eyes.

In the uneventful week that followed, Mike and I spent as much time as we could together. One night, we had a long, romantic dinner at the hotel. On another, I went over after I closed the house. On Sunday night, after closing, I packed an overnight bag and arrived at the hotel at 2:00 a.m. In the morning, he went to his chambers while I luxuriated at the hotel, sending downstairs for a big room-service breakfast with waffles and fruit. At noon, we set out on the long, tedious drive to Port Justice. We'd had rain for three days, but the sky was clear at last, and the sun poured down, hot and bright. The air had a fresh-washed quality to it. It felt good to slip my sunglasses over my eyes.

By the time we got down the last treacherous bit of gravel road and turned the car toward the sea, the sun was casting sharp-edged shadows alongside the shacks; even the dinghies shone dully, outlined by pools of shade. We parked as close as we could get to the thatched pavilion and climbed out of the car. Mike rested his hands at the base of his spine, stretching upward with a grimace. "Are you okay?" I asked.

"Fine," he said. "I don't unfold as easily as I used to."

The pavilion was obscured by a truck, and then a boat resting upside down on a wooden rack. There was a gash in the hull the size of a bucket. "Don't take that one," Mike observed. We picked our way around it, and then we could see the pavilion and, inside it, the objects of our quest. "Good God," Mike exclaimed softly.

They were seated at a table with a backpack between them. Carità had one elbow propped up, her cheek resting against her hand, the picture of despondency. But it was her husband who had caused Mike to exclaim. Ian sat oddly splayed in his chair. His left leg, stretched out stiffly before him, was sealed from knee to instep in a hard white plaster cast. A wide gauze bandage, looped over his head and under his chin to hold it in place, covered one side of his face. A pair of metal crutches leaned against the back of his chair.

"Looks like he's done with fishing," I said softly. Mike gave me a sidelong glance, registering dismay and accord. As we approached, Carità's head came up, and Ian turned toward us, watching indifferently.

"What the hell, son," Mike said, when we were under the thatch. "What happened to you?"

What happened to Ian was the following:

Four days after we left the newlyweds, Ian had gone out with his neighbors at dawn to do some hand-line fishing. The sea was choppy, but they had unusually good luck, and as the sun climbed steadily into the brightening sky, the deck came alive with slippery, flopping fish. Ian had snagged yet another and stood astride the seat, leaning over the gunwale, pulling in the line hand over hand. To bring the fish gradually up from the depths, he played it in and out until he could see his catch just beneath the surface. It was a big one. He got into position for a final yank over the side. The boat was tossing in the chop and had taken on water; the deck was awash, as were the fishermen, everything wet and slippery, with fish gasping and wriggling from stem to stern. At last, Ian had maneuvered his catch to where he could clear the gunwale, and he jerked the line straight up, hard and fast. The fish rose high before him, twisting and gyrating in the deadly air with such force that it managed to work free of the hook. As the liberated fish dropped smoothly into its element, the line snapped back to the boat, and the hook caught Ian in the fleshy part of his cheek, near his mouth. He staggered, clutching his face, dimly aware that his left foot was wedged between the seat and a built-in tackle box. Holding his cheek with one hand, he bent down to release his shoe. As he struggled, the boat rolled abruptly; he lost his balance and pitched backward over the side. The line caught on the rail, and the hook tore through his flesh all the way to his ear. At last, his foot came free of the shoe, but not before his ankle snapped from the pressure. He flailed in the water, aghast with pain, until his fellow fishermen pulled him out. Then he lay among the dying fish in the hull, moaning in agony all the way back to the shore.

Carità, sleeping fitfully in the sizzling shack, was awakened by the shouts of a neighbor who told her Ian was injured and, as there was no real doctor in Port Justice, they'd taken him to San Bosco in a truck. She spent a miserable few hours in the pavilion, listening to the locals recounting the details of the accident. It became clear to her that they all agreed. Ian was hopeless as a fisherman. He was, in fact, something of a laughingstock in the village. He was returned to her in the afternoon, bandaged, his leg bound in plaster. They'd gotten through the last three days of their residence and were now in a state of unrelieved gloom. Ian confessed that he just wanted to get out of Port Justice as soon as possible.

At the end of this story, Mike and I exchanged a thoughtful look. Then, to my relief, he said the right thing. "You poor kids!" he exclaimed. "Let's get you home."

In the next moment, no one spoke as we all asked ourselves where this home might be. Mike was living in a hotel room; I lived in a brothel; Carità was banned from the mansion. Carità stood up and pulled the backpack toward her across the table. "We'll stay at Bessie's," she said dejectedly.

"I'll take that," I said, relieving her of the backpack.

While his father held out the crutches to him, Ian struggled to stand. His face was gaunt; doubtless, he hadn't been eating much. His hair had grown out enough to look unkempt. The dye had faded, and the result was a shock of muddy gray curls with blond roots. His eyes burned with a zealot's fury.

"Can you get down the steps?" Mike asked him.

"I can," he said.

I slipped the backpack straps over my shoulders and offered my arm to Carità. Mike went ahead, followed by Ian, his long body slung pathetically between the crutches, jerking across the floor. At the steps he paused, lifted one crutch, shifted his weight to his good leg, and hopped awkwardly to the pavement.

Carità and I brought up the rear. As we made our halting progress to the car, I envisioned the sad spectacle we must present.

Carità, ever resourceful, had something else on her mind. "Could I borrow a set of sheets from you?" she asked. "We'll have to sleep on the foldaway couch, and Bessie doesn't have an extra full set in the apartment."

The drive back was gloomy and uncomfortable. Carità and I huddled in the narrow back seat. Mike got Ian arranged in the passenger seat and stowed the crutches in the trunk. We were off. Mike asked Ian a question or two and received sullen, monosyllabic answers. We bounced along in silence until we joined the main road. Carità leaned forward, directing her voice to Mike. "Could we have the radio on?" she asked.

"Definitely," said Mike, and with the press of a button the tense atmosphere was lubricated by a sultry female voice, reminding us that love was torture and betrayal a burning hell. In silence, the four of us listened to moody songs of passion and loss all the way to the city.

As we were forced to double-park, I waited in the car while Mike escorted Ian and Carità up the stairs to Bessie's apartment. I moved to the passenger seat. Mike didn't stay long. "Is Bessie there?" I asked when he returned. He slid in beside me and patted my shoulder as if rubbing an icon for luck.

"No," he said. "She's at work."

"She's in for a surprise," I said.

"I'll say," Mike agreed.

My house was dark but for a light in Mimi's bedroom. "Come in and have a drink," I said. "I'll get the sheets and we can go back."

"Right," said Mike. In the kitchen, I took the vodka bottle from the freezer and poured out two tumblers half full. Mike leaned in the doorway looking perplexed. "Do you think Carità is fed up with Ian?" he asked.

We heard the hall door open above and Mimi's quick footsteps on the stairs. She appeared in the doorway, nearly colliding with Mike. "Excuse me," she said, sliding past him.

"Mimi," I said, "this is Mike Drohan."

"Pleased to meet you," she said, putting out her hand. Her frank manner set Mike at ease, and he gave her hand a firm shake. "Likewise," he said.

"Did they come back?" Mimi asked, turning to me.

"They did," I said. "We left them at Bessie's. Ian had an accident, and he's on crutches."

"Crutches!" she exclaimed.

"Broken ankle," Mike added. "Also got a gash on his face."

"Was he in a fight?"

"Fishing," Mike said.

"They need sheets," I said. "They'll have to sleep on the foldaway. Bessie works late, so I said I'd bring over a set."

"I'll take them," Mimi said. "I want to see Carità."

"That would be helpful," I said.

She headed back up the stairs. "Shall I drive her over?" Mike asked.

"She'll take her bike," I said. I sipped the cool, stinging vodka, feeling a pleasant jolt to my brain.

"How will she carry the sheets on a bike?"

"The bike has a basket."

He glanced out the porch door. "It's getting dark."

"The bike has a light," I said.

"Okay," he said, bringing his glass to his lips.

"She's Carità's best friend," I said. "She'll find out what's going on with those two."

Mike pulled out a chair and sat down wearily. "That was a long drive," he said.

"It was," I agreed. "But we're done now."

Our eyes met, and we smiled the same smile of relief. "Shall we go to the hotel?" he asked.

"I think so," I said.

Mimi came lightly down the steps, carrying a set of sheets folded inside a pillowcase. "Is Carità upset about Ian?" she asked.

"She looks pretty depressed," Mike said. Then, yielding to me, "Do you think she's depressed?"

"She hardly spoke," I said. "She just wanted to listen to the radio all the way back."

"Carità does love the radio," Mimi said, and she was out the door.

"She seems an independent young person," Mike observed.

"She dislikes your son," I said. "She doesn't trust him."

Mike sucked an ice cube from his drink and cracked it between his molars. When he'd melted the bits and chased them with a gulp of vodka, he set the glass on the table with an air of finality. "My impossible son," he said.

I passed a luxurious night at Mike's hotel, sleeping deeply between bursts of half-conscious sex. We were practiced lovers now, quick to sense the ebb and flow of desire. By the time I returned to my house in the morning, Mimi had left for school. I didn't see her until the afternoon, when she came in to change for work. I was at the table, reading the society page of the island paper. She dropped her book bag at the staircase, came into the kitchen, and went straight to the refrigerator.

"How was school?" I asked.

"I just aced the midterm in poli-sci."

"Good for you," I said.

"I'm feeling celebratory," she said, taking a half-full bottle of champagne from the door. "Can I buy you a drink?"

"Please," I said. "It's on me."

She took down two flutes from the pantry. I folded the paper and pushed it aside as she sat my glass before me. "So how did you find Carità last night?" I asked.

She sat down across from me and took a swallow of her wine. "Not good," she said.

"What's going on?"

"I think the poor girl is at her wits' end," she said.

"She was stressed when we picked them up," I said. "But I didn't get a chance to talk to her. Ian was busy radiating gloom."

"He's definitely gone off the deep end," she said. "The whole time I was there, he was mumbling on the louvered porch."

"He's talking to himself?"

"He's praying."

"Jesus," I said.

Mimi lifted her chin, raising her glass to my apt response. "Exactly," she said.

"I didn't know he was religious."

"He thinks God spoke to him through a fish."

How much more of this fanatical husband could Carità stand? I thought. "Why did God do that?"

"Ian fell into bad company and committed a sin," Mimi explained. "The worst possible sin: he murdered a man, and now he must expiate that crime. Jesus, the fisherman, sent a fish and literally hooked him and knocked him down and broke his ankle. He got the message, and now he plans to change his life."

"Mike was right," I said. "He never should have sent him to that school."

"Carità doesn't know what to do. She says he's determined to disinherit himself and devote his life to serving the poor."

"She needs a lawyer," I said.

"He wants them to join an oblate order where a married couple is attached to a monastery and lives a selfless life, just like the monks."

"She told me he was having monkish thoughts," I recalled. "And that was before the fish."

Mimi shook her head slowly, as at a sad thought. She finished her glass and reached out for the bottle. "That fish was lying for him," she concluded.

When Mimi had gone upstairs to conjure her nightly transformation from serious student to exotic femme fatale, I sat at the table, thinking about the last couple of days. It seemed to me that we had arrived at an impasse—"we" being Carità and Ian and Mike and me. Ian, in the grip of religious mania, was beyond reason. Carità, ambitious and determined, understood that her improvident marriage might block the way to what she wanted, which was an education. Mike was in limbo. Claudia had agreed to destroy all the photos in return for his complete submission to the terms of the divorce settlement, which he fully expected to be harsh. He was telling himself he was madly in love and nothing else mattered. What he wanted was an escape hatch from the muddle he'd made of his life.

And then there was me. I was the only one who didn't want to change my life. I'd worked hard for the stability and independence I had in this tumultuous world. And I enjoyed life just as it was. I had no desire to marry Mike, but I didn't want to lose him. I felt reckless, alive, and free in his company. He excited me.

The sun was setting, and a light breeze freshened the warm,

still air. I heard the gate open and looked out to see Vivien and Charlotte coming up the walk. They greeted me pleasantly—Vivien had brought a bag of grapefruit from the bush in her yard—and proceeded up the stairs to change from their street clothes. I was piling the grapefruit in a bowl on the table when Jack came in, looking weary. He had a day job and two young sons he never got to see.

It was time to open the bar.

Three nights passed. It was the weekend, and we were busy; the girls stayed late and went home exhausted but uncomplaining, as they knew they'd have big cash packets on Monday, as well as a day and night of rest. I was closing too late and too exhausted to go to Mike's hotel.

On Monday, I slept late and didn't have breakfast until ten. Then I cleared the table and laid out my books to do the weekly tallies and prepare the packets for the girls. Liquor sales were way up, and I knew the girls would be smiling as they counted out the bills in their envelopes. It was hot already. I had the doors and windows open, the fan on, a glass of iced tea on a cork coaster next to the adding machine. I was so focused I didn't hear the gate open, or footsteps on the porch, so I started when a soft female voice said, "Good morning, Mrs. Gulliver."

It was Bessie, standing placidly at the screen as if she'd been there for some time.

"Oh, Bessie," I said. "You startled me."

"I'm so sorry about that," she said.

"Come in," I said. "Come in. Can I get you something to drink?"

"No, thank you," she said.

Mimi was right: Bessie was looking fine. I guessed she'd lost fifteen pounds, and she had her hair cut in a becoming style. Her complexion wasn't so flushed; she'd applied eye shadow and lipstick with considerable skill. She was dressed neatly in lime-green Bermuda shorts and a pale-pink cotton blouse, a mildly daring and pleasant combination. She gripped a straw bag with a faux-tortoiseshell clasp in one hand. She opened the screen with the other and stepped into the kitchen.

"Have a seat," I said. "How are you? You're looking very well."

"I'm fine, thank you," she said. "I came to see Mimi. Is she here?"

"She's not," I said. "She went off on her bike half an hour ago. Returning books to the library, I think. She should be back soon."

"Oh," she said, bringing her hands together over the purse with a wringing gesture I recalled from the first time I'd seen her.

"Do sit down," I persisted. "We can talk while you wait for Mimi. Let me give you a glass of iced tea. I'm curious to know how your sister is doing."

She focused on me, and I had the sense that she was weighing her decision, to stay or to go. I smiled. "It's good to see you, Bessie," I said, meaning it. "Mimi tells me you've been promoted, and things are going well for you."

She made up her mind. "Iced tea would be nice," she said, pulling out a chair. "It's awful hot out."

"It is," I agreed, getting up to fix her drink. When I'd set the sweating glass before her and resumed my seat, I closed my account book. "Tell me how Carità and Ian are doing," I asked. "When we dropped them off at your place, they seemed a little"—I searched for an innocuous word—"defeated."

"That's just it," Bessie said. "I don't know how they are. They stayed one night; the next day they left, and I haven't heard a thing."

"Do you know where they went?"

Bessie took two swallows of her drink, looking into the glass as if she saw something of interest there. I pushed a coaster toward her, and she placed the glass carefully in the center. "Ian decided he had to have a confrontation—that's the word he used—with his mother. He found a cab, and they went to his house."

I pictured Ian on his crutches, stumping along the street, flagging down a cab.

"Carità didn't want to go," she continued. "She said his mother had locked her up like a servant and then, when she escaped, forbidden her back in, so she wasn't interested to find out what she'd do next."

"What did Ian say?"

"Oh, he said it would be different, because Carità would be with him, and it was important that his mother acknowledge the marriage. Then he went on about how he was going to disinherit himself. Also, he wanted his mother to drop the divorce proceedings against his father, because divorce is a sin against Holy Mother Church."

"Poor Carità," I said.

"I feel so bad for her. I feel guilty, too. I didn't know a thing about Ian when they ran away to get married, and Carità didn't know much except that he was rich. I thought they were sweet together. He seemed to truly care for her. The priest hardly asked any questions; he said he'd known Ian since he was a child, so I thought, well, if the priest thinks he'll make a good husband, it must be okay."

"Don't blame yourself," I said. "You couldn't have stopped them. But how did Carità know Ian was rich?"

"She asked him his full name the first time he came here, and when he said Drohan, she recognized it. Then that poor Betone boy who got killed, he told Mimi Ian was the only heir of the richest family on the island. So Carità set her cap for him. And now all he wants to do is give all his money away."

"Maybe his mother will talk him out of that," I said. "She married for money, so she shouldn't look down on Carità."

"It doesn't matter how rich people got their money," she said. "They always look down on people who don't have any."

I gave Bessie a closer look. "That's a very astute observation," I said.

"It's what Uncle Peter used to say," she said.

"Right," I said. "Uncle Peter."

We heard voices, a laugh, steps on the porch. Mimi came in, followed closely by Mike. She hailed Bessie and pulled a chair up close to her. "How are you?" she said.

"I'm okay," Bessie replied. "Just worried to death about Carità."

We all looked at Mike, who leaned in the doorway.

"She's fine," he said. "Claudia sent her secretary to my chambers this morning. I asked her how the three of them were getting along, and she said Ian was angry and belligerent, but Carità was doing well. She was so courteous and smart, Claudia was disarmed. They agreed that Ian must be persuaded to return to college as soon as possible. At some point, they got on the subject of horses, and Claudia was a goner. She told the secretary she thought all would be well if Ian would just listen to his wife."

This story made me shake my head in admiration. "Carità is a force of nature," I said.

"Truly," Mike agreed. "I wouldn't want to get between her and anything she wants."

"And how is Ian?" Mimi asked.

"He's been to our doctor and had the dressing changed on his face. They cut the cast off, did an X-ray, and put a new cast on. The ankle is fractured in three places. When it heals, he should be able to walk on it, but it will always be weak."

"How do you know all this?" I asked. "Did you go with them? Are you back in Claudia's graces?"

He shook his head somberly. "No. I grilled the secretary. She was sent to tell me about a meeting with Dugan. Claudia told him about our divorce and Ian's plan to be the new St. Francis. He wants all four of us out there tomorrow for what he calls counseling and mediation."

"That's quite a lot of news," Mimi said.

"I think it's good," said Bessie. "Father Dugan is a kind man."

"He'll need to be a very wise man if he's going to talk some sense into my son."

"Maybe he won't want to," Mimi speculated. "If Ian wants to give his money away, wouldn't Jesus approve of that? Isn't that what he did, and what he told his disciples to do?"

"Jesus never had anything to give away," Mike replied. "His father was a carpenter. He didn't own any property. He slept on people's lawns."

I smiled at this idea, but I felt anxious about Ian's next move. I thought he was just obstinate enough to go through with his threat. "If Ian wanted to give his inheritance away," I asked Mike, "wouldn't Carità be entitled to half of it?"

"If he owned any property, she'd be entitled to half the sale price," Mike said. "Checking and savings accounts would be joint, but those are relatively small. Most of Ian's money is in a trust, and she would have no claim on that, even if they divorced."

Mimi and I exchanged looks of wide-eyed alarm. "Does Ian know this?" I asked Mike.

"Probably not. He's never shown any interest in money. But he'd find out soon enough if Carità tried to divorce him."

"So she could get cut out completely," Bessie said.

Mike nodded.

"That is so unfair," Mimi concluded.

Mike smiled at our naïveté. "How do you think rich people stay rich?" he asked, not unkindly.

Bessie covered her eyes with her hands. "I need to tell Carità this right away," she said.

Bessie and Mimi, eager to talk over the recent developments in Carità's increasingly complicated life, went out together. As they left, Mike undraped himself from the doorway and took a chair at the table across from me, smiling a Cheshire Cat smile.

"I thought you were in court today," I said.

"They settled," he said. "I've got a trial this afternoon; then I'm free."

"That's good," I said. "You can go to the family powwow tomorrow."

"I'm going," he said, "though I don't want to."

"Aren't you curious?"

He walked his hand over to mine and stroked my fingertips with his. "Not much," he said. "Unless dread is a kind of curiosity."

"Well, I'm curious," I said. "I want a full report."

"I'll take notes," he said. "Will you come to dinner with me tonight?"

"Yes," I said.

"Will you stay the night with me?"

"I will," I said.

He withdrew his hand and, resting his elbow on the table, propped his chin in his palm. "I'm feeling weirdly happy," he said.

"Why weirdly?"

"It's just new to me," he said. "And, frankly, it's a little scary."

"And to what do you attribute this frightening cheerfulness?"

"To you," he said. "I feel it when I'm with you."

"That's very sweet," I said.

"You think I'm a silly, shallow person."

"Aren't you?"

He rubbed his fingers back and forth across his forehead, as if feeling for an entry point. "I guess I don't know myself very well," he said.

"Most people don't," I assured him.

"Why is that, do you think?"

I tapped my forefinger to my brow. "It's dark in there," I said.

In the morning, as I watched Mike pulling on his socks, I thought he was about to find out a few things about himself that he probably didn't know. I had no desire to attend the family meeting with Father Dugan, but I would have liked to be a fly—or some other insect—on the wall. Each of them had a goal, no two the same, and reconciliation seemed unlikely. My view was that two divorces were in order, and what they needed was a couple of lawyers. But no one was interested in my view.

He pulled on a pair of loose-fitting beige trousers and took an indigo short-sleeved shirt from the closet, turning in time to see me scatter a cloud of muffin crumbs across the breakfast tray. He stood, fastening the buttons on the shirt. "Here I am," he said. "Dressed for mediation."

"Do you think Father Dugan knows how things stand between you and Claudia?" I asked.

"I'm sure he does. She tells him everything. And, of course, he's against the divorce. That's one of his reasons for calling this meeting."

"So this is double-barreled marriage counseling."

"Right," he said. "It's the all against the all."

After Mike left, I finished my breakfast and took a shower in the hotel's posh bathroom. I was thinking about the four of them, the Drohan family, and all the possible conflicts that must arise and accusations they might lodge against one another in the benign presence of the priest. Mike was sanguine in his conviction that his wife wanted only to be rid of him; Claudia was done. He made her out to be coldhearted, calculating, and a gold digger. But if that were the case, why wasn't her lawyer along on the junket to Father Dugan? Mike had hurt and humiliated his wife for two decades, so any thought of reconciliation on her part necessarily included a hard-earned appreciation of the unlikelihood that he would change. But if she could go from refusing Carità entry in the house to enlisting her in a campaign to send Ian back to college, she wasn't one to cleave too tightly to a principle.

The priest had a commitment to the sanctity of marriage; divorce wasn't an option he could even consider. Part of the conversation would have to touch on his opposition to a process that was already under way. How he felt about Ian's plan to refuse his inheritance was anybody's guess, but he would have to take a side.

Ian's hatred of his father would be the most volatile and potentially destructive force at the meeting. Carità was probably correct in her judgment that he feared failure and didn't much want her to succeed. He believed she must be indebted to him for rescuing her from prostitution. I'd noticed that he was fond of flinging the word "whore" around; clearly, in his view, it denoted a category beyond the pale, deserving of universal contempt. He had elevated her out of ignominy into the sparkling realm of his patronage, and he expected gratitude and submission, neither of which would be on offer from Carità.

And what did Carità want? I thought I knew the answer to that question. Carità just wanted everyone to calm down so that she could go to college and study economics. And of all the clashing wills that would be on display at Father Dugan's mediation meeting, I had no doubt that Carità's was the strongest and would prevail.

This made me smile as I toweled myself dry and worked a blob of hotel moisturizing cream into my hands. As I'd brought nothing else with me, I put on the dinner dress I'd worn the night before, took up my purse, and let myself out of the hotel room. A young couple smooching at the elevator separated sullenly, and we rode without speaking down to the lobby together. On the street, the bellhop flagged a cab for me. These hotel escapes were charming, I thought, but I was eager to be back in my house. We had a couple of afternoon regulars, and the linen delivery would be stacked up outside the kitchen door. The girls would be arriving in the afternoon, ready to take up their duties. The whores, I thought, using Ian's preferred term. I knew the argument. Payment for services rendered is a common enough practice in the world economy, but if the service is sex, the server can be dismissed as depraved and insensitive. A whore is paid to give a performance, and her skills deserve to be rigorously tested. Is there anything, sexually speaking, that a whore won't do for payment? And doesn't her willingness to take money and move on to the next customer prove that she is the most despicable creature on earth?

Sex, I thought. It makes hypocrites of us all.

The girls all knew we needed a replacement for Carità, so I wasn't surprised when Charlotte showed up early for the evening shift with a very attractive young woman who was interested in joining our staff. Her name was Teresa, and she was an aspiring actress, a difficult proposition on an island where the venues were mostly cabaret and dinner theater. Teresa was renting a room in the apartment house Charlotte lived in, and they had become friends. She was employed as a waitress, working for tips. The hours were long, and she didn't have time to go to the occasional audition that came her way. A night shift would suit her, she said. Charlotte and I assured her it wasn't easy work. "Sometimes," Charlotte said, "the clients are demanding and insulting. You have to turn off your brain."

"They're like that at the café," she said. "And the ruder they are, the smaller the tip."

Teresa had wavy black hair, flashing brown eyes, full lips, a knockout figure, and a saucy demeanor that made me think she would add interest to our evening gatherings. "Can you dance?" I asked.

She could indeed. Also, of course, she could sing.

"We don't have much call for singing," I said. "Do you want to start tonight?"

"Definitely," she said.

"You might want to use a different name," Charlotte suggested.

"I thought of that," Teresa said. "When I'm here, I'll be Carmen."

"Perfect," I said. "Charlotte will take you upstairs and show you the layout. We have a wardrobe you can use, or you can wear your own clothes, as long as they're colorful and sexy."

And off they went. I hadn't told her about the option of a room. Why? First, she had a room, so it wasn't urgent that she live in. Also, something in me still felt that spare room belonged to Carità, though of course I knew she would never return to it.

The Drohans would have arrived at St. Roch's by now, I thought. I wouldn't hear from Mike until the morning.

The evening was slow at the start, but after nine, four clients came in together—two regulars and two friends of theirs.

Sally was upstairs, and Charlotte, Vivien, Mimi, and Carmen were in the drawing room, so there were enough girls to go around. The music was sultry, as was the night, and they were all soon drinking champagne cocktails, whiskey, and vodka, dancing, joking, and flirting. Carmen comported herself very professionally, I thought. She had a teasing way about her, a quick smile, and a braying, contagious laugh. She danced in place, lowering her eyes dreamily and gently touching the forearm of whoever engaged her. She might be a real asset.

She was certainly the opposite of Carità, I thought. Carità, with her cool, faintly regal carriage, her voice like a velvet caress. As I watched Carmen, I missed Carità.

When the clients were gone, we gathered in the kitchen to finish up the drinks and canapés. Brutus quickly got into an easy, joking relationship with Carmen, and by the time we closed, they'd agreed to have a last nightcap at his bar. I locked the door behind them and went up to my bed in a hopeful frame of mind. I heard rain pattering at the windows as I drifted into a dreamless sleep.

That gentle rain turned into a fierce storm that overflowed the gutters, rattled the windows, and brought down a carpet of mimosa blooms onto my back porch. I was in my robe, sweeping the debris back onto the grass, when Mike pulled up in his spiffy car. He didn't get out at once, but sat gazing up at me through the open passenger window. I stopped sweeping, rested my broom against a trellis. He opened the door and climbed out, unfolding his long legs slowly, so that he appeared to be rising up on a platform, one hand raised in a half-salute.

I knew at once that the meeting hadn't gone well. His face was ashen, his shoulders drooped. As he neared the gate, he dragged his feet like a man approaching the gallows. I held the screen open and said nothing as he passed inside. He fairly collapsed at the table, holding his forehead between his hands.

"It didn't go well, I take it," I said.

He lifted his face, his eyes, wet with tears, finding mine. "My son has lost his mind," he said.

I pulled out a chair and sat sideways, facing him. "Is he still on about disinheriting himself?"

He gave me a bleak smile. "He's not on about anything. He's completely sedated in the infirmary at St. Roch. They'll move him to the psychiatric ward at DePaul General later today."

"My God," I said. Mike shook his head slowly, covering his mouth with his open hand as if to push back the news he'd just given me. "What happened?"

"It was all of a sudden," Mike said. "I thought the meeting was going well. Claudia and I weren't getting anywhere, but we were being civil, and Father Dugan was making some headway with Ian, or so I thought." He covered his forehead with his palm. "Why didn't I see it coming?" he asked himself.

"Sweetheart," I said, "I'm so sorry."

He brought his hand to mine, pressing my fingers together against his knee. "You are the dearest person in my life," he said.

"What can I get you?" I said. "Do you want a drink? Could I make you some tea or coffee?"

His eyes focused on me at last. "You're still in your robe," he said.

"It's early," I said.

"It's like the first time I saw you." His sentimental streak would come to his rescue, I thought.

"I'll make you a Bloody Mary," I said. "Just as I did then. Have you eaten?"

"No," he said.

"Did Claudia and Carità come back, too?"

"Yes. Claudia's arranging for an ambulance to bring Ian back."

"An ambulance!" I said.

"They need to keep him sedated."

I went to the refrigerator and took out the eggs, tomato juice, and a plate of crustless sandwiches from the night before. Then I pulled the vodka from the freezer and a tumbler from the dish rack. "I want you to tell me the whole story," I said. "Start at the beginning. Did you meet in Dugan's office?"

This is the story Mike told me.

It had started calmly enough. Claudia, Ian, and Carità were all in the conference room when Mike arrived. It wasn't the sparsely furnished office where Father Dugan had given us his homemade medicine, but a lounge in the faculty residence attached to the school. The furniture was all pine side tables and brown cushioned chairs. The chairs were arranged in a circle so that, though each person could see every other, none was close enough to touch. Mike took the only chair open, between Ian and Father Dugan. Claudia spoke to Carità, then went to a side table, where there was a pitcher of water, poured out two glasses, and brought one to Carità.

"So here we all are," said Father Dugan. "And I may say we have a great deal to work through."

Mike hadn't seen Claudia in a few weeks, and he was surprised at her appearance. Her face was drawn; she'd cut her hair short, wore no lipstick, and, he noted, her fingernail polish was badly chipped. Carità, on the other hand, was neatly turned out, her hair tamed by two clips. She had on her sunglasses.

Ian had cleaned up as well. He was wearing a black T-shirt and jeans, one leg cut apart to accommodate the cast. The gauze bandage around his head was gone, and a long line of black stitches held together a seam of flesh that, while still swollen and pink, was dry, healing. His beard and hair were neatly trimmed. But his eyes were eerily staring into space. He looked like an actor, unblinking, nerves on edge, waiting for the curtain to open.

Father Dugan began by explaining his motive for calling the family together, and his hopes for the reconciliation that might be achieved if they all spoke honestly and kept their hearts and minds open to one another. He first addressed Claudia, asking her frankly why, after so many years of marriage, she and Mike had made up their minds to break the vows they had made before God.

Claudia said the marriage had been in name only for many years. Her husband had made it clear that he held the vows they'd taken in contempt. She kept up appearances for the sake of the family, of her son, but he was grown now, and Mike had formed a new attachment that she simply couldn't tolerate.

"There was a bit more about Claudia's sense of betrayal," Mike said, "and then my turn came, and I said Claudia had never given me a chance, that she was more interested in horses than in me. She said my indifference and philandering had driven her to the horses. We went back and forth on that, adding details. I said I thought she was having an affair with one of the trainers at the barn, which is true, I'm pretty sure she is, and she said I was so depraved and faithless I assumed everyone else was.

"Then the priest steered us back to his view of divorce and the position of the Church, the importance of reaching some agreement about cohabitation or temporary separation, so as not to lose the benefit of the sacraments."

"What are the benefits of the sacraments?" I asked.

"Oh, you innocent," Mike said. "It's stuff like communion, last rites, and marriage. Baptism, too, I guess. The detail of interest to Claudia would be that a divorced person can't remarry in the Church."

"I get it," I said.

"I'm sure this guy knows I haven't been in a church in twenty years," Mike said. "So I figured he was talking to Claudia, and that he thought if she agreed to some kind of nonlegal separation, she could stay in the Church and I'd be fine with it. She looked so miserable I almost felt sorry for her, but then I thought of her locking me out of my own house, and how much happier I've been on my own. I didn't want her to reconsider.

She started all this, but now I really want to be divorced. So I said, looking right at her, 'I know it's going to be bloody expensive, but I want this divorce as much as you do.'

"Well, that set her off. She burst into tears. 'You never loved me,' she whined. 'You'd rather spend time with prostitutes. You've ruined my life. You've ruined your son's life.'

"I said she'd married me for my money and we both knew it."

"You said that?" I interrupted.

"I did. Then Ian started writhing in his chair. 'He thinks he can control us with his money,' he said. 'He thinks that's all we care about, because it's all he cares about.' Words to that effect."

"What was Carità doing during all this?" I asked.

"She was just listening, the way she does. Drinking her glass of water. Ian was ignoring her completely. He started in about how he didn't want anything to do with me or my money. He planned to give his inheritance to charity. He wanted to live a simple life and serve the poor.

"Father Dugan took him up on that and pointed out that having money and serving the poor weren't mutually exclusive. If Ian actually wanted to help, he could finance a charity foundation to assist the homeless to find shelter and put their children into Catholic schools. There was a great need for this on the island. And he pointed out that beggaring himself, as Ian planned to do, would just put one more poor, homeless person on the street, which was no help to the poor at all.

"I thought that was a pretty good argument, but Ian wasn't

having it. He said he'd committed a crime and God had shown him the way to expiate it. The fish told him somehow, and then God beat him up in the boat. He and Carità would join the oblate order of the Franciscans and live a pure life of service and expiation.

"Carità did a funny thing then. She raised her hand, high, like a schoolgirl who knows the answer in class. Father Dugan said, 'Carità?' She stood up and said, 'I have something to say.' Then she gave a little speech. I may not remember it exactly, but it was along these lines. The problem, as she saw it, is that Ian and I have money and property that was left to us, saved and invested for us so that we can do as we please. Whereas she and Claudia had no money to speak of when they married. In the event of divorce, she said, the law is straightforward: the wife is entitled to half of the estate. But the Church is clearer still: the marriage contract simply can't be broken. In the marriage service, the pledge is irrefutable. She quoted it: 'With this ring I thee wed, and with all my worldly goods I thee endow.' Then she stressed the 'all'—'with *all* my worldly goods.' I noticed Claudia was listening closely to this argument, a bit awestruck, as we all were.

"Carità said she understood this pledge to mean that, as much as Ian might want to disinherit himself or give his money away to the poor, he couldn't. She turned to face him, and she said, 'It's no longer yours to give away, my love. When you married me, before God, you gave it to me. And now it's mine.' "

" 'And now it's mine,' " I repeated.

"That part is exact," said Mike. "It was a stunning conclusion."

"That marriage service made quite an impression on Carità," I observed.

"Evidently, she memorized the important parts."

"What happened next?"

"I was watching Ian, and I could see he was about to blow. He was staring at Carità, and blood was rushing up his neck to his cheeks. 'Take it,' he said to her, very coldly. He was getting redder by the second. His eyes bulged; I think he was holding his breath; his jaw was clenched so tightly, cords of muscle stood out on his neck. He pulled at the collar of his shirt as if it were strangling him. He leaned forward in his chair until he was bent over his knees. 'None of it,' he said. Then he pulled the shirt off over his head and started unfastening his jeans. 'I don't want any of it,' he said. He realized he couldn't get the jeans off over his sandal, so he unfastened the buckle and kicked it free. Then he rolled to one side to get his weight on his good leg and pushed himself to standing, holding on to the back of the chair.

"He did all this so quickly we hardly knew what was going on. Carità said his name. She had no idea what he was doing. Father Dugan got to his feet and said to me, 'Keep him in this room,' and he charged out the door, but he failed to close it. Ian had wrested his jeans off and had his underwear around his knees. I said something ridiculous like 'Calm down, son.'

"Claudia was sobbing into her handkerchief, wailing that Ian was out of his mind. Somehow, he got the briefs off and the crutches in place, and before I could get between him and the door, he'd clattered past me."

"And he was naked?"

"Except for one sock, and the cast. He was raving and hissing like a snake. 'You're all against me,' he said. 'Even my wife has betrayed me. I want nothing to do with any of you.'

"He was heading down the residence hall, where the brothers had their rooms, and the racket brought a few of them to open their doors. I yelled, 'Stop him.' Two of them stepped out into the hall. I noticed one of them was wearing pajamas with sheep printed on them; odd that I remember that. They just stood there with their mouths open.

"Ian was moving fast, whacking a crutch against the wall. He got to the entry foyer and turned out of sight. I went after him, but that door was open, too, and he pushed through the screen. Then he was on the drive. 'Help me,' I begged the brothers as I passed. Two of them came out with me.

" 'Stay away from me,' Ian shouted.

"Then Father Dugan came running up from somewhere, and he signaled the brothers to surround him. Ian knew he was trapped. He gave a strangled cry and whirled around to face me. The cast got jammed against the crutch; he went down on his good knee. Then he just crumpled to the ground like he'd been struck, and he rubbed his face in the dirt and flailed his arms. Father Dugan got to him and kneeled over him, producing, to my surprise, a hypodermic syringe. One of the brothers got down beside Ian and held his arm so Dugan could get the shot in." Mike paused, taking a deep breath.

"My poor son," he said. "He was banging his head against the ground, literally frothing at the mouth."

"This is awful," I said.

Mike rubbed his temples with his fingers and thumb

stretched wide. When he lowered his hand, his eyes were wet. "The shot worked almost at once. His body relaxed, his face went slack, and his eyes closed. One of the brothers went to get the infirmarian, and they came back with a stretcher."

"Where were Claudia and Carità while all this was going on?"

"They had come to the doorway. Carità stood back while Claudia told her what was happening. Father Dugan stayed with them, and I went off with the group to the infirmary. I didn't see them again. When I got back, Dugan told me they'd taken the car back to the city so Claudia could make arrangements for Ian to be moved to the hospital. He should be here this afternoon."

"Then what?" I asked.

"Then, presumably, he wakes up at some point and he's still crazy. They do a psychiatric evaluation and probably put him away somewhere...." His voice broke then, and he stammered out the rest: "Someplace where they medicate him until he's drooling."

"He needs professional care now," I said.

Mike nodded, turning his glass around in his hands. "The doctor called it a psychotic break. I told him about the sudden marriage, and the shooting, and the hiding out, and the boating accident."

"And the visions," I said.

"He has visions?" Mike said.

"He thinks that big fish that got away was Christ telling him to expiate his crime by serving the poor."

"Right," he said. "I guess that counts as a vision." He looked off into the middle distance, as if he heard someone speaking. "I should never have sent him to that school," he said.

"Finish your drink," I said, pushing back from the table. "I'll make you some eggs and potatoes."

He gulped the drink dutifully, then absently helped himself to one of the sandwiches. "I haven't eaten since yesterday morning," he said.

I went to the counter and lifted a potato from the basket. "Where does all this leave you and Claudia?" I asked.

"I honestly don't know. I'll see her at the hospital tomorrow to talk with the doctors. We have an appointment."

"Do you think she'll back down on the divorce?"

"No. She detests me. She can hardly look at me."

"Because she loved you," I suggested.

"She doesn't know anything about me," he retorted. "How long have I known you—a few months? I've been married to Claudia for over twenty years, and you know more about me than she does."

I chose a knife and started slicing the potato, making no reply to his assertion.

"She's always been hypercritical and aloof," he said.

"What attracted you to her?" I asked.

"She's very beautiful," he said. "And she was so aloof."

I laughed.

"And then she trapped me."

"How did she manage that?"

"In the usual way," he said. "She got pregnant."

I turned back to the counter.

"She always expects the worst, and that makes me want to live up to her expectations."

"So," I said, "it really *is* all her fault." I cracked an egg on the rim of the bowl, and the viscous contents plopped inside.

He heard the irony in my tone. "I'm not saying I don't share some blame."

I cracked another egg.

"It takes two people to destroy a marriage," he concluded.

"Maybe three," I said. "But never less than two."

"It's a wonder we've lasted this long," he said.

"Did you fight a lot?" I asked.

"At first, yes. Especially after Ian was born."

I cut a large pat of butter and tapped it off the knife into the pan, turned on the flame.

"He was a colicky baby," Mike continued. "Nobody was getting any sleep. I started staying away as much as I could."

"Didn't she have help?"

"Sure. She had a full-time nanny and a houseful of servants, but she managed to stay worn out by it all for a year. She was cold to me; I couldn't touch her."

I slid the potatoes into the pan and spread them with a spatula. Mike was quiet while I tended the stove. I had the sense that he was going over what he'd just told me. The potatoes were sizzling nicely.

"I haven't thought about those years in a long time," he said.

"What happened next?"

"Oh." Though I couldn't see him, I knew he was shrugging, pushing it off. "She got well, Ian started walking, and she bought the first horse."

"Did things get better between you?"

"Never," he said. "They got steadily worse for twenty years. I'll be relieved if we can put an end to this torture."

I flipped the potatoes and shoved them to the side of the pan. "It sounds like she feels the same way," I said.

He ignored this proposition and rushed back to the past. "The one who got the worst of it was Ian. Claudia wanted total control, and I just let her have it. She turned him against me."

"It's true that your relationship with Ian isn't a pleasure to watch," I observed.

He was quiet again, while I tipped in the eggs and scrambled them with a fork. I reached for a couple of plates and turned toward him. He was slumped in his chair, his hands resting on his thighs, his head bowed so that I couldn't see his face. "When I saw him lying there in the dirt, naked and crippled and grinding his teeth, flailing one arm like an animal trying to crawl away from pain, I felt . . ."

A moment passed. "What did you feel?"

He raised his eyes to mine, frowning so forcefully that deep creases striped his forehead.

"This is my fault," he said.

I moved to the table, pulled a chair close to him, and sat facing him, resting one hand on his thigh.

"I was a shitty father," he continued. "From the start. I treated him like an obstacle."

I said nothing, as I thought this was probably a fair statement of the case.

"He gave up trying to please me," he said. "I drove his mother away, and then I blamed her for turning him against me, but he had plenty of cause to despise me without her help."

He took a sip from his drink, swallowing hard. "He was a feisty kid. He stood up to me. When he was ten, Claudia and I had an argument at dinner, and she stormed out in tears. He said to me, very calmly, 'You are a bad man, and you are destroying our family.'"

"What did you say?"

"I don't know. Something cruel, something dismissive." His eyes were damp, and he sniffed audibly.

So he knows, I thought. And if he knows, why does he keep doing it? I reached for my purse on the counter and fished out a handkerchief. "Here," I said. "Use this."

"Thanks," he said, applying the cloth to his nose and blowing hard.

I pushed my chair back and went to the stove. "Let's eat our breakfast," I said. "It's getting cold."

The rest of the week passed without event. We were busy over the weekend; the girls worked late. I heard nothing from Mike, nor did I expect to. He was occupied with his family and making arrangements for Ian's care. On Monday Mimi and I both slept late. We were eating toast and eggs at the table when I heard the gate and looked up to see Carità sweeping her stick across the walk to the porch. As Mimi had her back to the door, she shot me a questioning look.

"It's Carità," I said.

"At last," said Mimi. She pushed back her chair and left the table to open the screen. Carità came up the steps. The two young women greeted each other in a warm embrace. Then Mimi held the screen open and Carità entered the room she knew so well.

"Carità," I said, "it's good to see you."

"Hello, Mrs. Gulliver," she said.

Mimi was fussing at the coffeepot, filling Carità's mug, adding milk. "Sit down," she said. "I'll bring you coffee."

"Thanks," said Carità. "I will."

She was altered. Her hair was pulled back in a French braid, and she was wearing a simple boatneck dress with a full skirt and three-quarter sleeves, made of some light fabric that had a sheen to it. The color, a soft sea green, complemented her eyes.

Mimi set the mug near Carità's hand and held it until her fingers found the handle. "So . . . how are you?" she asked. "How is Ian?"

"I'm okay," she said. "Ian is not so good."

"Is he conscious?" I asked.

She nodded. "In a manner of speaking," she said.

Mimi slid into the chair next to her friend. "Is he still in the hospital?"

"He is," Carità said. "He'll be there until they get his medications adjusted; then they'll transfer him to the private sanitorium near the park."

There was a pause while we took in this information. Carità looked puzzled. "Hasn't Mike told you what happened?" she asked me.

"I haven't spoken to Mike since Wednesday," I said.

"Oh," she said. "You don't know about the scene at the hospital." She sipped her coffee, considering where to begin her story. "You know we had an appointment to meet with the doctor in the hospital on Thursday morning, right?"

"I do," I said.

"So that's where we met, in an office inside the ward. Right away it was creepy, because you could hear patients shouting on the way in. The doctor had a slight accent, maybe German or Dutch; his voice was harsh. Claudia told me he looked like a weasel, very sleek and beady-eyed. He said Ian had suffered a seizure, that they were slowly reducing the medication they'd used to stabilize him, and he should regain consciousness soon. If he didn't, that might mean there was more serious damage, and they would have to reassess his condition. Mike asked a bunch of questions; he was very polite but determined. The doctor basically repeated what he'd just told us. Eventually, Mike gave up, and the doctor said we could go see Ian.

"We went down a long hall, very medicinal, hospital smells—bleach and urine—people coming in and out of rooms, mechanical sounds, beeps and clicks, wheezing, wheels on linoleum. We stopped at a door and went into the room. Mike was ahead of me, and he gasped when he saw Ian. Claudia didn't make a sound. She told me afterward that Ian looked very bad. His skin was bluish, his mouth was slack and dry, they'd wrapped his head in gauze bandaging, and he had a drip going in one arm and a tube coming out under the sheet to a bag hanging at the end of the bed for urine. The smell in there was sickening, almost sweet. I don't know what it was. The doctor said Ian had been completely unresponsive, though his pupils dilated when tested. 'He may be able to hear you,' he said.

"Someone came in with an extra chair, and we all sat down facing the bed. 'There's not much to do now but wait,' the doctor said. 'If he doesn't come out of it in the next few hours, we may be dealing with something more serious.'

" 'What kind of serious?' Mike asked. He sounded terrified.

" 'It's hard to predict,' the doctor said. 'If he goes into a coma, it could be a long time.'

"Claudia started crying, but quietly. I could hear her digging in her purse for a handkerchief.

"I didn't know what to think. I asked if I could touch him, and they all started dithering about how of course I could. I think they'd forgotten I couldn't see him. Mike took my arm and brought me to the bedside. Ian's breathing was short, like he was panting. I leaned over him and put my hand out, found his shoulder, his neck, his cheek. I said, 'Sweetheart, I'm here.' I stroked his face around the gauze. Then I turned away, and Mike guided me to my chair. The doctor said he would leave us, and he showed Claudia the call button for the nurse. He went out.

"We sat there for a long time. The room was hot. Claudia went out to the bathroom. Mike paced the floor, stood by the bed making weird noises, like he was clearing his throat. Claudia came back and sat down.

"A nurse came in to check the monitors. She said Ian's blood pressure was very low. Mike asked what that meant, and she said, 'He's wearing himself out with that shallow breathing.' Then she went out, and I could hear Mike working his jaws. 'He's wearing himself out,' he said to Claudia. 'What does that mean?'

"Claudia said she had no idea. Mike said, 'I can't stand this.' He went to the bed and stood there for a few minutes. Gradually, I heard that he was crying. He was saying, 'I'm so sorry,' softly, over and over.

" 'Let him rest,' Claudia said.

"Mike stayed by the bed. I think he was leaning over Ian. He said, 'Please forgive me, son. Please don't die.' More sobbing. Then, 'Please forgive me.' "

"Poor Mike," said Mimi. "Way too little, too late."

"He'd gotten us all so worked up, we were terrified. Claudia said, 'Mike, stop it.' He stepped away. I heard Ian's breathing change. It caught in his throat, and I thought, Oh God, he's dying. I stood up and went to the bed. I said, 'Darling, I'm here.' He took in a long breath through his nose. 'Come back to me,' I said. I rested my hand on his cheek. He gasped, then breathed out a sharp puff of air. In the next moment he spoke, in a perfectly normal voice, as if he'd just arrived and was not surprised to find me there. He said, 'Carità.' I moved my hand and felt that his eyes were open."

"He woke up," I said, stating the obvious.

"Did he know what happened?" Mimi asked. "Was he himself?"

Carità shrugged. "Sort of. He seemed confused but not anxious. I told him he was in the hospital, and he said, 'Before I got here, I was in heaven.'

"I said, 'Maybe you almost were.' Then Claudia and Mike came up, and he said, 'Oh, why are you here, too?'

"Claudia told him he'd had a seizure at the school. He said he didn't remember anything about it. He seemed annoyed at her. Mike told her not to press him.

"Ian said, 'There was a door; it was midnight blue, and light was seeping out all around it, golden light, and then the door flew open, and all the light came pouring through like a liquid, a flood of glowing honey, and someone was calling my name over and over.'

"'You had a vision,' Mike said, and Ian said, 'I was in heaven.'

"Then the doctor came in. The whole atmosphere of the room changed. It was as if there had been music playing and someone just turned it off. He introduced himself to Ian and said he would be looking after him, and he shouldn't worry about anything, but just rest. Ian said that was okay with him, because he was very tired. The nurse came in. The doctor said they'd be doing some tests, and they shooed us out. We went back to the office and sat there for a very long time. Mike was agitated, though, obviously, he was relieved. We all were. At last, the doctor came back and told us Ian had suffered some motor loss—he can't close his fist or move his arm on the right side, and he has some cognitive function irregularities, whatever that means—but, with physical and psychiatric therapy he believed Ian could recover."

"That's such good news," I said.

"It's a huge relief," Carità said. "I was so scared."

"What will you do now?" Mimi asked her. "Are you staying with Claudia?"

"Oh yes," Carità said bitterly. "And I really want to get out of that house. Claudia thinks I'm some kind of interesting pet. She wants to sit around drinking wine in the evenings, telling me stories about Ian's childhood, and what a total failure Mike was as a father. Ian could be in rehab for months. When he gets out, we're not moving into Claudia's house. He would hate that, and so would I. School will be starting. Even if he does go back to college, which is doubtful, student housing isn't going to work for us. We need a place to live."

"I'll help you look at apartments," Mimi offered.

"Well, that's just it. I can't look for anything, because I don't have enough money. I have some savings, but that won't last long. Ian has a big account; money goes into it every month. I'm his wife; I should have access to it, but I don't, and he's in no condition to deal with bankers. I tried bringing the subject up to Claudia, but she just said she'd be happy to take me shopping."

"Do you think she doesn't want you to have Ian's money?" Mimi asked.

"I think she doesn't want me to leave," Carità replied. "She wants an audience. I need to talk to Mike, but I don't know where he is."

"He's at the hotel," I said. "I'll see him tonight. I'll tell him you want to talk with him."

"Please," she said. "Tell him I need help. Tell him I'm sick of living in other people's houses. I want a house of my own."

Later that night, over a plate of roast chicken and fries at the hotel restaurant, I told Mike about Carità's visit. "She's staying with Claudia, and she's miserable. Claudia treats her like a pet. She wants a place of her own."

He swallowed half a glass of red wine. "She should move out."

"She can't. She doesn't have any money. She can't get into Ian's bank account."

He set the glass down, picked up the fork, put it down across the plate. "I hadn't thought of that," he said. "She should be getting his allowance."

"Can you help her?"

"Sure. I'll make an appointment at the bank."

"Do it soon," I said. "She needs to be on her own."

"I'll do it tomorrow," he said.

I returned my attention to my plate. My mission was accomplished; Mike would help Carità. Why did I feel so dispirited?

"Carità is lucky to have you looking after her interests," he observed.

Was Carità lucky? I thought. Was it luck that brought her to my house? "I don't think she'd agree with you about that," I said.

"Why not? You helped her when no one else would."

"I think she would say I exploited her. I know that's what Ian thinks."

"Young people are always self-righteous."

"That may be true of Ian. But Carità has a pretty clear understanding of the world and her place in it."

"Maybe so," he said, giving me a look of puzzlement. "What is it? Do *you* think you exploited her?"

I recalled a conversation I'd had with Carità early in our relationship. She'd talked about how hard the work was, how the clients wanted to humiliate her, but because she had no other source of income, she would do it. As she faced her own powerlessness, I could see by the set of her jaw that she was determined it would not last forever. This brave, intelligent, beautiful, blind young woman who had been so thoroughly betrayed and abandoned that she'd turned up in desperation at my door.

I looked down at the remains of half a chicken, skillfully dismantled on my plate. I lifted my glass, sipped from it, letting the wine linger in my mouth, a little chalky and minerally, the way I liked it. I swallowed. Mike watched me attentively, waiting for my answer.

"Yes," I said. "I do."

Two days after that dinner with Mike, he met Carità at his bank, where she became co-signatory on both Ian's checking and savings accounts. To the surprise of both her father-in-law and his banker, when the time came to sign the agreement, Carità took up the pen and asked to have her hand placed at the beginning of the line. Then, in a clear script she had obviously practiced, she wrote her full name: Carità Lucia Bercy Drohan.

What did I expect then? Did I think Carità would stop by the house with a bottle of champagne and invite me to celebrate her triumph? I'd played a hand in it, surely. But the truth, and I knew it, was that Carità was not grateful to me. I'm not sure she even considered me a friend, though, as Mike pointed out, I'd helped her when no one else would.

Ian had accused me of exploiting Carità the first time he came to the house. He wanted to save her from me. But if I'd turned her away, she would have had to seek out the charity of strangers. Given who I am and what I do, what other option did I have but to offer her a job?

The phrase Mimi used—"those who have nothing to offer but their labor"—came to my mind. These were the laboring classes, who, according to Marx, were doomed to be exploited by the owners of the means of production. "That would be us," Carità had observed.

But I don't own the means of production; my girls aren't sex slaves. I'm an employer. They join the house, which offers protection and wages for servicing men's desires, however rude or strange or even disgusting they may be. We survive by gratifying male sexual fantasies. It's not a game, and it's not fun. A whore's first lesson, usually performed on a banana, is learning to overcome the gag reflex. Doesn't that just say it all?

When Carità appeared in my drawing room, what I saw was that her beauty, her blindness, and her poverty made her an object of desire, and she was thereby destined for destruction by the powers of this world. Without protection, she would be worn down and cast aside. Only money could protect her, and we both knew it.

I sat at my kitchen table and quietly plumbed the previously unexplored depths of my hatred of men—not in particular but in general, for everything they do, and everything they are, for their presumption of rights and power, for the privilege they enjoy without so much as a thought, for their peculiar and unjustified contempt for women. The world I live in isn't benign; it's the world men allow to women. They made it for us. They have all the power, and we work around them. They like to use our bodies, and our having minds of our own can get in the way of that. If we're smart, we find ways to make them pay, or so it seemed to me as a young woman, when I came to understand how many doors were closed to me simply because of my sex.

If anything, I thought, I'd saved Carità. It was through me that she'd realized the dream I hadn't known she had. She was rich, she was free, she was going to college.

Though, in reality, all I'd provided was a place where she might meet a man who could get her out of the soul-killing work I had to offer. Her uncle had sterilized her, a cruel, sweeping decision that well fitted her for service at my house. She had persuaded herself that this didn't matter, that she didn't want children. And in truth, I wasn't sorry to hear it. A girl who couldn't get pregnant was a distinct advantage.

Had I exploited Carità?

What other option did I have? She had come to me. Desperate and destitute.

What other option did I have?

In the months that followed, Carità visited Ian every other day. His recovery was slow, but steady. She told Mimi he seemed, at best, a muted version of himself. The doctors kept him medicated, and the therapists kept him busy. He recovered full use of his hand, and, once the cast was removed, he walked with only a slight limp. He began to imagine a return to normal life. He disliked group therapy sessions but took to art therapy with something like his old passion. His teacher was so impressed by a series of watercolors he completed that she asked an art professor from the college to have a look. He invited Ian to join an oil-painting class in the new term, leaving him with the mildly cryptic comment: "You should be encouraged."

Once he discovered painting, Ian was eager to leave the hospital. Carità and Bessie had been searching for a house with a studio. They found a fine old cottage not far from the college with an outbuilding that had been a woodworking shop across an untended garden at the back.

The house wasn't grand, but it was spacious and cool, shaded by a crepe myrtle tree on one side and a gallery porch on the other. The sisters spent a few weeks shopping for tables, chairs, couches, beds, linens, mattresses, pots, pans, and dishes, until the house was sufficiently furnished for Ian's return. Mimi went to visit them a week after his arrival.

"Ian's changed," she told me. "He looks different."

"Has his face healed?" I asked.

"The stitches are gone; it looks pretty piratical. His hair has grown, and he's pale from being indoors all the time. He's got an odd look in his eyes, kind of wary, but he's clearly pleased with everything Carità has done. He's affectionate with her; a little chilly to me. I think I make him uncomfortable."

"He doesn't want to share Carità," I said.

"That's true," Mimi agreed. "She's going to have to fight that the rest of her life."

We allowed a pause while the weight of this pronouncement settled in.

"Do you think Carità loves Ian?" I asked.

She gave it a moment's thought. "I do," she said. "He makes her impatient, but she has his interests at heart. She's trying to arrange everything in the world so that he can do what he wants to do."

"That's a good definition of love," I said.

"They've worked up this narrative that the cruel world tried to keep them apart, but they escaped together. He saved her from your house, and she saved him from his parents."

This stung me. "She was free to leave my house anytime she wanted," I said.

Mimi gave me the half-smile of an indulgent parent. "Of course," she said. "We all know that."

"And, anyway, you're the one who made it possible for her to go to college," I said. "He was against that. He wanted her to make nets."

"Well, he's over that now," Mimi observed. "He's all for her ambition. He wants her to manage his career."

"Do you think she knows how much he wants to control her?"

"I think she must. But she's not letting anything faze her.

She asked him to show me the studio. That livened him up a bit. He's just getting it set up, but he had a portfolio of work he'd done, watercolors and some pastels. Pretty impressive stuff. Kind of strange and visionary, full of light. He can't wait to start painting in oil. I think the painting is going to be his salvation."

"I had a hunch he was some kind of an artist."

"What made you think that?"

"Let's see," I said. "He's single-minded, humorless, driven, self-righteous, self-absorbed, passionate, and needy."

"That sounds about right," Mimi agreed. "Of course, the sad thing is that Carità can't see the paintings."

"That may be a blessing," I suggested, and we nodded sagely, wise to the ways of the world.

Mike's divorce from Claudia dragged on, but they managed to get past the accusations and settle down to a civilized division of property. To Mike's surprise, Claudia insisted on selling the mansion and dividing the proceeds. Later, it was revealed that she wanted to purchase a large horse property just outside the city, which she knew was about to come on the market. Also, as Mike suspected, Claudia was indeed having an affair with a horse trainer, and she married him shortly after her own divorce was final. "I don't know what she does about the sacraments," Mike observed. "But I hear they were married by a justice of the peace, and she's cooled on Father Dugan."

One evening, Mike asked me to meet him the next day at

one of the smaller department stores near the waterfront. He made it sound important and mysterious, so I dressed in my most presentable businesswoman style and took a taxi at the appointed hour. There he was, poised on the sidewalk, looking up and down the street for me, with that peculiar intensity that amused me. He was so self-possessed in public; passersby regarded him with interest. When I got out of the cab, he was quick to greet me—a kiss on the cheek, a hand at my waist. With an air of urgency, he escorted me into the store and directly to the elevator. He produced a small key and turned it in a keyhole next to the button for the fifth floor. This was curious, because the store occupied only the first four. "I have a surprise for you," he said.

The elevator opened onto a narrow hall covered in a trompe l'oeil scene of a beach with palms and seagrass and parrots partially camouflaged among the leaves. At the center was a double door, framed by two painted marble columns with ivy curling up the sides. Mike produced a second key from his pocket, unlocked the door, and threw one panel open with a flourish. "Ta-da," he said.

My eye was immediately drawn across the wide, empty room to the outer wall, which was glass, giving a view made up entirely of the sky and a glittering reflection of the sea. When I stepped inside, I noticed that the room gave on to other rooms at either side, that it was freshly painted, and that the parquet floor had been buffed to a sheen. Mike pressed me forward gently, his hand on the curve of my back. Our footsteps rapped sharply across the empty space. We reached the glass wall; there were six panels. He lifted a hidden latch, and the two at the center, mounted on tracks, slid open smoothly before us. We stepped through to a wide terrace that ran the length of the building. One end was enclosed by a tubular stucco outcropping, with a narrow door set in beneath an overhanging arch. While I gawked at the view of the port and the marina, Mike urged me along toward this mysterious door. "Now for the finale," he said, pulling it open before me. I was looking at a circular iron stairway, which rose from a dusty-blue-and-gold mosaic floor laid out in a design of a sunburst. "It's a tower," I said.

"You go first," Mike said. I grasped the rail and climbed the creaking, wedge-shaped steps toward the bright light that poured down from above. Mike was close behind me, and he laughed when he heard my gasp of delight as I stepped into the open air. Just to my left was a shiny, spindly structure it took me a moment to identify. It was the cross atop the tower of Our Lady of Good Hope Church. Standing on the ledge below it, the statue of the Virgin Mary—one hand resting on her pregnant belly, the other slightly raised as if in greeting—looked out over the harbor. I recalled gazing up at her from the balcony of my dingy apartment, where I had my first heady taste of liberty, which quickly dissolved into the deadening grind of The Tackle Shop. Now we were level with each other. "We meet at last," I said to her.

I turned to Mike, who stood grinning at the top of the staircase. "I've looked at this building a thousand times," I said. "I had no idea this was up here."

"You can't see it from the street," Mike said. He joined me, and we stepped to the rail, hand in hand, gazing out at the dramatic scene. "I bought it," he said. "It's ours."

The city unfolded below us in every direction, from the park to the port, all of it teeming and bristling with humanity, and beyond it—the sea, translucent aquamarine streaked with gold, endlessly rolling and churning and battering the shore, breaking over the rocks, caressing a long stretch of white beach to the east, pushing snakelike through the narrow channels that ran through a marshy area to the south.

"This is the highest point in the city," Mike said. He was right. As I looked from side to side, far and near, it was clear that we were standing high above it all.

That was two years ago. In the interim, much has changed. I have seriously mixed feelings about the invasion of the telephone, which began shortly after Mike bought the tower apartment. At first, every phone came with a party line, sometimes more than one, which meant you couldn't be sure you could make a call when you wanted to, and if you did, there was no guarantee your conversation would be private. A party line in a brothel was exactly what I didn't need. Brutus had one installed in his office at the bar; he thought it might be useful for making orders, but his party was an old woman whose relatives had provided her with the phone to keep her out of their hair. She was on the line from dawn to dark, gossiping about the relatives with her sister, who lived on the far side of the island.

It seemed to me that the telephones coincided with a general rise in crime, corruption, greed, and traffic on the island, but perhaps there was no connection. Sex tourism was becoming a problem, particularly near the port, where there were clubs that featured outrageous sex shows with underage girls and boys who were regularly arrested, only to appear at a different club after the brief respite of a night in a jail cell. I was something of a dinosaur in the field, with my canapés and my drawing room and my girls over eighteen, but business wasn't bad, thanks to regulars and locals. Carmen had proved competent and enthusiastic, eager to take over if I stayed away a night or two. She sensed that I was losing interest.

Carità was in her second year at the college. She worked hard; her grades showed it. In fact, she was something of a star student, admired by professors and fellow students alike. She was in her element. Ian changed his major to art and found friends among the ambitious and pretentious young painters and sculptors who lounged about at the student center all day, and at night moved to certain bars on the waterfront, where they could drink cheap beer and agitate one another until they passed out.

Bessie married her sous-chef, Ralph, an agreeable working-class young man with ambitions to open his own restaurant. When a small café near the park came on the market, he confided his dream to his sister-in-law. If he could come up with a loan to buy it, he and Bessie could run it together. Carità talked to Ian and her banker. The result was a large loan backed by Drohan money on the most generous terms. After the basic renovations were completed, the café was christened "Ralph's." Within a year, it was widely considered a feat to book a table.

Once Mike got the tower apartment minimally furnished, I began to spend most of my free time there. He was in an acquisitive mode, spending his afternoons at furniture stores and auction houses. Gradually, the rooms filled with couches and tables and expensive art. Two of Ian's oil paintings hung on either side of the terrace doors. They were big, four feet square, and, as Mimi had said, full of light. Dim figures could be glimpsed through an aura of intensely swirling white and gold. It was like looking at the sun.

One night, as we were drinking white wine in the tower, looking out at the black sky studded with stars, the sea below, just as black and ribboned with white, the streets, empty but for a thin stream of cars, like rodents with flashlights for eyes, racing through the sleeping city, I said to Mike, "I'm thinking of offering Carmen a half-interest in the house and easing my way out of running it."

"You're giving up your house," he said, keeping any element of surprise out of his tone.

"No," I said. "I'll still own it, and I'll still manage the finances. I'm good at that. Bessie and Ralph are thinking of adding a bar, and they don't have a clue how to run it. I could keep the books there as well, make sure their bills are paid and the bar is properly supplied. I don't much enjoy the drawing-room ritual at the house anymore. It depresses me. And I don't want to hire and fire staff. It's just too much drama. Carmen will enjoy doing that."

"That means you could keep your own hours," he said. "And maybe spend more time here."

"Yes," I said. "Would you like that?"

"I would," he said. "More than I can say."

I smiled at his controlled enthusiasm.

"But only if *you* would like it."

"Right," I said. "No pressure."

We sipped our drinks, gazing at the sea.

"I'm thinking of making some changes myself," he said.

"To the apartment?"

"To my life," he said.

"What will you do?"

"Get off the bench, for one thing."

This surprised me. "Can you just do that?"

"I can phase it out. There's a young judge in the pipeline, very eager to take my place. He's competent. He loves the work. I can do some senior jurist stuff and gradually walk away."

"Then what would you do?"

There was a pause. He sipped his drink and looked toward the park. "I'm thinking of buying the *Banner*," he said.

"The newspaper?" I was frankly astounded. Why would Mike want to own a newspaper, and especially the *Verona Banner*, which was barely more than an advertising flyer?

"The Bilchard family owns it. Frank Bilchard is a complete idiot, and he's run it into the ground, so now it's for sale."

"The Bilchards own half the port," I said.

"They do indeed, and they're turning a good part of it over to the thugs who are filling the gap Joe Shock left. But no one knows a thing about it, because they control the news."

"How do you know it's for sale?"

"I know the managing editor. I've known him since we were in college together. We ran the student newspaper—we

were both crazy for journalism. Ernest Hemingway was our
god. I read his books and followed him in his travels. I just
wanted to light out and live dangerously in a war zone."

"But you didn't."

"It was made very clear to me that the Drohan family
needed a lawyer. Law school was a way to get off the island,
so I agreed. It wasn't a mistake; I'm not sorry I went. Yale
was eye-opening. I worked hard and made Law Review, so
I was part of a prestigious journal. I figured I'd come home,
be a dutiful son, practice law a few years, and look out for an
opening."

"What was your friend doing then?"

He looked puzzled for a moment, then recalled where he'd
started. "Ed," he said. "That's his name. Ed Latour. He was
working for an alternative paper that died some years ago.
Then he moved over to the *Banner*. In those days, it wasn't a
bad paper. They paid their wire-service fees, which they no
longer do, so there was an international-news page, also a lot
of local-news coverage, a little human interest. The circulation
was never large, but it was respectable. Ed tells me Frank Bilchard has been steadily firing serious journalists and replacing
them with fluff writers, so it's all recipes and society gossip. He
expects the axe any day."

"It's been a disgraceful rag for some time," I agreed. "I
read it for the restaurant reviews."

"I never look at it," Mike admitted.

"But you're going to buy it."

"I think so. It's not worth much now, and Frank knows it,

so the price won't be high. I'll make Ed the chief and give him a decent salary. Then, once I get free of the court, I can take a more active interest."

I sipped my wine, pondering this sudden and radical proposition. Mike's close, unwavering attention was focused on me, waiting for my opinion of the plan. It dawned on me that he very much wanted my approval and feared that I would make some scoffing, dismissive remark.

"What do you think?" he asked doubtfully.

"I think it's brilliant," I said. "You can make a real difference on the island. If people are informed, they can make better choices."

He took in a slow breath of air and laid his hand over mine on the rail. "That's the hope, isn't it?" he said.

I could feel relief washing through him. This is so touching, I thought. And who would believe it? Mike Drohan is an idealistic guy.

We looked out at the city spread beneath us, dark now, with patches of light near the waterfront. The stars were fading, and a waning moon carved a bright "C" into the velvety black of the night sky. It was clear, damp; a light breeze came off the water, carrying the briny scent of the sea.

"We're changing our lives," Mike observed.

Far off, I could make out the flickering lights of a steamer anchored at the entrance to the bay.

"We're changing our lives," I agreed.

Mimi, having completed her studies, graduated from the college that spring. She had secured a fellowship for graduate studies at a prestigious university on the mainland. Her future was bright, and she was more than ready to embrace it. The graduation ceremony was to be held in a small, open stadium on the edge of the campus. I was gratified, maybe even teary-eyed, to receive an invitation to this event. As she was moving out her few possessions from my house, Mimi stopped at the kitchen table, placed her palm flat on the wood, and said, "I learned a *lot* at this table." This touched me, and I realized how much I would miss her solid, practical presence under my roof.

As Mike, Ian, Bessie, Ralph, and Carità were also invited, it was agreed that we should meet on the quad and walk to the stadium together. It was one of Mimi's peculiar strengths to bring together friends from all walks of life, and our group was certainly a testament to that skill.

Mike and I drove to the campus in good spirits. His relationship with his son still wasn't warm, but it was amicable. Ian tolerated Mike because Carità insisted that he should. And he tolerated me, just barely, because I had not, as he would have preferred, languished in his father's affections. To the world's astonishment, and my own, we were an entity now—the judge and the madam—so widely known that we no longer sparked comment when we entered a restaurant, or even strolled hand in hand across the manicured grounds of the college. Ahead, near the reflecting pool at the convergence of four walkways, Ian, Bessie, and Ralph stood together, occupied in a conversation in which Ralph had taken the lead. He was a high-spirited, amusing young man, full of anecdotes about his café staff and the vicissitudes of the kitchen. He was short, squarely built; he could have been a wrestler or a stevedore, and his too-loud laugh somehow suited him. Bessie's affectionate eyes followed his patter as if it were both new and hilarious, though neither was likely the case. Ian, towering above them, his head lowered so as not to miss the punch line, wore the vague, indulgent expression of a nanny supervising a wayward child. He spotted our approach over the heads of his friends and raised one hand in a listless salute.

We joined them. The conversation quickly turned to the perennially safe topic of the weather, which all agreed was perfect for the planned event. Mike asked Ian if we were meeting Carità on the walk over, and he replied that she was with her tutor in a building abutting the quad, and would meet us where we were, very soon. He pointed to an ivy-encrusted hall with arched windows and a stone staircase. "It's Becket Hall," he said. "That's where the program offices are."

As I considered this solid edifice, enjoying the sheer unlikelihood of finding myself on a college campus, the tall carved door at the top of the stairs opened, and several young people emerged from the dark interior. The first two, a boy and a girl in conversation, were followed by a boy on his own. Then, as these three ambled down the stairs, Carità appeared squarely in the door frame, one hand finding the stair rail, the other gripping the harness of a large, solemn-looking dog, who paused until, with a subtle pressure, she urged him on. Ian, who was standing behind me, said in a voice that contained no small element of awe, "There she is."

Carefully and confidently, Carità descended the stairs.

Two boys came out behind her, and one of them took the steps quickly to come down beside the dog. He spoke to Carità, and she replied, saying something that made him laugh. They arrived at the sidewalk and stood for a moment, continuing their conversation. Another boy and a girl, passing on the sidewalk, called out to Carità as they approached. She turned to reply; the dog stood stolidly at her side. The first boy went down on one knee to pet the dog, holding his big head between his hands, looking up at Carità, who bent over him, briefly touching his shoulder with her free hand.

My brain buzzed with recognition. Where had I seen this configuration before? Then it came to me: the statue of St. Roch in Father Dugan's front hall. The saint, loving and merciful, bending to bless a supplicant, the dog standing on alert. The strange, heady aura of sanctity that had confounded me then enveloped me now, and I stood speechless as before a vision.

"Carità!" Ian called out joyfully.

Carità. I recalled that first day, when she sat on the couch in my drawing room, with her wild hair and her broken teeth, and as I noticed the otherworldly, glacial gleam of her eyes, Bessie informed me, "She's nineteen years old. She's blind from birth."

Later, Bessie told me their mother had lived just long enough to name her infant daughter.

Carità.

Was it a name? Or was it a plea?

Carità.

"It means 'mercy,'" Bessie said.

Author's Note: On Marriage Vows

Vigilant readers will surely note that the phrase "with all my worldly goods I thee endow," which Carità Bercy memorizes so flawlessly and employs in self-defense to preserve her husband's fortune, is part of the marriage service found in the Anglican Book of Common Prayer and does not appear in the Roman Catholic liturgy. Though I was raised in the Episcopal Church, where weekly readings from the Shakespearean English of Cranmer's prose created a music all its own, I was educated by Carmelite nuns, during the period when the Latin mass was banned and the flat modern English translation offered few delights to the ear.

When it came time for Carità to marry her mad suitor, Ian Drohan, I wanted the ceremony to give her something to think about, something to arm her in the battlefield of church and state, and the words from the service I knew so well sprang to mind. It is the vow that Shakespeare himself would have taken when he brought his pregnant bride, Anne Hathaway, to the altar in 1582.

Shakespeare's Juliet Capulet is a tragic heroine, doomed to

die for love. But Verona Island is a world of my own creation, and I intended my Juliet to survive. More than that, I wanted her to triumph. Thus, at an important juncture, Carità reminds her young husband of his vow. "With all my worldly goods I thee endow," she repeats, stressing the word "all."

And the plot thickens.

Acknowledgments

I would like to thank several friends and colleagues who read and commented on early drafts of this novel.

First, and foremost, I want to express my continued gratitude to my agent, steadfast friend, and tireless advocate, Molly Friedrich, whose confidence in this manuscript was genuine and heartfelt from the start.

Thanks also to Amy Bloom, who offered trenchant suggestions early on, and to Hannah Westland and Rebecca Gray, at Serpent's Tail in Britain, for invaluable notes and questions.

I am indebted to my brilliant editor at Doubleday, Lee Boudreaux, for her many pages of single-spaced editorial questions, remarks, and thoughtful suggestions, which took me on a guided tour of my own novel and resulted in a deep revision of the enterprise.

Thanks and respect are due to Terry Zaroff-Evans, my copyeditor, for her impressive vigilance and flawless accuracy.

My continued thanks to my daughter, Adrienne Martin, who, in spite of a crushing schedule of teaching, children, pets, and her own writing, took time out to serve as my patient and highly competent first proofreader.

During the writing of this novel, John Cullen, my partner and first reader for thirty years, suddenly passed away. He was with me as I set out, and he read the first forty pages with more than his usual enthusiasm. As I knew enthusiasm to be one of several emotions he was incapable of faking, I carried on with a goodwill. After he was gone, finishing a project he was excited about pulled me through some very dark hours. His memory lives on, having influenced and now inhabiting this book. I wrote it for him.